PRAISE FOR THE CAIT MORGAN MYSTERIES

"In the finest tradition of Agatha Christie, debut author Ace brings us the closed-room drama, with a dollop of romantic suspense and historical intrigue." —*Library Journal*

"Cait's enjoyable first outing should earn her a well-deserved encore." —*Publishers Weekly*

"If you're a lover of classic mystery, this Cait Morgan novel is for you . . . murder with touches of Christie or Marsh but with a bouquet of Kinsey Millhone." —*The Globe and Mail*

"A sparkling, well-plotted, and quite devious mystery in the cozy tradition, all pointing to Ace's growing finesse at telling an entertaining story." —*The Hamilton Spectator*

"Perfect comfort reading. You could call it Agatha Christie set in the modern world, with great dollops of lovingly described food and drink." —*Crime Fiction Lover*

"A really good story . . . suspenseful mystery."
—*Cozy Mystery Book Reviews*

THE Corpse WITH THE Emerald Thumb

CATHY ACE

TouchWood Editions

TouchWood Editions
touchwoodeditions.com

LIBRARY AND ARCHIVES CANADA CATALOGUING IN PUBLICATION
Ace, Cathy, 1960–, author
The corpse with the emerald thumb / Cathy Ace.

(A Cait Morgan mystery)
Issued in print and electronic formats.
ISBN 978-1-77151-063-9

I. Title. II. Series: Ace, Cathy, 1960– Cait Morgan mystery.

PS8601.C41C65 2014   C813'.6   C2013-905977-6

Editor: Frances Thorsen
Proofreader: Cailey Cavallin
Design: Pete Kohut
Cover image: dbvirago, canstockphoto.com
Author photo: Jeremy Wilson Photography (jeremywilsonphotography.com)

 Canadian Heritage Patrimoine canadien Canada Council for the Arts Conseil des Arts du Canada BRITISH COLUMBIA ARTS COUNCIL

We gratefully acknowledge the financial support for our publishing activities
from the Government of Canada through the Canada Book Fund, Canada
Council for the Arts, and the province of British Columbia through the
British Columbia Arts Council and the Book Publishing Tax Credit.

MIX
Paper from
responsible sources
FSC   FSC® C016245
www.fsc.org

The interior pages of this book have been printed on 30% post-consumer
recycled paper, processed chlorine free, and printed with vegetable-based inks.

1 2 3 4 5 18 17 16 15 14

PRINTED IN CANADA

For the man who saved me from a scorpion, poolside in Bucerias. My hero.

Seven Days

THE JUMBLED MOUND THAT BUD had dumped out of his pockets sat on the breakfast bar of our vacation condo. I said, lovingly of course, "You need a manbag."

"I think the correct term is a *murse*," replied Bud, looking endearingly smug.

"Fashion-speak from a retired cop who owns just three jackets?" I gave him a friendly poke.

He grinned. "Now all that dead weight's gone, I'm off to get supplies. I saw a bodega across the road when we arrived, and I need a beer, or three. You'll let me back in, right?" He grabbed a handful of cash as he made for the door, grinning.

"So long as there are treats for me too." I was still recovering from being squashed into an unreasonably narrow seat on our flight from Vancouver to Puerto Vallarta, followed by an hour in a tiny car where "air conditioning" meant opening the windows. Treats were definitely in order.

"Okay. I'll see what I can find to make you smile. Back soon," was Bud's parting shot.

I grappled with the shutters in the main room, which eventually flew open to reveal a narrow road and some white stucco buildings below, beyond which glittered the Bay of Banderas. I hoped that the ominous clouds gathering on the horizon wouldn't spoil our exploration of the resort's supposedly "lush" gardens. Our first real vacation. A whole week of just Bud and me. Wonderful!

As I repeated the shutter-wrestling process in the bedroom, I spotted Bud leaving the bodega holding a promisingly bulky carrier bag. He popped into a flower shop next door. I smiled inwardly as I unpacked my suitcase. A distant bell chimed noon. *Idyllic.*

It was the scream that drew me back to the bedroom window.

I looked out again to see a wailing woman holding open the door to the florist's store. Though the lights inside the store provided only partial illumination, I could make out the shape of a body lying on the floor. Its throat was being gripped by a kneeling male figure— he looked up and mouthed something at the screaming woman. I couldn't hear what was said, because just then a pickup truck roared by. But in that instant I recognized the face of the figure who was throttling the person on the ground.

It was Bud.

Slack-jawed, I stood at the window as the scene below me played out. Two men in almost farcically elaborate blue and gold uniforms rushed out of the bodega next door to the flower shop: a short, portly guy, and a tall, lean one. The short one attended to the still-screaming woman, who was now swaying and clutching at the air, while the tall one pulled open the door she'd allowed to swing closed. A weapon had magically appeared in his hand, and he pointed it into the building. In the gloom, I saw Bud raise his hands and clamber to his feet, then turn, ready to be handcuffed, which he was. I felt as though I were watching a movie: fascinated, yet disconnected.

The tall man, who was quite obviously a cop, dragged Bud out of the store into the midday sun. I could see that Bud's shirt, arms, and knees were covered in blood. Not his, I hoped. The tall cop appeared to bark instructions at the short one, who propped Bud's distraught discoverer against the side of the building. He ran off and returned a moment later in a police car that must have been parked around the corner, at the end of the building. As Bud was manhandled toward the vehicle, he pushed out his bloodied chest, pulled himself up to his full five ten, turned his face skyward, and shouted with all his might,

"Jack...Jack...Petrov...Cartagena..." Then he was gone—shoved unceremoniously through the back door of the sedan. The tall cop spoke to his shorter colleague, waved his arms around a bit, then took off his hat and jacket, tossed them into the trunk, and jumped into the driver's seat. The car shot off down the road, throwing up dust and small stones in its wake, its wailing siren slicing the humid air.

I breathed in for what seemed like the first time in many moments. I found I still couldn't move. I was trying to process what I'd seen. What on earth had just happened? None of it made any sense. Well, given the circumstances in which he was discovered, what had happened to Bud *did* make sense ... but how had he managed to get himself into that position in the first place? He'd only been out of the apartment for five or ten minutes!

I tried to give my attention to the scene in the street below. A switch flipped somewhere in my brain, and I worked out that pretty soon there'd likely be the arrival of a coroner, or the Mexican equivalent, then the body would be removed, the crime scene secured, and an investigation would begin.

I knew, instinctively, that the person on the floor was dead. It seemed to me the tall cop had been pretty sure that Bud had done it. There would be an investigation into *why* Bud had done it. But there could never be a resolution to such an investigation, because Bud *couldn't* have done it.

I sat down, hard, on the edge of the bed and wondered what to do. My instinct was to run to the short policeman, who was managing the gaggle of people milling about outside the florist shop, and tell him who I was, who Bud was, and that Bud couldn't possibly have killed anyone. My own background as a professor of criminal psychology at the University of Vancouver might not carry much weight, but I was sure that Bud's long career in law enforcement would speak volumes. We'd worked together for quite a while, when I'd been his hired "victim profiling" consultant, and we'd been dating now for a few months short of a year. So *I* knew him. *They* didn't. All I had to do was go down there and point out the mistake they'd made.

But I remained seated on the edge of the bed.

What had Bud shouted? It must have been important. I didn't need my useful, but largely secret, eidetic memory to recall what he'd called out.

"Jack. Jack Petrov. Cartagena."

I concentrated. I didn't know anyone called Jack Petrov. Nor, as far as I knew, did Bud. The only Jack I could think of was Jack White—Bud's old mentor and colleague, who'd given us the use of the apartment where I was sitting. He and Bud had worked together for decades. It was not only his condo that we'd been loaned for a week, but also his little car, which we'd driven from the airport. Jack was looking after Marty, Bud's tubby black Labrador, on his acreage in Hatzic, back home in BC. As I visualized Jack's kind, pale face and his tall, spare frame, which always seemed to be in motion, I could feel an indulgent smile play on my lips. I decided that since I couldn't ask Bud himself what to do, Jack was the next best person to speak to.

But how? I dragged my cell phone out of my carry-on bag and checked the directory. No, of course I didn't have Jack's numbers back home. I spotted Bud's phone on the counter, where he'd dumped it with all his other bits and pieces. I didn't like the thought of checking his phone, but it seemed the only option. I scrolled through names and acronyms, most of which meant nothing to me, then, finally, I found "White Cell" and "White House." I dialed the house to start with. After several rings, I disconnected and punched the button to call the other number. An instant later, I heard Jack's voice, echoing on speakerphone.

"Hi—Jack here. I'm driving. Sheila's in the truck with me, so be careful what you say, whoever you are."

I could hear giggling and Jack's adorable, if sometimes overly fussy, wife saying, "Oh, you're wicked, Jack White. Don't say that; it could be anyone."

I could picture them both quite clearly. The perfect pair. Happily heading out somewhere in the truck on a Sunday afternoon. My mouth dried as the seriousness of Bud's situation jangled my nerves.

"It's me, Cait," I managed to squeak out.

"Ah, get there okay? Everything alright with the car and the condo?" Jack sounded cheery.

"Um . . . yes. Everything's fine. Well . . . no, it's not really. Look, Jack, something terrible has happened and I don't know who else to turn to." As the words left my lips, I knew I sounded pathetic and useless. I hated myself for it. *Buck up, Cait!*

"Hang on a minute," replied Jack. After a pause, "Okay, I've pulled over. It sounds like you need my attention. This can't be good news. Where's Bud? Is he okay?"

I took a deep breath. "No, Jack, he's not. He's been hauled off by the police. I think they believe he killed someone."

The words hung in the air. I heard Sheila gasp and Jack curse.

"Tell me exactly what happened, Cait." Jack's tone was grim.

I did. Briefly.

When I finished, Jack said, "And his exact words were Jack, Petrov, and Cartagena, right?"

"Yes. Does it mean something to you?" I hoped it did, though I couldn't imagine what.

"Sure does," said Jack. "It means you have to clear out every-thing, and I mean absolutely *everything*, that you and Bud brought to the condo, get it back to the car, and drive back to the airport. The apartment must look as though neither you nor Bud has ever been there. Find a cloth, a towel, anything, and wipe down the surfaces and objects you've touched. Lock up behind you. And do it fast. *Now.*"

"Do *what*?" Jack wasn't making any sense.

"Look, Cait, just do as I say. It's important. What Bud shouted out was a message, to me. You did exactly the right thing calling me, because the message wouldn't make any sense to most people. But it makes sense to me. There must be no connection between you and Bud at all."

"Now wait a minute, Jack. I'm not leaving Bud here, alone, in the hands of the police, suspected of a crime he didn't—*couldn't*—commit. No way!"

Silence again. Then, "Jack, she's not used to this. She might not even know. You should tell her." I could hear Sheila quite clearly, despite the fact that she was trying to whisper in the background.

"What don't I know, Jack? *What* should you tell me?" I knew I sounded angry. I was.

"Did Bud have any ID on him when he was picked up?" was Jack's reply.

I sighed impatiently and spread out the mound that Bud had created on the counter. "I don't think so. His credit cards, his wallet, his passport, his phone—I'm using it now—they're all here. I think he just had some cash with him."

"Which passport is there?" Jack snapped.

"What do you mean 'which passport'? His *Canadian* passport, of course. How many has he got?" I sounded as puzzled as I felt.

"Well, I don't know how many he's got now, or which ones he brought with him or traveled on, but he's often had several, and I'm guessing that, even though he's retired, he's still got his Swedish one."

I could hear myself splutter, "Why's he got a Swedish passport? He's *Canadian*."

"You've got a British one *and* a Canadian one, right?" Jack sounded very sensible.

"Yes, but I'm Welsh. I kept dual citizenship when I emigrated, so of course I have a British passport. Bud was born in Canada; why would he have a Swedish one?"

Jack hesitated. "You know that his parents are Swedish?"

"Yes." I knew in my gut that a shoe was about to drop.

"Bud was born in Sweden and brought to Canada as a baby, but he sometimes used his Swedish ID for his CSIS work. Well, his Swedish one and some alternate Canadian ones with a few different names on them. I think one of them even used his real name." *Okay—so not just a shoe dropping, but an entire collection of heavy boots.*

I sat down on the corner of the sofa and felt my multi-purpose right eyebrow shoot toward my hairline. "*CSIS?* The Canadian Security Intelligence Service? Bud's a *spy?*"

"Don't be silly, Cait." It was Sheila's voice cooing at me from my distant homeland. "Look, over the years, Jack and Bud have worked on some cases that needed CSIS clearance, that's all. Right, Jack?" I pictured Jack nodding at his wife, or else glowering at her. "So they have all these special papers for when they travel doing stuff like that. Of course, Bud's last job meant he had to use them a lot, but maybe he's told you all about that?" She sounded hopeful.

"Not a word," was all I was able to say, though I suspected that my tone alone spoke volumes.

Sheila and Jack cleared their throats. In unison.

"Well, we're not really supposed to talk about it. I guess Bud stuck to that. Better you don't know," said Jack, a little too quickly.

"What, in case somebody arrests me, too, and points shiny lights at me till I talk?" This was all sounding quite ridiculous. Bud, and Jack, working for CSIS? And Sheila knew all about it? And me? *Not a thing.*

Jack paused, clearly trying to decide what to say next. "So, back to the question of passports. If one of his Canadian ones is there, the chances are that's the one he traveled on. So he's got no ID on him. And I know he won't say a word. Literally."

"How? How do you *know* that?" I was beginning to panic. The world I knew was melting around me.

"Petrov, Cartagena, that's how I know," replied Jack. "It's a case we studied during a CSIS training course. How to deal with being picked up by the locals when you're in a highly compromising situation. Petrov was a Russian operative who was found on the roadside next to a dead street vendor in Cartagena, a port city in Colombia, back in the 1980s. He tried to talk his way out of it, then tried to bribe his way out. It's used as a case study of what *not* to do. Rule of thumb: say nothing. That's what Bud will do. If he hasn't got a passport, they won't know where to start. They won't be contacting any consulates, because they won't know which one to talk to. That gives us time. Where did they take him, by the way? I'm going to guess they started by dumping him into the cells at the local police station, but do you know if that's the case?"

I was grappling with everything that Jack was throwing at me. "What? *Where?* I don't *know.* They bundled him into a car and took off. How on earth would I know *where*? I'm not leaving. I'll find him somehow. I must. I have to save him—"

"Cait! Stop it!" Jack shouted at me. His voice echoed in the cab of his distant truck.

"Jack . . . shh . . . don't speak to her like that," hissed Sheila.

Jack sighed. "Cait, listen. This is serious. Very serious. You *must* get out of there. Clear out. Completely. Do *not* connect with Bud, don't even try to. Find a flight and get back here as soon—"

"I'm *not* leaving him, Jack, and that's that. There is no way I'm running away from this. From Bud. I'm staying, and I'm going to help him. When it comes to fight or flight, you'd better realize that we Welsh do not run—we stand our ground, and fight it out if necessary . . . if we can't talk our way out of it, of course." I was close to tears, but every molecule of my body was determined that I would stay in Mexico to help Bud. Somehow.

Jack sighed heavily. "Right. New plan. Cait—I still need you to clean up the apartment, clear everything out, drive back to the airport, and wait there until another flight comes in from Vancouver. Then get back in the car and drive to . . . have you got a pen handy?"

"Hang on." I scrabbled in my purse, hunting for my always-disappearing reading-cheats, and ruing the fact that I needed them at all. Finally, I found them, shoved them onto my nose, and got ready to take notes.

"When you eventually leave the airport, drive as though you're going back to the resort, but stay on the main road for about a mile beyond the turn you took to get where you are now. You'll see a sign on the right for the Hacienda Soleado, got it?"

"Got it."

"Turn there. Once you drive off the main road, you'll have to get yourself along a pretty poor track, up into the hills, until you come to the place itself. It's an agave plantation where they make tequila. One of the owners is a buddy of mine and he's got a place there. All the owners have. I happen to know he left for his home in the States last week. I'll make some calls. Tell him a friend of mine wants to borrow his place for a week. When you get through the entrance, you'll see a big adobe building: that's the tasting room and restaurant. Go there. They'll have the keys and codes you'll need, and someone will tell you where to go. Clear?"

"Clear."

"I'll get myself down there as fast as I can. In the meantime, just get to Henry's place at the ranch and lay low. His full name is Henry Douglas. If anyone asks, you are who you are, he's a friend of a friend, and you're there for some sort of—I don't know—academic retreat or something. Okay with you?"

"Yes, okay." I could hear my voice quiver. "Jack, what happened to Petrov?"

Silence.

"I'll get this sorted, Cait. The fact that Bud was covered in blood makes me think he was trying to help someone who'd been injured."

"*Of course!*" I blurted out. "It was the victim's blood, not Bud's. Why didn't I think of that?" I felt so relieved, but dim.

"Because you're not thinking clearly, dear," came Sheila's overly soothing tones. "Just do as Jack says, and he'll come down and help straighten everything out. It doesn't need to become some huge international incident."

"No, it doesn't," butted in Jack. "That's exactly what we don't want. *None* of us. Down there the municipal cops don't deal with murders, so they'll be looking to hand Bud off to their federal colleagues as soon as they can. As it's a Sunday today, maybe I can get there before they pack him off to Tepic or Guadalajara, which is likely what they'll do. From your descriptions, Cait, it must have been Al and Miguel at the scene. Al's the tall one. Nice guy. Though why they were in their dress uniforms, and in Bob's Bodega next to Margarita's flower shop, is beyond me."

It had completely escaped me that, with Jack being a "local" in Punta de las Rocas for part of the year, he would know all the people involved. It also dawned on me that he might even know the victim.

"Who might it have been, Jack—on the floor?" I asked as reasonably, and gently, as I could.

Jack tutted. "I don't know. I can't be sure. It's Margarita's store. She's the florist, and a wonderful plantswoman. She can grow pretty much anything. She has a nursery up in the hills, not far from the plantation I'm sending you to. In fact, her father, Juan, is the jimador at the Hacienda Soleado—he's the one who cares for the agaves there. He's also the mayor of the municipality, the intendente. Important guy, in his own way. If it's her—well, I can't imagine what happened, or who would have wanted to harm her. I've always thought of her as well respected in the area, and all she does is grow plants and sell flowers. It's puzzling. And worrying."

"Jack, look, I'll do as you asked, and maybe I can call you again when I get to the hacienda?" I was looking around the apartment and beginning to focus on my tasks as I spoke. This was better. There was something I could *do*.

"Sure. By then I'll have made some calls, and I should be able to tell you when I'll arrive."

I had a thought. "Hang on a minute, Jack—why would I have your car? I mean, if I'm not supposed to be connected to Bud, then should I be connected to you? Why would I be driving from the airport in *your* car? Wouldn't I just get a cab?"

Jack didn't answer immediately. "You make a good point, Cait, and you're right. I'll need to think through whether or not it might be alright for us to 'know' each other. I'll tell you when we speak again. Meanwhile, park my car in the short-term parking lot and leave the ticket in the glovebox. I'll collect it from there when I fly in. I've got my keys here; you've got the spares. You have the keys, right? Bud didn't keep them in his pocket?"

I double-checked. "They're here. No worries." *Huh! No worries!*

"Okay, Cait, when you're at the airport and you see a flight getting in from Vancouver, keep an eye open for when folks are leaving the baggage area, join the crowd, and jump in one of the government cabs that park right outside the terminal. There's no point you dragging the luggage across the road to get a city cab, even though they're a bit cheaper. Have you got local cash?"

I checked in my purse. "Yes, I brought a fair amount with me, so I should be fine."

"Good. And how's your Spanish?"

"My comprehension's excellent. Speaking it takes a bit of time, but I can get there." I allowed myself a wry smile as I thought about the book of conversational Spanish that Bud had given me when he told me about this vacation. He knows how lazy I am when it comes to languages, but he told me I had to learn Spanish before we left, which isn't as easy as it sounds, even for someone like me who has an eidetic memory. Language isn't just about remembering stuff; it's about putting all the right bits together in the right order and making it sound right. Now I was glad that I'd applied myself.

"Good," replied Jack, "you might need it with the cab driver. Use the details I've just given you. You'll be fine out at the Hacienda Soleado. Everyone speaks English there. You'll be a bit isolated at the plantation, of course, but that fits better with the idea that you're trying to get away from everything. Just lay low. You know, just be quiet and generally uncommunicative. Act like a brain-box taking a break."

I felt another wan smile creep up on me. "Okay. I'll keep a low profile. And I'll peer at people over my sunglasses to make myself appear more forbidding."

"I know you're a quick study, Cait. Bud's always boasting that you belong to Mensa. Which reminds me—there's something you *can* do that could help Bud. Do that memory thing he's told me about—you know, when you recall the exact details of an event, or a place, or a person. You might have seen something that could help."

"Bud told you about that?" I was surprised. I had thought that Bud respected my choice to keep my special skill set private. Then again, the last fifteen minutes had been full of surprises about Bud, and none of them, so far, had been pleasant.

"Yes, he told us, but he also told us not to tell anyone else, and we won't, right, Sheila?"

"Oh, of course not. I know lots of things I don't *really* know." Sheila sounded conspiratorial.

"Is there anything else I should do? Or *not* do?" I thought I'd better check. This cloak and dagger stuff was all new to me, and seeing Bud hauled into custody, leaving a corpse in his wake, was a new and frightening experience.

"Cait—concentrate, and call me when you're settled. Go on, get going. We'll head back to our place now. It'll be a better base for getting in touch with the people who can help Bud. Talk to you in a few hours or so. And Cait?"

"Yes?"

"Don't panic. This *will* be sorted out. Bud will not be held, or charged, or incarcerated for something he didn't do. Right?"

"Yes, okay. Jack, you never told me what happened to Petrov in Colombia. Tell me. Please?"

"Cait, it was a case study of what *not* to do, so don't give it any more thought."

"Jack, *please?*" I needed to know.

Jack sighed. "He was tried, found guilty, and executed. He did everything *wrong*, Cait. That won't happen to Bud. We won't let it. *He* won't let it. Now stop thinking about the idiot Petrov and get going!"

"Yes, Jack. I'm on it." We disconnected from each other, and the silence closed in around me.

I looked around, stood up, and got busy shoving toiletries back into my suitcase not an hour after I'd taken them out. I felt as though the firm ground upon which I'd believed my relationship with Bud was built was disappearing from beneath my feet. Bud was *Swedish*? Cleared by CSIS? Jack had said that one of Bud's passports bore his real name. Was "Bud" not even Bud's real name?

I wondered if this was how Alice had felt, when she went sliding down the rabbit hole.

No Time to Waste

PUTTING THE APARTMENT BACK TOGETHER took me longer than I had thought it would. I grappled, alone, with the luggage that Bud and I had hauled up to the condo together, and awkwardly dragged it all the way back to the car. As the cases thumped down the stone staircases, I realized that my bag weighed almost twice as much as Bud's. That said, it was a good deal more attractive. His was navy with orange plaid—*so ugly*—and mine was black and white houndstooth—*very classy*. I was pretty sure I'd managed to make my way about unnoticed. The resort was quiet. I guessed that was due to the time of year: before the schools let out for the summer, but after most of the snowbirds had departed for their other homes. With all the action that was taking place at the crime scene in the street, the parking garage, which was on the other side of the resort, was hardly going to be the center of attention.

By the time I pushed the keys into the ignition of Jack's borrowed car, I was sweaty and breathless. Forcing myself to focus on the matter in hand, I reversed the route Bud had driven us along earlier in the day, but now, instead of joyfully heading toward a vacation promising togetherness and relaxing hours in the sun, I was running away from a crime scene at the behest of Jack White, a man I hardly knew at all. I could feel my turmoil presenting itself as an acid tummy, as I stuck to the speed limit and let the idiots in the fast lane scream past. By the time I got back to the airport, parked the car, and hauled two suitcases plus my carry-on tote back into the main terminal, I was a wreck—physically, and mentally.

I checked the Arrivals board and noted that a flight from Vancouver was due to land in just over two hours. I looked around and spotted a small coffee shop where I could wait. Managing to avoid making eye contact with the hordes of salespeople trying to offload timeshare condos quickly became a priority, so I kept my head down, rolled the luggage along as best I could, and grabbed a couple of innocuous-looking wraps, a chocolate bar, a bottle of water, and a bucket-sized cup of coffee.

Finally, surrounding myself with baggage, I plopped onto a plastic seat that faced a wall decorated with photographs of the seawall promenade, the Malecón, in Puerto Vallarta. Ironically, one of them featured a whimsically surreal sculpture entitled *In Search of Reason*, by Sergio Bustamante. Looking at the triangular-headed figure at the base of a ladder that led unsupported into the sky, where two smaller figures teetered, I thought I understood what the artist had been trying to say. When nothing makes sense, you'll do anything, however dangerous or hopeless it might seem, to find a way to reach the freedom that reason, and understanding, offers. I felt trapped in a bubble of un-reason. Of non-sense.

What I'd seen earlier in the day only made sense if Bud had been helping someone who'd been gravely injured. *Okay.* What I'd then been told about Bud, by someone who'd known him for a heck of a lot longer than I had—decades, in fact—only made sense if . . . if Bud didn't trust me enough to tell me about his work, or his true self.

I dwelled on that as I munched on a chicken and salad wrap. It might as well have been shredded paper and shoe soles wrapped in carpet for all the pleasure I got from it, which, for me, is unusual. However bad food might be, I always at least *notice* it, but this? It was gone before I'd realized I was eating it. Of course I was trying to manage the shock of seeing Bud in such a terrible situation, but my mind wasn't reeling because of that. It was whirring and clicking because I was wondering if, once again, I'd chosen to open up to someone, to let someone into my heart, who was less than truthful about themself.

I'd done it with Angus all those years ago in Cambridge, when I was studying for my master's degree in criminology. He'd been handsome and charming, but as soon as he knew I was his, he'd subjected me to the pain, and shame, of beatings and—possibly even worse—a complete undermining of my self-confidence. Getting hauled out of my own home in handcuffs, accused of having beaten him to death, after finding him dead on my bathroom floor a few weeks after I'd officially kicked him out just highlighted how bad a choice I'd made, in more ways than one.

Had I done it again? Picked a "wrong-un," as my mum had always liked to refer to the boys I'd brought home—*they'd all been "wrong-uns" according to her, of course.* Given that at forty-eight years of age I am still single, maybe she'd been right. No question Angus had been bad. Bad through and through. And certainly bad for me. But Bud? No. Not Bud. Whatever Jack had said, I *know* Bud.

Since Bud's wife, Jan, had died so tragically, we'd talked and talked. About nothing at all, and about all the important stuff. I know Bud Anderson through and through. I believe that. I *know* he is a good man. A man who'd dedicated his life to law and justice, and not a man who would harm, hurt, or deceive me. He is warm, funny, and loving. Okay, so he has pretty questionable taste in clothes— well, no taste at all really, material things not mattering to him. And Bud *can* be very sure of himself, in a quiet way. Years as a police officer will do that for you. There's an air that never leaves you. I see it in all his retired colleagues. True, he sometimes doesn't agree with my point of view on certain matters, but everyone's entitled to their opinion, and we usually end up with a truce that holds—until the next time the topic comes up. My being a criminal psychologist and his being a cop sometimes leads to some juicy up and downers: usually ending with us both having to agree that psychology might explain some activities, but it doesn't excuse them.

Crumbs from the wrap had landed on the shelf that is my more-than-ample bosom. As I wiped them off, I dragged myself to a more reasoned outlook.

Bud was being held by the Mexican police for a crime I knew he did not commit. As I stirred my coffee with my chocolate bar— *don't judge till you've tried it!*—I came to a decision. I would do as Jack had asked, and show up at the Hacienda Soleado, but, beyond that, if a chance presented itself for me to help Bud in any way, I'd take it. The first comforting taste of melting chocolate spurred me to realize that I could use the time I was stuck at the airport to recall the exact events surrounding Bud's arrest, rather than dwell on my anxiety about not knowing his real name, or where he was born—or the fact that CSIS had issued him multiple passports over the years.

I took in my surroundings. The airport concourse was as noisy and chaotic as you'd expect—groups of people jostled past each other, looking up, or back... anywhere but the direction in which they were moving; announcements were being made over a *boing*-ing loudspeaker system; and the shrieks of invisible children echoed off the marbled and tiled surfaces. I drained my coffee, pocketed the remaining wrap, shoved the bottle of water into my bulging carry-on tote, and headed toward an exit. I had to pass one of those we-sell-everything stalls as I left, and I knew that they'd have cigarettes there. I'd promised Bud I'd give up smoking, and I'd done really well on the nicotine gum for the past three weeks. I even had a big stash of it ready to get me through our vacation. I hesitated and imagined lighting up, taking that first long draw. I rational-ized that I was under tremendous stress, and that Bud wouldn't know... but I realized that my addiction was just winning out over my willpower. So I gave in. I bought five packs of my regular tiny, super slim light cigarettes—just to be on the safe side; they don't sell them everywhere, and in Mexico, who knew where I might find them again—and all but ran out of the building to find a spot where I could get my fix. I found a bench and lit up.

Once the dizziness subsided, and I managed to get used to the strangely bitter taste, I felt much better just holding a cigarette. I couldn't help but smile when I realized that I kept glancing around, thinking that Bud might suddenly materialize and give me at least a filthy look. I told myself not to be stupid, and that's what finally got me to the right place to be able to settle down mentally and recall, in detail, everything I'd experienced that morning. It's not a process I totally understand—it's just something I've always been able to do. If I close my eyes to the point where everything goes a bit fuzzy, and hum to myself, I'm able to recall, in every one of my senses, what I've experienced. Of course, the psychologist in me knows that it's not a perfect ability: sometimes I get it wrong, and sometimes I misinterpret what I've seen, smelled, felt, heard, or even tasted. We all do that, all the time, with every stimulus we perceive—we apply our own knowledge, our own attitudes and expectations to it all. And that's what we "remember."

I was partially shaded by the trunk of a towering palm, and a slight breeze cooled the sweat that the sun and humidity had squeezed out of my still-pale skin. May and the first two weeks of June in Vancouver had been the usual—wet and mild, but certainly not sunny. I made sure I was touching every piece of luggage before I screwed up my eyes, and then I was back in Jack's condo in the Rocas Hermosas Resort . . .

The Beginning?

I AM PULLING AND PUSHING at a red-painted wooden shutter as the door of the condo closes behind Bud, heading to the store. When the shutter creaks and flies outwards, the light dazzles me. My eyes adjust, and I immediately look out to the sea, which heaves and glints beneath the midday sun. I smell its salt in the air; I feel the freshness of the breeze on my skin. *Delightful!* I don't like the look of the dark clouds in the distance. I've been looking forward to exploring the "lush gardens and multi-level pools" promised by the resort's website, so don't go and rain on me today! I look down at the scene beneath our borrowed condo. I have opened the French doors inward to their full extent, and the shutters are now wide open. There's no balcony, just a chest-high rail that prevents me from falling to the ground thirty feet below. I can't look straight down, it makes me nauseous and dizzy, so I only glimpse the green, shrub-filled beds that surround our complex. I can, however, look out, and I see the red-brown, dusty stone road that lies between our temporary home and the buildings that sit between us and the sea. Two low white stucco and glass buildings with flat roofs sit back to back, parallel to each other, with a lane between them.

The building facing our condo houses three establishments. On the left is Bob's Bodega—it takes up about half of the building. It's almost totally glass-fronted, with large double doors and a clear view inside. I can see racks of groceries, toiletries, vegetables, and breads, as well as items of clothing, swimwear, and row after row of bottles of booze. *I hope they've got some ice-cold beers in a fridge somewhere.* The right-hand wall of the store houses the counter area, where I can see a cash register. I cannot see anyone inside.

Next door to the bodega, beyond a pillar of stucco, is a florist shop: MARGARITA FLORES is painted in vivid yellow on the sign. It is a very narrow store. Most of its frontage is the single glass door, with a glass panel on either side. The panels are covered in photographs of floral displays, a few of which are faded. That's a shame—they look like pretty arrangements, but without color, they lack appeal. The door is backed with some sort of covering that makes it dark, impossible to see inside. I guess it's to stop the light from getting to the stock and wilting the blooms

On the far right of the building, filling the rest of its length, is Serena Spa, with a gold and brown painted sign above a glass door. The glass walls, which are interspersed with stucco columns, are covered with photographs. Some show lurid, highly decorative manicures—how anyone can function in the real world with nails that long is a mystery to me. Others display women with beatific expressions whose perfect bodies are being massaged with glistening stones. On what planet is it pleasant to have boiling hot rocks dumped on your back? There are also models with glamorous hair and alarmingly large white teeth, grinning inanely at passers-by— porcelain veneers have a lot to answer for. As I am looking, and thinking, a woman comes out of the door of the spa and waves back to someone inside.

It's the woman who screamed when she saw Bud. She's wearing loose white capri pants, flip-flops, and a royal blue tee. The color looks good against her tanned skin. Her long, dark hair is pulled up, hanging loosely in a ponytail. She must be about thirty, is slim, and moves as though she's in good shape. Lithe. She's speaking to the person inside the spa, and she's holding . . . what is it? It's a cake box. I can't imagine this woman eats a lot of cake. She's too slim to indulge in that sort of thing often. Just as she turns away from the spa, I see Bud go into the bodega. The sunlight flashes on the glass door as he pulls it open. A seagull cries above me, and I glance up.

The woman in the capris calls to someone on the same side of the street as our complex. I cannot see the person, I do not look down, but the woman in the capris is beckoning to them with her free hand, and smiling. She's got a kind face, I suppose, and I shouldn't judge her too harshly for having the willpower to stay slim. I can see that she's starting to cross the road toward our condo.

As I pull my head back into the apartment to go into the bedroom, I catch a flash of something out of the corner of my right eye. It's a flash of white and glinting gold, popping out from beyond the gleaming white-painted end wall of the building. I don't know what it is, but it's human height, and moving. *Now I know it must have been one of the policemen in their fancy outfits. Yes, gold braid, white feathers in their hats . . . that must be it. That's where the police car emerged from.*

Now I am moving to the bedroom. I see my suitcase on the floor and I lift it, awkwardly, onto the bed. *Good grief, it's heavy, but I've hardly brought anything at all!* I try to not make the bedcover dirty. The bedroom and bathroom are small, as is the entire condo, but I don't care. Bud and I are going to have a wonderful time. No students or papers to grade for me, and a total break from familiar surroundings, all of which are saturated with memories of his dead wife. After nine months of dating, we're finally going to have some time alone together, where I won't be hemmed in by things and places that remind us of Jan . . . though I wish we could have brought Marty on the trip.

I am opening my suitcase as I am thinking this. I am not really looking at what I am doing. When I do look down, I realize how dark the bedroom is with the shutters closed, and that it's stuffy, with a smell of fresh linens, but aging potpourri. I leave the suitcase, pull open the second set of French doors, and begin to wiggle at the fastenings on the wooden shutters, which are as difficult to open as those in the main room. With fingers that have learned a new skill,

I open these more quickly. As I fiddle, in my mind's eye I am seeing Marty, Bud's gentle amber-eyed black Lab, as he jumps and gambols when we run him on the beach. He loves to run in the surf. *Oh, but all that sand that sticks to him!* He's staying with Jack on his acreage in Hatzic while we're away: Marty loves that too—three German short-haired pointers to play with, and new toys into the bargain.

The bedroom shutters fly open, and again I am dazzled. Once more I look across the road, and now I see Bud leaving the bodega, a red-and-white-striped carrier bag in one hand—it looks bulky. He holds open the glass door for the woman carrying the cake. A man has joined her. The man is taller than Bud, so the older guy must be about six feet tall. He's thin and wiry and is wearing shorts, a golf shirt, socks with his sandals—*oh dear!*—and a sun hat. It looks like a Tilley hat, so maybe he's Canadian? Once the man and the woman have entered the bodega, Bud lets go of the glass door. He's smiling as he walks the few steps to the next store, adjusts his baseball cap to shade his eyes from the sun, and then pulls open the door to the florist shop. *How romantic,* I think. Men have never bought me flowers. I'm just not that type.

My eyes wander back to the sea beyond the buildings, and I notice again the ominous clouds bubbling on the horizon. The air feels more humid than it did just moments ago. As I scan back to the road from the sea, I see a man in the lane between the two parallel buildings. He's leaning against the back wall of the building that faces the sea. It, too, is long and low; the back wall is entirely white stucco. He's noticeable because he's wearing a vivid red, double-breasted shirt with black pants. He's standing beside a door that's in two halves, like a stable door: the top half is open wide, the bottom half is ajar. Inside, the building is a big, black cavern, but I can see a glimpse of daylight on the floor . . . the building must open to the sea view. *Nice spot.* He's holding something: a glass of water and two sticks. *Why do I think they are chopsticks? Ah, I understand.* I can just make out a white chef's hat pushed back on his head—I almost didn't notice it against the snowy white of the stucco. So he's a chef. Taking a break from a hot kitchen? I can't smell any food on the sea breeze.

I take one last look at the horizon, wishing the clouds away, then turn my attention to my suitcase and the Ziploc bags full of toiletries. As I pull out the carefully packed plastic bags, I hear a bell. Twelve distant, almost mournful, chimes. I imagine they are coming from the gold-coroneted tower of the Church of Our Lady of Guadalupe in Puerto Vallarta, but then reason it's probably too far away for me to hear across the bay and the bell must be sounding at a local clock. I feel the stress of having taught an intersessional semester—which has all the work of a full-length semester squashed into half the time—lift from my shoulders. I had a particularly tough group for the Deviant Criminal Behavior: Background and Insights course, and there'd been a few temper tantrums when students had seen their grades. Now, with Bud buying beers and flowers—perfect— and me able to forget about students and grades, the next week will be wonderful. I know it.

I have just balanced a second can of hairspray on the edge of the bathroom counter when I hear a scream. It's a long howling scream. I immediately rush the few steps out of the ensuite bathroom, past the bed to the window, and look to the street below. The woman in the capris and the blue tee is holding open the door to the florist shop with her left hand; her right is raised above her head, its fingers splayed wide, as though to catch a large ball. She is looking down and away from me, but the noise that she is making fills the midday air.

At first, I cannot see what she is looking at. My eyes are adjusting to the stark contrast between the sunlight and the comparative gloom inside the store. I have a clear line of vision, and I quickly make out a figure, lying on the floor, its arms wide. The floor is shiny and black. The splayed-out arms seem thin and pale. I cannot see the whole body, because there's a bulk kneeling over it, their hands around the victim's throat. The chin of the person on the floor hides the hands from me, but I know they must be there because I can see the kneeling person's arms. Now the kneeling person raises their face to the screaming woman, and I see their mouth open: a big O, then teeth bared in an E shape. I realize it's Bud's mouth and face.

A truck roars along the road between the condo and the stores. It's a blue pickup, battered, old, with a roaring exhaust. The driver's window is open and I see an elbow. That's it. The tires spit up dirt and stones as the truck heads toward the road that leads from the resort. These two things happen simultaneously. My eyes are on the face of the man I love; the truck is in the lower periphery of my field of vision. *Have I missed something? Is the truck important?*

My eyes haven't left Bud's face, but then the screaming woman in the white capri pants loses her grip on the door and it swings shut, obliterating my view of Bud. As the door to the florist's closes, the double doors to the bodega swing out into the street, one person pushing open each door. *I know now, thanks to Jack's local knowledge, that these are policemen, that the tall one is called Al—which strikes me as a pretty odd name for a Mexican policeman—and the short one, Miguel.*

Miguel rushes to catch the woman in the capris just as she's about to collapse. She's flailing, grabbing the air; he supports her as she falls, helping her to rest against the stucco wall. Simultaneously, the tall cop, *Big Al, as I now think of him,* draws his weapon and shouts at the door. He pulls the door open and points his gun down toward the body, then at Bud, who I can see once more. Big Al holds the door open with his left foot; he has both hands on the gun. He's shouting—*I can tell by the way his shoulders are heaving*—and he's waggling the gun at Bud, indicating that Bud should stand.

Bud is shaking his head. *His body language says . . . defeat. He is beaten. Giving up.* He removes his hands from the throat of the body on the floor and holds them above his head, showing the cop he has nothing in them. First he puts his right foot flat on the floor, and then he pushes himself up from a kneeling position to a standing one, his hands still above his head. *Now I realize his hands aren't in shadow; they are dark with blood.* Big Al pulls a set of handcuffs from beneath the royal blue tunic bedecked with gold epaulets that's just a little too tight on him. Clearly a dress uniform.

The surreal vision of a blood-soaked Bud being handcuffed by a man with gold-tasseled shoulders, wearing a tall antique-style, white-feathered hat, will, of course, always be with me. But it will never be as bittersweet as it is at this moment . . . because it is now that I recall, for the first time, the look in Bud's eyes as he casts them toward our condo. He sees me standing in the window, I realize now. For a second, he looks right into my eyes, and I can see his expression: love and dread. Oh Bud!

Having checked the body on the floor, Big Al pushes Bud out of the store. Bud blinks in the sunlight. The tall cop speaks sharply to the short one, Miguel, who pats the capris woman on the hand and abandons her, leaving her propped against the wall. He heads toward the spa. He doesn't exactly run, but he walks smartly with an odd skip and a stuttering gallop thrown in—the way unfit people, like myself, move when they're trying to hurry along but can't really make that much of a sustained effort. I see him disappear around the far corner of the building out of the corner of my eye. *I only see him in this way because I am still looking at Bud.* Now in broad daylight, I see that the front of his favorite blue and white squiggly-patterned shirt is covered in blood. Ruined! I can just about see his bloodied forearms pulled behind his back, and I know his hands are in the same state. His knees below his khaki cargo shorts are dripping with blood. *Poor Bud.*

A white saloon car, marked clearly as a police vehicle, squeals around the building and pulls up in front of Bud and Big Al. Miguel jumps out of the driver's seat and draws his weapon, *quite unnecessarily!* Big Al, who's about six feet, with a spare, athletic frame, grabs Bud by the shoulders from behind and begins to steer him toward the rear door of the car. Bud stands up straight, pushes out his chest, preventing Big Al from moving him farther forward, and turns his head to face the sky. *Bud doesn't want the cops to know he's shouting to me. Of course!*

"Jack ... Jack ... Petrov ... Cartagena ..." The effort of making his voice carry as far as possible means his breast heaves with each word. Big Al regains momentum and shoves Bud, head first, into the back of the cop car—Miguel is holding the door open, his gun pointed at Bud's back. That is my last glimpse of Bud. I cannot see him inside the car. *It's as though someone has switched off a light in my life.*

Big Al moves to the driver's side of the vehicle, talking and waving his arms at Miguel, who is nodding and trying, somewhat unsuccessfully, to re-holster his weapon. He doesn't use that gun very often—he's not comfortable with it at all. He's fat, sweaty, and unfit; he's all dressed up like something out of a musical-comedy movie from the 1930s; and he's been pointing a weapon he's unfamiliar with at the man I love! Big Al is throwing his jacket and ridiculous hat into the trunk of the car. He slams the trunk shut. *He's angry. Very angry.* He's still shouting at Miguel and gesticulating as he jumps into the driver's seat, starts up the engine, and accelerates. Dust and small stones shoot from the tires. Miguel flaps his hands in front of his face, waving the dust away. I can imagine how the grit will stick to the sweat trickling along the folds of his flabby face.

With Bud gone, I breathe. My eyes follow the police car along the road, until it's out of sight. Its siren is piercing, without any musical tone; it lashes into the humidity of the afternoon and bounces off the moist air, a dead and mournful sound. By the time I look back down to the street, more people are on the scene. The man with the Tilley hat is helping the woman in the capris to her feet. He's being helped by another woman. This is the first time I've seen her: she's short and round, wearing a floor-length traditional dress. She's about sixty, dark skinned, with black-but-graying hair pulled into a bun on top of her head. She's offering the woman in the capris a glass of water, and I suspect she's something to do with Bob's Bodega, because, together with a dark-skinned man, also in his sixties, she is helping the woman into the bodega in a solicitous manner.

The skinny, pale-skinned man in the Tilley hat is now being joined by two other women, who are rushing from the spa. One is as tall as he is, so she must be about six feet, and I'm guessing she weighs about three hundred pounds, though it's difficult to tell because she's wearing a full-length bright orange, voluminous dress, topped with a matching broad-brimmed orange sunhat. I can't judge her age at all. Beside her is a shorter, trimmer woman, maybe in her fifties or sixties. She's blond and smartly dressed—preppy. She seems to be with the tall, thin Tilley man—their body language screams "couple" when she greets him. The large orange-clad woman clearly knows them both. Everyone seems to know everyone else.

Just as the women join the thin man, they are met by the chef I'd seen in the lane between the buildings. He comes from the end of the building that houses the bodega. It is clear that he knows Miguel, who is waving everyone away from the florist's store, but is, apparently, keen to share information. There is a great deal of breast clutching and head shaking. The women hold their hands to their mouths in horror. The chef shakes a fist at the heavens. Another woman rushes around the bodega end of the building: she's very short, very thin, dressed as though for tennis, and her complexion suggests she's of African descent. She might be in her fifties or sixties. She makes for the short, blond woman. They embrace. They share shock and horror. The large woman in the orange robe waves her arms about, the chef in the red shirt beckons to everyone, and gradually, with Miguel encouraging them, they all go inside the bodega. Just as I decide that I need to think about what it is that Bud called out, I see a tall, overweight man of African descent, wearing a vivid Hawaiian shirt, come barreling around the spa end of the building. He's smiling broadly and opens his arms toward Miguel in a welcoming manner. Miguel speaks to him rapidly, and the big man rushes into the bodega, a look of concern clouding his face.

That's when I call Jack. While we are on the phone I hear a distant siren—probably the vehicle sent to collect the corpse. And that's it. That's all I can recall that might help Bud.

I opened my eyes, adjusted my sunglasses, and lit another cigarette. I realized I'd managed to catch quite a bit of sun on my nose: it was a little tender. So, other than getting sunburned, what had I achieved? I gave my recollections some analytical thought.

Between the time I saw Bud enter the flower shop and the moment I heard the woman scream about three minutes must have elapsed, that's all.

Had Bud fought someone off inside the store? Had he had to kill to save his own life in there? Who lay dead on the floor? How had they died? When had they died? Was there maybe even more than one body in there? And why did Bud have his hands around the person's throat when he was discovered? What had he said to the screaming woman? Would he really not say a word to the police?

Damn and blast! Questions . . . more and more questions!

I looked at my watch. The flight from Vancouver was due to land soon, so I grappled with the luggage again and made my way toward the entrance of the airport. It was busy. I managed to push my way inside—always more difficult when you're trying to get in to the arrivals area—then I hung about, waiting until I could see the pale, stressed faces of Canadians looking forward to a week of sun and margaritas begin to appear. I took my cue, managed to grab a cab without too many problems, made sure the driver knew where I was going, and we set off. This was my third trip along the Jalisco/ Carretera Federal Highway 200 that day, and I was beginning to get the lay of the land. Unfortunately, this was by far the most rapid version of the trip, so I buckled up, tried to hang on, and hoped the cabbie would at least slow down a bit when we came to the Punta de Mita exit. *He didn't.* The reddish-brown hills covered in scrubby green and the fields of blue-green agave planted in rows streaked past in a blur beneath the clear blue sky. The air rushing into the cab smelled of dust, exhaust fumes, and just a little of the sea. I missed Bud's smell. I missed Bud. And I was terrified by my imaginings of what might be happening to him.

Start All Over Again

BY THE TIME WE ARRIVED at the Hacienda Soleado, I was glad to get out of the cab. Bud says I'm a hopeless passenger because I'm a control freak—maybe he has a point. I wrestled with my conscience about a tip—"Drive slower!" didn't seem appropriate—then I balanced the two suitcases and my carry-on tote as close as possible to the doors of the delightfully rustic adobe building that Jack had told me to look out for. The sign beside the door announced AMIGOS DEL TEQUILA. I pushed open one of the heavy wooden double doors and felt the tingle of air conditioning on my damp skin. Lovely!

The place was deserted. In front of me was a long, high bar, behind which were a myriad of glittering bottles, a great number of which were of a similar design—stumpy, with dimples and fat stoppers. Dotted around the cool, red-tiled floor were high marble-topped tables and leather-upholstered bar stools; the white plastered walls were adorned with atmospheric photographs of rows of giant blue agave set in a luminous landscape. I took a moment to decompress.

"Hello?" I called. My voice echoed.

Somewhere beyond the bar a door swung open and smacked against a wall.

"Coming!" A young man appeared around a corner: a tousled mop of unruly blond hair, a lopsided grin, chef whites, and a pair of large hands being wiped on a red cloth. "Can I help?"

I smiled. "Yes, I hope so."

"I'm Tony, Tony Booth," said the charmer, waving a still-damp hand. "I won't shake." He grinned. "Prepping the meat for tonight.

Not quite finished." His accent was American. He didn't look Mexican at all. *Odd for a chef at a Mexican restaurant—in Mexico.*

I suddenly felt nervous. I'm really not used to living a lie. "I'm Cait. Cait Morgan. I'm here to collect the keys for Henry Douglas's place. Do you know about that?" I couldn't be sure that Jack had managed to get through to his friend, or, indeed, that word would have reached the hacienda.

"Yep. Henry called about half an hour ago. Nice for you to be able to get away at such short notice. He said you're a prof. Is that right?"

I forced a smile. "Yes, that's right. At the University of Vancouver." *Stick to the truth whenever possible, Cait.*

"Gimme a sec . . ." said Tony, as he disappeared in the direction from which he'd arrived. He was about thirty, in good shape, with a breezy manner and a surprisingly good tan for a chef—they're usually so pasty. Tony Booth looked as though he'd be more at home on a longboard, riding waves off the Californian coast, than in a Mexican restaurant's kitchen.

"I wrote down the security code," said Tony jauntily, as he handed me a single key on a leather lariat and a scrap of paper with four digits written in what I trusted was red ink.

"Thanks," I said, as cheerily as I imagined a person would if they were arriving for a week's vacation.

"Henry's place is Casa LaLa—you know, 'cause he's from LA? He thinks it's funny. But I guess you know all about his so-called 'sense of humor'?"

"Henry's a friend of a friend, really," I replied. Rather sheepishly as it turned out. *Embrace the lie, Cait.* "But the friend that he's a friend of is quite a . . . unique character."

Tony looked puzzled and a bit concerned. I wondered what my face was doing as I tried to be convincing in my role.

"I guess you could say that about Henry too—well about *all* the FOGTTs."

"FOGTTs?" That wasn't an acronym I'd ever heard before.

Tony smiled and nodded. "The Friends of Good Tequila Trust. That's what these guys are called—the owners here. They each own a share of the place, each have a house on the hacienda; they've each paid their money, and, when we finally make a profit, they'll each get their cut. I don't think it'll be long now: the way this place is set up, and with some good PR in Puerto Vallarta, I reckon the next season could see us break through. The Tequila Soleado they make here is doing pretty well back home in the States."

I tried to look as though I was interested in what the young man was saying, which a casual visitor, whose partner hadn't been locked up for a murder he didn't commit, probably would have been.

"So what do you do here, exactly, Tony?" was all I could pull together by way of small talk.

Tony looked down at his chef whites, resisting the temptation to make a smart crack. "Um, I'm the chef." He smiled and waved his arms as if to signify "Ta-da." I mirrored his smile and felt my eyebrow arch at the inanity of my own question.

"Sorry—it's been a long day already," I said, by way of an excuse.

"Hey, don't worry! I also design the menu and do the shopping at the local markets, so I know how long days can be. If I'm not down in PV—that's what we all call Puerto Vallarta around here, saves us a lot of time in a day," he grinned, "if I'm not there by 6:00 AM, I'm not gonna get the best stuff, so I'm up and at 'em every day." He looked proud.

"And what sort of dishes appear on your menu, Tony?"

"Depends on what's good, and what's freshest, of course," he replied, "but today we'll be having . . . hang on a minute." He scrabbled in the deep pocket in the front of his apron. "Here you go, today's menu. All small plates, you understand. Open 5:00 PM to 11:00 PM, daily."

The young chef handed me a grubby piece of paper upon

which he'd scribbled, almost illegibly, "Roasted ancho, or green tomatillo, salsa with blue corn chips; red snapper ceviche; smoked mussel ceviche tostadas; barbequed pork quesadilla; mushroom empanadas; chicken mole tamales; hahas." I was familiar with most of the items that were listed.

"I didn't realize I was so hungry." I smiled, as my tummy rumbled aloud. "What's a 'haha'? I don't think I've heard of them."

Tony smiled. "The FOGTTs love them. Sort of a coconut, pecan, and chocolate macaroon, and they're rich, small, and very popular with coffee. I won't be making them for a couple of hours yet. Will you come to eat, or at least nibble, this evening?"

With my mouth watering, and the wonderful smells coming from the kitchen making things even worse, I realized that I didn't have a plan. Not a clue about what I was doing, or where, when, or what I was going to eat. It also occurred to me that I was going to be hunkering down in the house of someone who'd left their place for the summer and hadn't expected any guests, so there might not be so much as a bottle of water in Henry's place. *Damn and blast!* I should have thought ahead and brought supplies.

As I stood there, silently accusing myself of rank stupidity and imagining the pathetic little cardboard-flavored chicken wrap I'd stuffed into my pocket, both of the huge doors behind me flew open and a voice bellowed, "Where's Juan? Tony—have you seen Juan?"

I turned and was confronted by a huge figure, black against the brilliant sunlight outside.

"They should bring back the death penalty. It's disgusting that they can get away with this sort of thing! Where's Juan?" *Bossy voice, booming—someone used to getting their own way.*

As my eyes adjusted, and the figure stepped forward, I recognized the large woman dressed in orange I'd seen outside the florist's store earlier in the day.

"I'm sorry, Dorothea," said Tony, fluttering to the woman's side, "I haven't seen him all day. But it *is* Sunday, so he'd probably be in church, or at home . . ."

I took another look at Dorothea. She towered over me, at about six feet to my five three—*five four on a tall day*—and was proportionately large in every way: a big orange hat was stuffed onto a headful of red curls; a voluminous, full-length orange cheesecloth dress was gathered beneath her huge bust. Her flabby, heavily freckled arms were bare—*not a good look*—and, below puffy ankles, her feet were encased in, of all things, gold ballet flats. She looked like one of those wobbling toys that's never supposed to fall down . . . though she looked alarmingly top-heavy and seemed to teeter on her tiny feet.

As I was sizing up Dorothea, it seemed she was doing the same to me.

"Who are you?" she asked imperiously, peering at me over her sunglasses.

"Cait. Cait Morgan." The peering was working. I felt intimidated.

"Well, Cait, that's nice for you. Why are you here? Those your bags outside? Staying somewhere here? Friends with one of the FOGTTs? Have you seen Juan? Do you even know who he is?"

It was like being fired at by a machine gun. I decided to give as good as I'd got.

"Vacation. Yes. Casa LaLa. Henry Douglas is a friend of a friend. No, and no."

I smiled as sweetly as I could when she seemed taken aback.

She gave me a look that informed me she was ignoring me. "So, Tony, no sign of Juan? We have to get hold of him. Can't you phone him?"

"You know he never answers the cell phone he has, *and* you know his house doesn't have a phone," replied Tony, as patiently as a saint. "Why do you need him . . . on his one day off?"

Dorothea gave me a sideways glance. "There's news he must hear. Not good news. Haven't you *heard?*" She seemed incredulous.

Tony shifted uncomfortably. "No, Dorothea, I haven't heard anything. You know that Sundays are busy for me. I've been out at the market, then in the kitchen all morning. What's happened?" His patience seemed to be wearing thin.

I judged Dorothea to be a woman who would always want to be whispering some tasty tidbit of gossip to a confidante—loud enough so that everyone in the room could hear.

As she planned her next words, she brushed imaginary motes from her arm and adjusted her hat. She was preening.

"It's awful. Juan's daughter, Margarita. *Dead.*" She uttered her final word with all the dramatic import you'd expect from a Wagnerian diva, shaking her head tragically, her arms falling limply to her sides, as lifeless as the woman about whom she was speaking.

"*What?* Margarita? Dead?" Tony sounded shocked. "What happened?"

Dorothea took off her sunglasses and looked me straight in the eye. "I'm not sure I should talk about it in front of a stranger." Her gaze was not kind. Her face made me think of a frowning pug.

I sensed a critical moment. "Oh, don't worry, I'm just leaving," I said, as pleasantly as I could. "I'm going to be here for the next week, Dorothea, so if this tragedy is a local one, I'm sure I'll hear all about it from someone else." I knew she wouldn't be able to resist.

She gave it a split second's thought and took the bait. "You're right, so you both might as well hear it from me." Dorothea drew conspiratorially close to us. I noticed that she wasn't just completely outfitted in orange, but she actually smelled of the fruit too. *Weird.*

"It's terrible. *Godawful.* Don't panic, my dear," she said, looking down at me, and even daring to pat me on the shoulder, "they've got the guy who did it. She had her throat slit, poor woman. He just walked into her store, bold as you like, in broad daylight, and slit her throat. Serena saw him do it. And Al and Miguel caught him red-handed. Literally. He was *covered* in poor Margarita's blood. Oh my sweet Lord. Just awful."

"You say someone saw a man slit this Margarita's throat?" I couldn't help but jump in.

"Well, *as good as,*" replied Dorothea grudgingly. "Serena opened the door to Margarita's place and there he was, strangling her on the floor."

"I thought you said he cut her throat?" Tony seemed confused.

"Yes. *And* he strangled her." Dorothea spoke with authority.

"Who *is* he? Why would anyone want to kill Margarita? Let alone cut her throat *and* strangle her?" Tony was asking all the questions I wanted answered myself. Excellent.

Dorothea looked annoyed. "I don't know who he is." She sounded terribly disappointed. "No one's seen him around before, and Miguel told us he didn't say anything. Nothing at all. He'd been in Bob's Bodega just before he did it. There he asked, in Spanish, for roses. Which Bob didn't have, of course. The man picked up some beers, some chocolate bars, some chips, paid in cash, and left. Seems he went right into Margarita's store next door and killed her, just like that. Oh, by the way, dear," Dorothea addressed me directly, "just so you know, Margarita is the daughter of the guy who looks after all the agave plants here, our jimador." She emphasized the H sound at the beginning of the word—*even her breath smells of oranges.* "Margarita's a florist . . . well, I guess you'd call her a plantswoman, really. Lovely girl. Real green thumb, you know the type. Can grow anything. And she did great flowers. Did that arrangement over there, in fact." As she made her surprisingly generous comments, she waved her arm toward a tall, slim vase holding one perfect Bird of Paradise flower, a palm frond, and some stones. It didn't look as though it would take an enormous artistic talent to put those elements together, but I reasoned that maybe simplicity was a virtue.

"I can't believe it. She was just here—yesterday," said Tony, shaking his head. "She brought over her accounts for Callie to work on last night. I know that Margarita and Juan didn't get along, but this'll hit him. She's still his daughter, after all. Hey—I'd better call Callie. She's got a meeting with another of her accountancy clients down in PV this afternoon, so she won't have heard. It'd be best if she got the news from me. Callie and Margarita get . . . *got* along real well. Oh, this is awful. My poor wife'll be beside herself. So, what's the full story, Dorothea? Callie's bound to ask. When did all this happen?"

"Eleven. Almost on the dot. *Terrible*," replied Dorothea, pushing an escaping curl of suspiciously red hair under her hat.

Luckily, given that I wasn't supposed to know what had happened, I managed to stop myself from telling her that everything had kicked off just after noon—*I heard the clock strike twelve myself.* I began to wonder why Dorothea would lie about Margarita's time of death. My thought process was interrupted by the arrival of two more people I'd spotted at the crime scene: the tall, thin man in the Tilley hat and the short, slim woman who'd greeted him so warmly outside the florist's store. They entered the restaurant together, and rather less dramatically than the flamboyant Dorothea.

"Ah, you're here, Dorothea. Of course," said the woman.

"Yes, Ada. I thought Juan might be here. He should be told what's happened."

"I see . . ." said Ada. She looked at me and offered her hand. "Hello, I'm Ada Taylor, and this is my husband, Frank. Are you, umm . . . ?" Her non-question hung in the air.

I shook her hand—*cool skin, well moisturized, firm grip; she smells of a light, floral scent.* I smiled. "I'm Cait Morgan. I'm going to be staying at Casa LaLa, Henry's place, for a week." I was getting quite used to using my unknown host's name.

"Nice to meet you. Though what a day you've chosen to arrive," replied Ada. She gave Dorothea a sideways glance and added, "I expect you've heard the bad news?" Her expression told me she was in no doubt about my answer, and her accent had already informed me that she was Canadian.

I nodded. "Yes. It sounds awful. Though Dorothea here was just telling us that the police have got their man. Do you know where they've taken him?" I had to take this chance to find out what I could.

Ada opened her mouth to reply, but Dorothea jumped in before she had a chance to utter a word. "Off to the local cells, Miguel said. Came into Bob's Bodega all flustered, saying they'd have to keep him there for a few days. He didn't like the idea of working extra hours to keep an eye on the murdering . . ." She paused and shook her head, as if to rid herself of the expletive she'd mentally managed to delete. "Apparently, some major drug thing went down this morning, and all the prisons from here to Guadalajara are full of gun runners, drug dealers, and the like. Hang the lot of 'em, I say. Though hanging's too good for some. They've completely spoiled the country for people like us."

"You have a point, Dorothea, but maybe they've spoiled it even more for the Mexicans themselves?" responded Ada quietly. "They're the ones who *really* suffer. We can all come and go as we please, after all. This is their home, dear."

Dorothea shrugged, as though the undeniable problem that Mexico faces when it comes to drug-running, and the terrible violence that accompanies it, was designed to specifically inconvenience her, and her alone.

"Hey, we don't talk about all that stuff, right, Ada?" said Frank Taylor. He'd removed his Tilley hat to reveal an almost bald head, which still sported a crescent of well-trimmed gray hair. He wiped the top of his head with his free hand, then held it out toward me. I hesitated for a moment before shaking it warmly. *Firm shake, kind brown eyes, a rather officious, outdoorsy air, and an incongruous whiff of cigars.*

"Hello, Frank. Nice to meet you." I smiled. "So why aren't the *local* cells full of the drug-runners?" I wasn't going to be sidetracked, so I looked directly at Dorothea as I spoke.

"Oh, it's too old. Quite cute, but old." Dorothea's reply was intriguing.

"What Dorothea means to say," added Frank, "is that we have some municipal jail cells in our very own police station, which, unusually, is housed within our very own town hall. I don't know how much Henry's told you about our little haven, but it's got quite the unique history you know—"

"Oh, come on now, Frank," interrupted his wife. "Cait's obviously come here on vacation. Let the poor woman get on with it. I'm sure she doesn't want one of your lectures on Punta de las Rocas's history. Want a hand to Henry's place with those bags you've got outside? How long are you staying, by the way?"

I decided to go with the flow of the conversation, for the moment. "Oh, just a week," I replied.

"All that baggage outside for a week!" replied Frank. Ada gave him a sideways glance that clearly communicated, "Don't be so rude!" Frank had the good manners to look sheepish.

I didn't have to respond, because our group was joined by yet another arrival. And this was someone I was relieved and terrified, in equal measure, to see.

The policeman I'd come to think of as Big Al entered the restaurant. No longer in his fancy uniform, his light gray pants and short-sleeved, crisp white shirt seemed much more practical, though his heavy gun belt and the glittering gold epaulets on his shirt definitely marked him out as law enforcement. He was hatless, and pulled off his sunglasses as he walked in.

He stopped just inside the doors, allowing them to close behind him. He squinted for a moment, then nodded to each of us. As his gaze rested upon me, I noticed a puzzled expression pass over his face like a shadow. "I can't find Juan. Any of you guys seen him?" His voice was a light tenor, not unpleasant. What was most surprising was his accent—not a hint of Spanish about it. As I took in his appearance, I noted other unusual features: his hair was fine and light, his eyes were a definite green, and he had excellent even, white teeth. I put him in his mid-thirties. *Really not a bad looking guy, if you like that sort of thing . . . very young, of course.* But that accent? Those eyes? How could a municipal cop in Mexico look and sound so American? I was beginning to realize how un-Mexican the whole place felt. I reminded myself that this was a hacienda owned by a group of ex-pat investors, but, surely, the cops would be locals?

"None of us has seen Juan," replied Dorothea on behalf of the group.

"I thought he might be at home, or in church?" offered Tony, who'd been quiet for a while.

"I tried both places. No sign. Thought he might be here," replied Big Al.

"Unlikely, on his day off," responded Frank Taylor, his wife nodding her agreement.

Big Al nodded and put his hands on his hips. "I guess you know what all this is about?" he asked, looking directly at me. Once again he had an unusual look on his face. Clearly the man was thinking about something other than our main topic of conversation. He might be facing a grim task, but he was distracted.

I felt a blush well up from somewhere deep inside me. *Oh dear!* "Dorothea told us," I replied, as truthfully as I could. I'm not really cut out for lying to policemen.

"Al, you don't know who our guest is. She's going to be staying at Henry's place for the next week," announced Dorothea, with obvious glee. As I looked at her again, I felt some sympathy for the woman begin to creep over me. Dorothea seemed compelled to make herself the center of attention, which spoke to my internal psychologist of a child who'd been ignored or, maybe because of her size, had been the center of attention for all the wrong reasons. Either way, I felt I should make an effort to temper my judgmental attitude toward the woman.

Big Al shook his head and held up his hand, indicating that Dorothea should be quiet. She was, but she looked crestfallen. Tapping his teeth with the end of an arm of his sunglasses, Big Al looked sternly at Dorothea. "Don't tell me, Ms. Simmonds. Don't tell me!" He returned his attention to me. "I've seen this woman's face somewhere before, but I can't quite remember where it was. Just give me a moment . . ."

I could feel my heart thump in my chest. What if he'd looked up from the crime scene and spotted me in the window? What if I'd already given away my link to the resort on the coast, and my connection to Bud?

We all waited while Big Al narrowed his eyes and sucked on the arm of his sunglasses. *Yuk!*

"Got it!" he exclaimed. Every face conveyed anticipation. I suspected mine portrayed something closer to fear, however hard I tried to look like the rest of the group. "I know exactly who she is." He smiled at me, enigmatically, as he spoke, looking me up and down. "This is Doctor Caitlin Morgan, a professor at the school of criminology at the University of Vancouver. A specialist in criminal psychology, she's done some fascinating work in the still-controversial field of victim profiling. I must say that her arrival here, today of all days, is . . . very interesting."

His words hung in the air as all eyes turned toward me.

Getting Into It

I'M RARELY SPEECHLESS. I THINK the general opinion among my students would be that I'm *never* lost for words. But as the group took in the announcement about who I was, and what I did, I felt my mouth dry up. I swallowed, hard, and mustered a weak smile.

"How on earth do you know all that about me?" I asked the now much more menacing policeman. *Had* he seen me at the condo window? Even if he had, how would he know who I was?

As Al peered at me, he nodded. "I know a great deal more about you than that," he replied ominously.

"*Really?*" I squeaked.

"But I am being rude." He smiled. *Shark teeth.* "I know who *you* are, but you don't know who I am. Allow me to introduce myself," he saluted, hand to his forehead, "Alberto Jesus Beselleu Torres, captain of law enforcement for the municipality of Punta de las Rocas. If folks around here are feeling especially formal, they call me Captain Al. Of course, if someone's feeling intimidated by my presence, they tend to call me Captain Torres. At your service, Doctor Morgan." He stood to attention and bowed at the waist.

"Oh, please, Cait. Call me Cait. I'm not that keen on being *Doctor* Morgan inside the university, let alone when I'm away from the place. So please, everyone," I tried to catch each member of our group with what I hoped was a winning smile, "it's just Cait. Cait Morgan. Thanks." I tried to maintain the smile as I added, "So how did you come to know who I am?" *No point beating about the bush.*

Al relaxed his formal stance and smiled broadly, and more genuinely, I thought. "I wish I could say I possess cop-telepathy, Cait, but I recognized your face from a photograph on your university's website. I am taking some criminology classes at the university in Guadalajara, and yours is a very good school, with a reputation to which our little department aspires. Your work on victimology, and the theories that came out of your school some years ago on geographic profiling, is fascinating."

Again, I could feel a blush rise on my cheeks. I'm not very good at accepting compliments. *Not really used to them, I suppose.*

"Thanks," was all I could summon. *Thank heavens that's the only place you've seen me,* was what flitted through my mind.

"So what brings such a well-known criminologist to our little out-of-the-way bit of paradise?" Al asked the obvious, if undesirable, question.

"She's a friend of a friend of Henry's," butted in Dorothea, aiming to re-establish her position as local know-it-all as rapidly as possible. "Isn't that right, Cait?" She beamed at me, glowing with proprietorial pride.

"Yes," I replied. Monosyllabic responses seemed safest.

"Well, it's auspicious," observed Al. "We've all suffered a great loss this morning, as you've heard. A valued and much-loved member of our community, Margarita Rosa García Martinez, a wonderful and irreplaceable woman, was found murdered. I have the perpetrator in custody, a circumstance I would like to boast was due to excellence in police work, but, really, I just happened to be on the scene at the time."

I have to take my chance!

"That's certainly our good fortune, Al. I've been told that the man in question . . . do you have his name yet, by the way?" I tried to make it sound like a throwaway question that had just occurred to me.

Al shook his head. "No," he replied, looking grim.

"Oh, right," I said, trying to make sure I didn't give away my relief, then continued, "I've been told that the man in question cut the throat of your, um, friend, and then strangled her. Can that be true?"

Al's face cracked into a wry grin. "I know it seems unlikely, but Margarita's throat was certainly slashed, and the man was found with his hands around her neck. One could surmise that he was finishing off the job, to be sure she was dead . . . or maybe he thought better of his actions and was trying to save her—"

"Oh, come off it!" interrupted Dorothea loudly. "Serena said he was throttling the life out of her!"

"He *could* have been trying to save her," said Tony.

"Rubbish!" exploded Dorothea. "If he wanted to save her, then why did he cut her throat in the first place?"

"Maybe he didn't." It was out before I could stop myself. *Damn and blast! Shut up, Cait.*

"What do you mean, Cait?" asked Al, as everyone once again gave me their unwanted attention.

Yes, what do you mean, you stupid blabbermouth? I composed myself as much as possible. *Think! Deflect!* In a split second I decided upon a course of action, then threw myself into it.

"Forgive me," I said, as gently as I could. "I know I'm a new arrival here, and I am mindful of the fact that you all knew Margarita and have feelings for her. As Al has told you all, I'm a person who focuses on victims—I consider their life and lifestyle, their habits, their history, their families and friends to help me, and those in law enforcement, build a better picture of why and how they might have ended up becoming a victim. None of this is to imply that they chose to become a victim, of course," I added hurriedly, as this is one of the criticisms of my discipline that I hear most often. "Certainly I have colleagues whose life's work is to look into the backgrounds of the criminals. But I look to the victim. Now, in this instance, you might not know anything about the man you have in custody, but you all know a great deal about the victim. And that knowledge could lead us to discover who the murderer really is . . . and why Margarita, apparently, had her throat slashed *and* was strangled."

"But we *know* who the killer is," shouted Dorothea. I wondered if she had any idea how to use a normal speaking voice. "It's that *horrible* man!"

I didn't like to hear Bud spoken of that way: I worked hard to prevent my expression from betraying my feelings toward Dorothea. My sympathies toward her were evaporating.

"I think that Cait means we can find out who the killer *really* is, rather than who the *real* killer is, isn't that right, Cait?" Frank Taylor leaped to my defense.

He was totally wrong, of course, but I didn't want anyone to know that. "That's exactly right," I said as brightly as possible.

"Ah, if only we could afford to retain the services of the famous Professor Morgan," said Al, watching my eyebrow rise, "but Cait Morgan, the private individual, is here for a vacation, not to work on a case." He looked a little disappointed.

I decided to go in for the kill. Obviously this man was ambitious, otherwise why would a local cop in one of Mexico's smallest municipalities be a part-time criminology student? He must want to better himself. I saw how I could insert myself into the case, find out who had really killed Margarita, *and* clear Bud. I had to be careful to go about things the right way. I didn't want to appear to be too keen to get involved, but I also didn't want to put him off to the point where he'd feel guilty about accepting my insights.

"You know what," I opened, "it sounds like a fascinating case. With all due respect to the late Margarita and you, her friends, I think I would find it an interesting challenge, that is if you don't mind me asking you lots of questions about Margarita, her life, and maybe even your lives?"

There were general shrugs around the room. I noticed, out of the corner of my eye, that Al had the look of a hungry man eyeing up a meal.

"I wouldn't want to impose," he said quietly.

"So you think you can work out who this murderer is, just by asking us all a bunch of questions?" asked Frank Taylor hesitantly.

Al managed a weak smile—and a slight eye-roll—in my direction. I stepped up. "Not exactly. What I do is try to understand the life of the victim, because this often opens up possible reasons for them having been killed. You see, without giving you the full lecture on the subject, more often than not there is some link between a victim and the person who killed them. This is especially the case when it comes to premeditated murder. Most murders are carried out by someone very close to the victim—a spouse, family member, or very close friend. That's where most investigations start, and where I'd start too: with the victim's closest family and friends."

"But Margarita couldn't possibly have *known* the man that Al has in custody, or someone would have recognized him. Oh!" Dorothea dramatically clapped her hand to her forehead. "Of course—he's a hit man, that'll be it!" She looked triumphant for an instant, then crestfallen. "But why? Why would a hit man come here to kill Margarita?"

"We don't know *everything* about Margarita," said Ada Taylor quite timidly. She seemed surprised to discover she'd spoken aloud.

Frank took his chance to leap to his wife's defense. "That's true, Dorothea. We all knew her, to some degree or other, but that's really just her professional life, you know, her flowers, her plants, and her photography."

Photography? Interesting.

"Yes," agreed Ada, spurred on by her husband's support, "I've never even met her at a social engagement when she wasn't involved in the event in some way—doing the flowers or taking the photos.

In fact, I have no real idea about the woman, or her interests, outside of her jobs."

Dorothea looked ready to shout something at us all when Tony spoke up. He had a way of disappearing into the background that I suspected came from having been in the food service industry for years. "Callie knows . . . *knew* Margarita quite well. She liked her. It's funny, though, we were saying only the other day how very private she was. She wasn't chatty when she was doing her floral work, or her photography, or even on occasions like last night, when she brought all her accounts for Callie to work through. In the past year of their being what folks would call 'close,' Callie's only ever been inside Margarita's home once, and that was because she'd offered to help carry some equipment to her van."

I allowed the conversation to develop. It was interesting to see this group gradually realize that they'd hardly known the woman who a few moments earlier they were sure they'd all understood.

I noticed that Al's eyes were darting around the group as people spoke. He was nodding his head. "You're all right, of course," he said. "Even as I was driving her killer to the police station, I thought about how little people here knew of the real woman." *An interesting choice of words.* He looked at me. "Cait, it's clear that in just a few moments you've made people think about this in a way that we might never have done. If you feel you could bear to give up some of your free time to help me gain some perspective on this, I'd value your input. It won't be for long. I'll be handing the guy over to the Federales the day after tomorrow. They reckon that by then they'll have cleared out enough of the people they rounded up in the dawn raids this morning for there to be room in the system for him. Since I'm stuck with him until then, it would be a great comfort to our community if I could use that time to maybe work out who he is, and why he killed Margarita."

And it wouldn't be too bad for your career, would it Captain Torres? I thought, as I smiled sweetly.

"I'd be grateful for the chance to get to Casa LaLa, maybe wash and brush up a bit, and unpack a few things first, but I don't see why we can't just dive straight in," I replied.

Al beamed. "I'll give you a hand with your bags, then I'll go find Juan and break the news. How about I pick you up here at 5:00 PM?"

I checked my watch.

"Okay, that would be great. Thanks. Do I walk to Casa LaLa from here . . . ?" I wasn't really sure how to finish my sentence as I didn't know what my alternatives were.

"No need to drive, it's the nearest building to this one. Just a five minute walk," replied Tony. "You have the key I gave you?" I nodded. "And the code is for the alarm, which has a pad right inside the front door. The water boys will be there tomorrow, so would you like to take some bottles for now?"

"The water boys?" I was puzzled.

Tony smiled. "Yeah, every Monday, Thursday, and Saturday morning they bring water for the water coolers in the houses and take the used containers. Since Henry wasn't expecting you, he didn't hold on to any containers, so they'll bring you two tomorrow—I'll sort that for you. Then you'll have a spare. If you can be at home around 8:00 AM the guy can show you how to put the bottle onto the unit that cools and dispenses it. It's not complicated. You just put the empty where he tells you, and they replace it next time they call. If you need extra, just let me know. But, like I say, I'm guessing there won't be anything at Henry's place at all, so why not take a few bottles now, to pop in the fridge? I'm sure you'll find your way around his place okay. The pool boy comes on Friday and Monday, so he'll show up tomorrow morning, but you don't need to be there for him. He has a key and his own code."

Oh, my very own pool! The thought gave me pleasure. Even

though I can't swim, I enjoy the way a pool catches and plays with the light, and, if it's shallow enough, I can always have a little dunk. Then I immediately remembered poor Bud's plight, and my priorities—*no dunking for me!*

"Thanks, Tony. Maybe I'll see you later for a bite to eat. We'll see how my time goes with Al, okay?" My smile was genuine as I was remembering the menu I'd read.

"Sure thing. If no one else needs me right now, I'd really like to call Callie. I think I've got the full picture. She'll be devastated by the news, but it'll be worse if she hears it from someone else." Tony was trying to get Dorothea, Frank, and Ada to leave, and they took the hint.

"Absolutely, Tony. You've got a busy day ahead of you, I'm sure," said Frank, as he began to usher his wife toward the door. "Come along, Dorothea, we'll let this young man get on with his work. We retired folk have nothing better to do with our time than sit about, but he's got to get ready to feed us all tonight. It would be great if you could join us, Cait. We all eat here most evenings, even if it's just to see each other and catch up on the gossip." His expression changed from jovial to embarrassed as he uttered his last words.

"Oh, Frank," remonstrated his wife.

"Everyone knows what I mean," replied a red-faced Frank. Looking at me he added, "It's always fun to have the chance to catch up with a fellow Canadian. Did you know our place is called Casa Canuck?" He grinned. "You a hockey fan, Cait? Get to many of those Vancouver Canucks games?"

"Not on my money, and with the prices of the tickets," I replied, maybe a little too quickly.

"Quite right," said Ada. "We watch most of the games here, on satellite," she added. "Sometimes it feels like we live in a very sunny Prince George, almost like we never left home."

"So you're from Prince George?" I attempted to sound politely interested.

Frank replied, "I had a brewery there, family business. Ada was the local butcher's daughter. It was a match made in heaven: beer and beef! The kids wanted nothing to do with it, so I sold up. Now I'm spending their inheritance. They didn't want to put in the work, so they won't get the profits. Besides, if our son wants to be an eternal kid and our daughter wants to double the world population with that tofu-eating husband of hers, good luck to 'em, but they can do it on their own. I worked my way up from the bottom—my father made sure I did every job there was before he let me have any management responsibility. But kids these days . . ."

"Oh come on, Frank. Cait wants to get settled, and she doesn't need to hear all about how our son and daughter have, apparently, let you down. Not now, and probably not ever." She patted her husband's arm, then looked at me. "Our children wanted their own lives, Cait, and that's that. If you start talking to him about hockey, or anything else remotely Canadian, then you'll only have yourself to blame if you're trapped for several hours." She smiled at me, then at her husband. "Don't say you weren't warned. Come on now, Frank, let's get home and get a few laps in at the pool before we change for appies." She led her husband out into the blinding daylight.

As Dorothea trailed behind them, a performer without an audience, Al looked at me and said, "Okay, let's get you installed, then I can go and do my very unpleasant duty."

We walked outside, the wooden doors closing heavily behind us, and we both shoved sunglasses onto our noses. Al wheeled my suitcase, I wheeled Bud's.

"You don't travel light, do you?" Al observed, smiling.

Two Days

THE EXTERIOR OF CASA LALA promised rustic comfort inside: vivid pink bougainvillea clambered up the adobe walls, almost reaching the terra-cotta tiles of the roof. Geckos scuttled as we approached. However, once inside, it was clear that Henry Douglas, the home's owner, had a preference for the minimalist approach to decor. *Shame—in my book clutter is joy.* White walls floated, unadorned, between a very dark wood ceiling and floor. The furnishings, such as they were, popped in cream or white against the flooring. I found the bedroom, with its en suite facilities, dumped Bud's suitcase into the closet, and then riffled through my own to find something that wasn't in need of an iron. Fifteen minutes later I was fresh from the shower, with clean hair pulled back into a pony-tail, sporting cream capris, a cream and lemon over-shirt, and cream sandals. I transferred everything I thought I might need from my carry-on tote to my cream crocheted purse—a Christmas gift from my crocheting/knitting sister in Australia, who knows that all my fingers become thumbs when needles or hooks are involved—and allowed myself a few more moments to explore the outdoor areas of my temporary home.

I noted that almost every flat surface inside the house, as well as the stark metal table on the stone patio outside, had a heavy glass ashtray on it. Clearly Henry was a smoker. But it still didn't seem right to me to smoke inside his home, so I plopped myself onto an angular steel chair next to the patio table and lit a cigarette. The outdoor space was even more minimalist than inside: stuccoed walls, painted in vivid, clashing colors, and one giant blue agave in a painted pot were all that surrounded the small, perfectly square pool. It all seemed somehow familiar. *Got it!* Luis Barragán, the famous architect from Guadalajara whose garden designs were almost a legend. Given that Barragán had died in the 1980s, and this renovation of an old building hadn't been undertaken until a few—maybe five—years ago, based on all the technology that was wired into every minimalist corner, it must be the owner's homage to the man. Or that of his designer. It was oddly pleasant, this vivid nothingness, with the shadows cast by one wall onto another providing ever-moving angles of shade against light. I was seeing the design in the light that Barragán had grown up with, had designed for. I hadn't understood it before. It reminded me that context is critical.

That had been the case that morning. The woman who'd screamed had seen Bud in a situation where she believed he was killing her friend, so she *saw* a killer. I, on the other hand, knew that if Margarita had suffered a slashed throat, then Bud had been on his knees with his hands around her throat trying to save the poor woman. *Context.* And context comes from knowledge that you do, or do not, possess. Sitting at that table I understood, as never before, that Barragán's designs worked for gardens within the context for which they'd been conceived. As light played against shade, the striking palette of the walls allowed my brain to conjure up floral displays, without there being any. I had gained a unique insight from a new experience. I might not be able to go around telling everyone that I knew that Bud was innocent, but I could, maybe, change the context of his discovery.

I unscrewed the top of a bottle of chilled water, scrabbled in my purse for a notebook and pen, put my reading specs on, lit another cigarette, and got to work. Before I called Jack White, I needed to get a few things straight. I wrote down a list of key points from my recollections at the airport.

I now knew that Margarita had had her throat slashed and realized that if Bud had thought he could help her, she must have received her injury moments before he stepped into her flower shop. The severing of a carotid artery means that the heart pumps blood out of the body fast. *Very fast.* With a reduced, or no, supply of blood returning to the heart, the body shuts down very quickly. Depending on whether she'd received a nick to one carotid or had had both completely slashed, she'd have been dead in anything from one and five minutes or so. The killer must have been very close by when Bud discovered her.

I'd been looking out of the window when Bud entered the bodega, and I hadn't noticed any activity inside Margarita's store at that time. I had seen Bud go inside her store. I had to assume that Margarita was already fatally injured by that time, and that Bud had immediately tried to help her. So the killer had struck sometime during the period when Bud was inside the bodega. That meant that either the killer had been hiding somewhere inside Margarita's shop when Bud was hauled off, or they had exited by another door.

I again pictured the street where it had all happened. I hadn't been looking at the scene every moment, but I could make up a timeline of activity. I could also list everyone I'd seen in close enough proximity to the flower shop that they could be a legitimate suspect. *And* I could eliminate some people from that list. That would be a start. I checked my watch. I had fifty minutes before I was due to meet Captain Al at Tony's Amigos del Tequila restaurant, so, rather than making more lists, I decided to call Jack. I was anxious to find out what was happening at his end of things, though I felt a lot less stressed knowing that I had a plan in place to help Bud.

Before I dialed Jack, I gave some thought to what I should, and shouldn't, tell him. Given that he'd been all in favor of me fleeing the country, I couldn't imagine he'd be enamored of the idea that I was now going to work on the case with the police. I decided to make up my mind when I got a sense of his mood, so I glugged my water, then called him.

Sheila answered the phone. She sounded breathless. In the background I could hear barking, and I was pretty sure I could pick out Marty's operatic woofs within the din.

"You sound busy," I observed.

"Oh, Cait . . ." was all Sheila managed before she burst into tears.

The pit of my stomach knew even before my brain did that this wasn't a good sign.

"Sheila—what's wrong? What's happened?" It was foolish to speculate, but it's amazing how many disastrous scenarios you can run through in the time it takes someone to blow their nose.

"The ambulance just left. I couldn't go with them because of the dogs. Sandra is on her way over to look after them, then I'm going to meet Jack at the hospital. They're driving him to the ER at Abbotsford Hospital. It's his heart. Oh, Cait, I'm so frightened."

So was I. But for different reasons.

I took a deep breath. I owed it to Sheila to give her what she needed, instead of looking for help for Bud.

"Sheila, if Sandra's coming, could she bring her daughter with her—you know, the eldest one? She could look after the dogs, and maybe Sandra could drive you to the hospital? I'm not sure you should be behind the wheel right now." Sheila's wonderful, and capable, but a bit prone to fuss. I could imagine how much of a state she must have been in at that moment. "Can't you leave the dogs alone for a while? I'm sure they'll be fine if they've been fed. Just put them out in their compound like usual." I knew the dogs would cope—Marty loves to run and play with Jack and Sheila's three animals—but I hadn't counted on her response.

"That's just it, I can't. Daisy, you know, our biggest girl, went and got herself caught on the compound fence somehow, and Jack was cutting her out when the whole thing collapsed and he fell down the bank to the creek. It wasn't until the dogs came rushing in that I realized anything was wrong. If it hadn't been for them, I wouldn't have looked for Jack until his dinner was ready, and by then he might have been . . . oh dear. Anyway, the dogs are all completely freaked. When I found Jack, it was clear that he'd done more than broken his arm—"

"Jack's broken his arm?" *Poor thing!*

"Yes, I could see the bone . . ."

My toes curled at the thought. Put me in a room with buckets of blood and I'm fine, but there's something about bones poking through flesh, or even the thought of it, that turns my stomach and makes my feet go all tense and tingly.

"I didn't notice his ankle. They think it's broken too. It was his face that frightened me, Cait, not his body. He was gray. And yellowish. *Terrible.* I thought he was . . . oh dear. So I called 911. I stayed with him. The dogs were all over us, licking him and fussing. Of course they were clambering all over me, too. Oh, Cait, I didn't know what to *do.* By the time the paramedics got to us, I thought for sure they were too late but they said he's stable. They aren't sure how big a heart attack it was, because he might have lost consciousness due to a concussion. But the dogs? They're going nuts. I can't leave them, because the fence is down. I swear they wanted to get into the ambulance with Jack."

Knowing that Marty had almost been killed by a bullet when he tried to save Bud's wife, I could well understand how four dogs could become more than a little fractious if their beloved human was injured and taken from them. I got Sheila's point. Bless her, she was putting the dogs' needs ahead of her own, because she must have yearned to be in that ambulance beside the man she loved.

I faced a dilemma. Jack White had cheated death after a nasty accident, it seemed. The man I loved was still locked up for a crime he hadn't committed. Jack had been a lifeline for Bud that I'd been counting on. Did I dare ask Sheila if Jack had managed to do anything on Bud's behalf before he'd been injured? I was torn. Poor Jack. Poor Sheila. My poor Bud. I made a decision.

"Sheila, I'm so sorry to hear what's happened. And I'm sorry I'm not there to help. I know your friends will rally around to support you—and I know you have a lot of friends. You deserve them: you guys are so giving and selfless. But—I have to ask—since I'm not going to be able to talk to Jack, do you know if he managed to speak to anyone about Bud? Is there *anything* he told you? I'm sorry to ask, Sheila, at a time like this, but I have to. *For Bud's sake."* I felt guilty, yet driven.

Sheila blew her nose again. "Don't be silly, dear. *Of course* you have to ask. All I can tell you is that Jack sent you an email. He said that it was best to get everything in writing, so he did all that before he realized that Daisy was tangled up in the fence. She's fine, by the way. No damage. Lord knows how she managed it. So check your email, and there'll be something from him there. I know he booked a flight to Puerto Vallarta tomorrow afternoon, but, of course, he won't be coming now. And . . . oh, there's Sandra coming up the drive now, dear. I have to go, okay?"

"Go, Sheila. Give Jack my love—give him *our* love. And don't give us another thought. Tell him I'm on it. I'm more than capable of sorting this out. He's not to worry about Bud, or me, and he's to concentrate on getting better. And Sheila, that goes for you too, *right?"*

"You're a good girl, Cait. I'll let you know how Jack is when I can. Bye for now."

Being referred to as a "girl" made me smile, but that was all I had to smile about. Of course, I felt sorry for Jack, and I hoped he was going to be alright, but honestly, this additional disaster could not have happened at a worse time.

I sprang up, darted inside Casa LaLa, and checked for a computer. Bud and I had agreed to not bring any equipment on vacation except our phones, so it was all well and good that Jack had sent me an email, but I had no way to access my accounts. *Typical!*

I checked what might be referred to as the usual places for any sort of computer, and even hunted in the cupboards and drawers—*you're clutching at straws now, Cait Morgan*—but I couldn't find a computer anywhere. All I came up with was a wireless keyboard, tucked into a drawer in the unit that sat beneath the huge flat-screen TV, which was suspended on the wall in front of the cream leather sofa.

I managed to work out how to turn on the TV, fiddled about with the remote control, and finally established that there *was* some way to get the keyboard working with the TV, and that maybe, if I just hung in there, I could find a way to get to the internet and then my email. But it wasn't to be—*of course!*—because just then someone knocked at the door.

I put down the keyboard and tried to look as smiley and polite as possible as I opened the door. There stood Frank and Ada Taylor with their hands full of carrier bags. Frank's Tilley hat was perched on his head at a jaunty angle, and Ada was looking almost manically cheerful.

"We brought supplies!" announced Frank jovially.

All I could do was invite them in, take the bags, thanking them profusely and telling them that they "shouldn't have," and pack everything into the fridge and cupboards. They were so sweet, and Ada was the epitome of the sort of woman you rarely notice, until you spot the fact that order reigns supreme thanks to her efforts. She reminded me of Sheila, but without the element of "fusspot."

"We know you're meeting Al later, but we thought you could do with a proper welcome," said Ada, shutting a cupboard door one last time, and presenting me with a dish of nuts, and some sliced fruit.

My polite gene kicked in. "Would you like a drink?" I asked. I grinned as I added, "Some very kind Canadians I know have supplied me with juice, wine, soda, and beer—so you have a choice."

Frank and Ada smiled at my attempt at humor.

"Juice for me, thank you, dear, though I usually prefer tea. Unfortunately, we didn't have an unopened box I could bring you, I'm so sorry. I find tea very soothing and even cooling, don't I, Frank? I'll have juice for now," replied Ada. "Shall I help myself?"

I nodded. "And you, Frank? Can I tempt you into having a beer with me?" *What are you thinking, Cait Morgan? You need a clear head!*

Frank glanced at his wife. "No thanks, Cait. Juice will be fine for me too," he half nodded toward Ada, "at least, I'm sure that's what the wife thinks."

"True," replied Ada as she poured a second glass. "And for you, Cait? Do I take it you fancy a beer?"

I looked at the bottles in the fridge and gave it some serious consideration. I knew I shouldn't. "Thanks, but I'll stick with juice too. I'll want a clear head for my conversations with Al about Margarita."

I wanted to get to the subject of the murder as quickly as possible. Bud didn't have time for me to be engaging in chit-chat.

"Are you sure you don't mind giving up your spare time to do this for Margarita?" was Ada's opening gambit.

Frank obviously picked up on the same aspect of Ada's question as I had done. "Cait's not really investigating to help Margarita, dear," he said. "We all know who killed her."

"Yes, dear, but we don't know why," was Ada's sensible reply.

"That's what I think I might be able to help with," I said, maybe a little too quickly. "Were either of you 'on the spot,' so to speak?" I asked, knowing the answer.

"Oh yes, both of us," Frank said, smiling. Ada tapped him on the arm. Frank's face rearranged itself into a more serious expression.

"How about we sit on the patio and you can tell me about it?" I asked, waving in the general direction of the glazed wall that I'd folded back on itself to offer almost entirely open access to the garden.

"Can I smoke?" asked Frank hopefully.

"Only if I can too," I replied.

Frank brightened. Ada tutted.

"He doesn't need any encouragement, Cait," she admonished me. "Him and his cigars. They're all the same around here. In fact, I think it's why he wanted to come here to live: when Greg told us about the place, he kept going on about how wonderful it was to be able to sit outside and puff on a cigar anytime."

"Greg?" I hadn't met Greg.

Ada smiled. "Of course, Greg's in PV today, you won't have a chance to meet him until this evening. Greg is Greg Hollins. He's the one who told us about this place. Lovely man. So tell me, are you single, Cait? Greg is. A bit older than you, of course, but he's single."

Ada's change in topic, and her knowing look when she mentioned that Greg was unmarried, threw me for a moment. I saw Bud's face flash upon what Wordsworth would call "my inward eye."

"Yes, I'm single. Totally single," I replied, with as much conviction as possible.

"What, never married?" The look on Ada's face told me I might as well have been growing a second head. I decided to laugh it off.

"Yes, just turned forty-eight and never married, no children, *and* no boyfriend." I smiled and waited for the inevitable look of pity that always creeps across the faces of married women with children after I make such a statement.

"Gay?" asked Ada brightly, and somewhat surprisingly.

It was Frank's turn to tut. "Just because she isn't married and doesn't have kids, it doesn't mean she's gay. From what Al said earlier on, she's made a very successful career for herself. Besides, kids—who'd have 'em? Ungrateful little—"

"That's enough, Frank," said Ada quickly. "I hope I haven't insulted you?" she asked me. The genuine concern on her face deserved a thoughtful response.

"It happens that I'm not gay, Ada, but I certainly don't take your question as an insult. And Frank might have a point, my career *has* been the biggest part of my life. That said, not everything's for everybody." I didn't add that the only person before Bud with whom I'd ever been in a long-term relationship had turned out to be a sociopathic alcoholic who'd beaten me and ended up dead on my bathroom floor. *Not the time, or the place, Cait.*

"And now you live in Vancouver?" asked Ada, still bright. I felt as though she was the one pumping *me* for information, when it should have been the other way around. I resolved to try to move ahead on a more quid pro quo basis.

"Do you know the Lower Mainland?" I thought I'd check. They both nodded. "I live in a little house on Burnaby Mountain, about half way up, on the way to the University of Vancouver's Burnaby campus. That's where I teach. I like it very much."

"But your accent's from Britain, isn't it?" asked Ada.

I smiled. "Yes, it's a Welsh accent. I'm from Wales, originally."

Ada looked delighted. "Frank's granddad was Welsh, isn't that right, Frank?" Frank nodded patiently. "But he wasn't a Taylor. Where exactly are you from, dear? Might we have heard of it?"

"I'm from Swansea . . ."

"That's where that Zeta-Jones girl is from, isn't that right, Frank? And Tom Jones was from near there too, I know. Fabulous voice. Jones was Frank's grandfather's name and he was from . . . I think it was Aber-somewhere. Was that it, Frank, dear?"

Frank didn't seem to be very engaged. "Yes, dear, that's right," he replied. I had no doubt that he'd hardly heard what his wife had said, and that mentally he was somewhere else. He rolled the end of his fat cigar in his mouth, then rested it in the large ashtray on the patio table.

"That murderer was in there killing Margarita when I was right next door, you know." Frank made the statement with grim determination. "Imagine. I was that close to him that I could have stopped him, if only I'd known."

Ada shook her head. "Don't start that again, Frank."

I took my chance. "How close were you, exactly, Frank? Were you literally next door to the flower store?"

Ada opened her mouth as if to answer on his behalf, but Frank gave her a firm look, picked up his cigar again, and manipulated it in his fingers as he replied. "I'd gone down to the Rocas Hermosas Resort on the seafront, right opposite Margarita's flower shop. I wanted to see a guy who works in the bar there. He's great at getting these things for me at a reasonable price." He looked almost lovingly at his cigar. "Anyway, I'd just left him, and I was wandering through the gardens, waiting for this one to finish at the spa. What was it today, dear? Mani, or pedi, or both? I lose track."

"Both." Ada nodded and wriggled her neat French manicure by way of evidence.

"We'd agreed I'd pick her up when she called me. You never know how long Serena's going to be, do you, dear?"

"No, not really. She's very much a mañana person, Cait, so you're never quite sure when she'll start on you, or finish. Once you've got your feet in that basin, well, there's not a lot you can do about it really, eh?" Ada shrugged. For two retired people, I couldn't imagine that a small delay when you were getting a pedicure would be a big issue, but Frank struck me as the sort of man who liked a schedule for his days.

"So there I am, hanging around waiting for Ada, when Serena comes out of the spa and calls over to me."

So far, Frank's account agreed with my own observations, and augmented them. Serena was the name of the woman in the capri pants who'd come out of the spa. The spa she obviously owned. And it *had* been Frank that Serena had crossed the road to greet.

"She came toward me, and she had this big cake box with her. Then she told me it was Bob and Maria's wedding anniversary, and would I join the celebration—"

Ada interrupted her husband. "Bob and Maria are the couple who own the bodega next door to Margarita's flower shop. Bob's Bodega. Lovely couple. Married forty years. Wonderful."

"I was getting to that," responded Frank. "They own Bob's Bodega, as Ada said, and they *are* very nice. Of course I said I'd join her, though I have to admit that I was a bit puzzled about Ada. I mean, if Serena was in the street, what was Ada doing?"

"I told you I couldn't leave, Frank. Serena had finished me, but I had to wait another ten minutes for my toes to dry properly. There's no point getting them done if you're going to ruin them, right, Cait?"

I nodded and smiled, though my personal experience of pedicures is non-existent. Just the thought of someone touching my feet makes me squirm. I suspect I'd knock out someone's teeth if they tried to grind down my hard skin and paint my toenails.

"While Ada was sitting around waiting for her toes to be ready for the world, I went into the bodega with Serena. That man—the murderer—even held the door open for us. Can you imagine? I was *that* close to him. There he was. All smiles. And he was just about to kill that poor woman." Frank and Ada both shook their heads, disbelief and anger on their faces. "Al and Miguel were already in the bodega. They'd known about Serena's plans for a while, and they'd agreed to get all kitted up in their dress uniforms to make it something special. Of course Bob and Maria were delighted, and they wanted to cut the cake there and then, but

Serena said she knew that Margarita wanted to be there for the cake-cutting and had agreed to take photos, so she said she'd go next door to get her since Margarita was late. A minute later we all heard the screams. I'm pretty sure anyone within a mile could have heard her. She's got one heck of a pair of lungs on her that Serena. Luckily, Al and Miguel were right on the spot, though they were a bit hamstrung by their silly outfits. And that's when all hell broke loose."

"I heard the screams too," chipped in Ada. "It frightened the life out of me. I popped my sandals on, carefully, and rushed out into the street."

"Were you on your own in the spa?" I asked, quite innocently I thought.

"Dorothea was in the back having a massage," replied Ada. "Well, I guess by then she'd have been getting dressed after her massage. Serena runs the place alone, and she'd just given me the final coat on my fingers, then gone outside with the cake that she'd brought through from out back."

"Is there more than one way in and out of the spa?" I asked.

Ada looked puzzled. "There's a door that goes to the lane behind, but that and the front door, that's it. Why?"

"No reason," I lied.

So Ada and Dorothea had been close to each other, but not together, during the critical few minutes between Serena leaving the spa and Bud going into the flower shop. *Interesting.* Could I picture Ada slashing a florist's throat? It seemed unlikely. There again, my years in the business of criminal psychology have taught me that you really *cannot* judge a book by its cover. Some of the most warped, evil minds have been possessed by perfectly *average-looking* people. I wondered how big a woman Margarita had been. If she was a plantswoman, and used to working the land, the chances were that she'd been physically capable. There was Ada, sipping her juice, about five feet five, around a hundred and ten pounds, looking like your typical well-groomed sixty year old, a happy wife, mother, and grandmother. Not an obvious suspect. Of course, there was still Dorothea to consider . . .

"What brought you two to Hacienda Soleado?" I asked, thinking I'd take my chance to gather a bit of background now that I'd established that at least one of my guests had, indeed, had the opportunity to murder Margarita.

"That was Frank," replied Ada. "And not just because he could sit about and smoke his cigars all day. In fact, we came here because he was bored, didn't we, dear?"

"Bored?" I asked.

"I'd sold my brewery in Prince George, and we'd been on a few cruises, taken a couple of trips to be with the grandkids, redone the bathroom *and* the kitchen. You know the sort of thing. But I missed the work." He smiled wryly. "Before I sold up, I couldn't wait to pack it in. The business changed so much in the last few years I was running it, with all the big players squeezing out our type of small operation. The day I walked out of there, I thought I'd be happy to never work another day in my life. Of course, then the wind changed and everyone started looking for the small brewery products, so if I'd only hung on . . ."

"Come on, Frank. You know the time was right," said Ada.

"Yeah, it seemed right at the time, and I got a good price. We met Greg on one of our cruises. We palled up and kept in touch afterwards. He mentioned this place he was investing in. It seemed like a good fit. I get to dabble in the tequila business and use all those years of knowledge about bottling, distribution, and all that, and we live in a home we got to design as we wanted, right here, at the hacienda. We moved in four years ago, and, I have to be honest, it's worked out great. Greg's quite a driving force for the business. He and Juan, poor Margarita's father, organized all of the distillation and bottling construction before we got here. Dorothea was the next investor. She met Greg on a safari in Africa. Then we came along. I get involved in just enough of the business stuff to keep my mind sharp, and we get wonderful weather pretty much all year. We don't miss the weather in Prince George, do we? Ada's never bored, are you?"

Ada shook her head. "So long as I've got my books, I'm happy." She smiled.

"Any books in particular?" I asked politely.

"Murder mysteries," she replied.

Time to Talk

I STOOD TO COLLECT THE glasses we'd used. I didn't want to hear what either of them was going to say next, because I knew what it would be.

"Ada always solves the crimes in her books before they tell you whodunit," said Frank.

There you go!

"I bet she could help you work out who this guy really is," he added eagerly.

Oh dear.

I smiled. "Why thank you, Frank; I'm sure Ada would be a very useful ally in the case, but, of course, if Al is going to be giving me any sort of confidential information—you know, autopsy results and that sort of thing—then I probably shouldn't share it." I hoped that would stall them.

"But we don't need to know all of that to work out who that awful man is, right?" commented Ada. "We know *he* did it, and we know how, where, and when, so an autopsy won't help at all. I'm pretty sure everyone here wants to help Al crack the case before the Federales get involved. We don't see much of them around here, but when they do anything at all, it's all flash and bang, sticking their noses into things that don't concern them, and off they finally go. We should all pitch in."

Nip this in the bud, Cait!

I sat down again and gave them each a meaningful look. "I know you want to help, but in a case like this, which hinges on gathering and interpreting information, the more people who get involved, the more opportunities there are for miscommunication, or misunderstanding. As psychologists we learn about various theories relating to the human psyche: the way the individual operates within groups and society, and the way that all of this might have some bearing upon behavior. If Al and I are trying to work out who this man is, and why he killed Margarita, I need to understand what it was in Margarita's life—whether that be an incident from many years ago, or a trigger word she might have innocently used that day—that set her killer in motion. If he is a hit man, who might have hired him, and why? If he's not, then how did they know each other, and why kill her now? I suspect that the best way you can help is to start by telling me what you knew about Margarita. That would be good. But I really would prefer it if you would let me help Al alone. Is that okay?"

Ada looked crestfallen. "I suppose," she said quietly.

"Margarita never got over the deaths of her mother and her siblings," said Frank, diving right in. "They died when she was about ten, I think. That's what her father, Juan, said. Their house burned down. The mother died, *and* her two brothers, and Margarita was left with that terrible scar."

"Scar?" I was curious.

Ada jumped in. "Of course, you never met her. Poor Margarita had a very bad burn scar up her neck and onto her face. There was no way she could hide it, so she didn't bother trying. Some people reacted to it quite badly. I know a couple of brides who were happy for her to do their flowers, but didn't want her taking photos at their weddings. Sad really. I mean, she couldn't help it."

I took my cue. "About her being a photographer—how did that play a role in her life?" I couldn't imagine how being a florist would put Margarita in danger, but photography offered a whole host of possible scenarios.

Frank answered. "She'd always taken photos of her arrangements, and her gardens, you know, to show them in albums, to help her sell her services. I think I'm right in saying she had a keen interest in nature photography in general, right, Ada?" Frank's wife nodded. "Then, when they built the new resort about six years ago, she took the store opposite. The one where she was killed. They have weddings at the resort, *and* they need their own floral decorations *and* garden maintenance. She had all those contracts. She kept the gardens looking good, brought in flowers for the public areas, looked after the plants inside, and, when brides were planning their weddings there, she was right on the spot. I think it was then that she saw the chance to do a bit more business, and she started being a wedding photographer. I'm pretty sure she was doing well at it. We've never heard any complaints, have we, dear?"

"Oh no," replied Ada. "She was very good at the photography thing. She had this way about her: you never felt as though she was in the way. Afterwards, when you saw the photos, which were always very good, crisp and clear, you wondered why you hadn't noticed her. But it wasn't just a job to her: she took her cameras— big, lumpy things—with her wherever she went. I know she took some wonderful shots of the flower market in PV, for example. You should check out her website."

Ah-ha! I pounced.

"I wish I could, but I didn't bring my laptop, and I can't work out how to get the wireless keyboard to work with the TV here." I was hoping Frank might be able to help.

"I think it's the same as ours," said Ada. "I can show you. Frank's not good with that sort of thing." She smiled indulgently at her husband. "I'm the one who does all that stuff, aren't I?"

Frank nodded. "Why don't you get her to show you? I can't be bothered with it all. Can't see what's wrong with picking up the phone, or writing a letter. It was one of the things that annoyed me about the beer business at the end: a bunch of twelve-year-olds telling me we had to build an 'online platform,' whatever that might be!"

Ada smiled again. "Our son is a software designer for video games, so he and I keep up to date on technology quite a bit, when we talk using our webcams. Frank's not quite so involved." She got up and brushed imaginary crumbs from her lap. "Come on, let's see what Henry's got here." She walked inside.

"Games! Games! *That's* what my son does for a living. A grown man, with children of his own. It won't last . . ."

I walked away from the irate Frank. Now about sixty-five years old, he'd quite possibly been born that age.

Ada was standing in front of the TV, the remote in her hand, scrolling through a menu I hadn't even been able to find—*maybe Frank isn't the only one a bit out of synch with modern technology*—then she pushed a few buttons and said, "Yes, it's the same as ours. Let me show you."

A few minutes later I was happily surfing the net. It was a relief: I was a big step closer to retrieving Jack's email.

Ada made sure I understood how to switch from TV to internet, and I turned everything off. "I'll start when you guys have gone," I said, as kindly as possible.

"She wants us to leave now, Frank. Put that cigar out, and she can get on with her investigating," called Ada to her husband.

I felt badly. I didn't mean to kick them out, but I was desperate to get to that email. I looked at my watch. I only had five minutes before I was due to meet Al. *Damn and blast!*

"Don't worry, you've got plenty of time, dear." Ada's voice was pitched to soothe, but I heard annoyance as an undertone. "When people around here say that something will happen at a certain time, it's just a vague suggestion. You'll get used to it. Most things happen eventually, just not when you thought they would. Like I say, you'll get used to it. In the end, it won't even annoy you, though you've just arrived, so you're still thinking like a Canadian rather than a Mexican."

"There aren't really a lot of Mexicans here, are there?" I ventured. "Considering we're in Mexico, that is." I wondered how Ada would react.

She smiled. "You mean that the Hacienda Soleado is a bit like a theme-park version of the country, right?" I nodded. "We're all imports here, dear, and we've decided how *we* want it to be, and we've made it that way. When we bought into the place and started building our houses, we all made an agreement that this would be our own vision of the world as it should be. All the best bits of Mexico, without any of the horrible things, you know. That's how we like it. We're a bit of a mixed bag, I suppose. We're Canadian; Greg is from Australia originally, though he hasn't lived there for a very long time; Dorothea, Henry, *and* Dean and Jean are all American—oh, you haven't met them either, have you? Nice couple. African American. Three grown sons, all in the service. He had some sort of job with the government, something to do with supplies. Dean's always very vague about exactly what he did—maybe it was a very boring job. They moved around a lot over the years with his job. Funny life, I should think. He says he enjoys being away from a desk. He helps Greg with the logistics for the FOGTT, you know, the Friends of Good Tequila Trust. He's very . . ." she searched for the right word, "effusive. Always telling jokes. Big man. Big character. Big laugh. She's not so talkative, but very nice. Keeps herself to herself a lot. They only moved here last Christmas. They bought out a nice couple from Seattle who said they wanted to move back there to be closer to the grandchildren, but, I don't know, there was something fishy about all that. I think they needed the money so sold up fast. Anyway, when Dean and Jean arrived he threw himself into the tequila business, didn't he, Frank?" Frank nodded dutifully. "Frank isn't involved that much, really, just enough to stop his brain from frying in the heat, but Dean seems to love it. Taken to it like a duck to water. And Jean? She goes into PV to do that tae kwon do boxing thing. Volunteers at the American hospital in PV too. Like I say, very nice. Their house is called Casa Nova. Dean thinks that's hilarious." She raised her eyebrows as she spoke. "So, yes, Hacienda Soleado is a bit, well, *fake*, if you like. If you go down to the seafront, you'll find that the village there is a little more authentic. It's small, of course, and dwarfed by the new resort. I suppose these days you really have to go way up into the hills to find the old way of life. Along the coast here it's newer developments, tourism and a mish-mash of expected Mexican-ness, and then poverty: the ones who play up to the tourists attract the pesos, the ones who want nothing to do with them live a subsistence lifestyle that we outsiders always look at and pity. But it's their choice, right?"

For a woman who liked a mani-pedi, and a good murder mystery, Ada Taylor seemed to have quite a lot to say for herself. I imagined that her desire to chat, and impart information, was often stifled by the domineering presence of Dorothea, and that her down-to-earth approach to life had been honed by decades of child rearing and husband wrangling.

"Come on, Frank; let's go now, dear!" she called.

Frank harrumphed his way toward the front door. "Told you she could sort out all that technology stuff for you," he said, with guarded pride. "How about we meet you at the Amigos del Tequila later on for a bite? You could bring us up to date after your meeting with Al." Frank looked hopeful.

"I'd enjoy that," I said, half-truthfully, "but I don't quite know what Al has planned for me, so I can't say."

"How about you take our cell number, and we can keep in touch?" suggested Ada.

"Good idea," I said. We exchanged numbers. *Thank goodness Bud made me buy a cheap roaming plan for our week here.*

We waved to each other as they set off toward Casa Canuck. As soon as it seemed polite, I nipped inside, shut the door, and pulled up the internet on the TV screen. A few clicks and I managed to access my email. I waded through the long list of sales offers from plus-sized clothing companies—it's so depressing when most of your inbox looks like that—and finally, there it was! Jack's message.

I opened it and read as fast as I could, which, given that I'm a speed-reader, was pretty quick.

Hi Cait—I won't beat about the bush. This is bad. I've spoken to an old CSIS colleague of mine in Ottawa, and he's promised to get in touch with an associated operative in the area, with whom I can liaise when I arrive. Funny thing is I know the person, kind of, and I never knew they were "in the business." Good cover. Ottawa's not happy about the situation. None of us are. I'm on a flight at 3:00 PM tomorrow. I should be at my condo by about 9:00 PM. I'll phone you when I get in. Meanwhile, here's some advice: don't get involved, keep your head down, stick to your cover story, and don't let anyone know what you do for a living, especially your role as a consultant with the Integrated Homicide Team here in the Lower Mainland. Henry thinks you're a friend of ours, that's me and Sheila. Stick to that. Be vague. Act as though you're on vacation. If you mix with the folks at the hacienda, be careful not to give yourself away. Steer clear of the cops and the crime scene, and, above all, make absolutely no effort to contact Bud, or even find out anything about him. I'm guessing that this murder will become a hot topic there: stay out of the conversations. If you need to, just hunker down next to Henry's pool and read a book or something. I trust you to do this. I know it's what Bud would want. He's following protocol, and you need to follow it too. Bud will hope that you've left. He'll probably think you have. So be as good as not there. Not to put too fine a point on it, but Bud's probably pretty safe if he's at the local cop shop. Once he's in the general population, if anyone finds out who he is, given his role in the gang and drug-running task force, he could be in grave danger. No one can know his name, or his background. I'm sure you understand. If you go anywhere near him, the chances of someone making a connection increase. So don't. I know the next day or so is going to feel like a long time. Call me if you want. See you soon. Jack.

So that was that. There was no information about Bud, his "colleagues," or what the heck was going on with regard to possible CSIS involvement, nor was there a single useful suggestion from Jack that might save Bud. *Nothing.* What was the point of telling me to keep out of it until he arrived? Especially now that I knew Jack wouldn't be arriving at all! There were *no* contact details, *no* names. Not a number or an email address. Nothing that would allow me to follow up on Jack's actions. Just a series of warnings to steer clear of Bud. And that one ominous comment about how Bud would be in danger if he was dumped into the general police holding system. The thought had been gnawing at me since Al had handcuffed Bud, so it didn't help at all to see that Jack felt it necessary to spell it out. *Damn and blast!*

What could I do? I hadn't outed myself—Al had done that for me. The cat wasn't just out of the bag, it was running willy-nilly around the place, yowling as it ran! I *couldn't* stay out of it now. No matter what Bud might have expected, and no matter what Jack had hoped, I was on the case. Not so much on it as up to my neck in it, in fact.

I was about to meet the cop leading the inquiry into discovering Bud's identity, and I'd promised to help him do just that, while I was being implored—*okay, instructed*—by Jack to do the exact opposite.

What could possibly go wrong?

Power Hour

I CLOSED UP CASA LALA and headed down the slight incline of the rocky track that led to Amigos del Tequila. It was well past 5:00 PM, but the sun was still pretty high, and the humidity was almost unbearable. As I walked, I kicked up dust. It stuck to my sweaty legs. *Lovely!* I don't do humidity. What was I thinking, agreeing to come to Mexico at this time of year? If I'd said no, then Bud wouldn't be in this predicament.

I was at the adobe restaurant and bar in a matter of moments. It had seemed to take a lot longer when I was dragging the bags up to the house, even with Al's help. Once again I pushed open the doors to the building where I'd made my fateful decision to help out the cops, and, once again, the place was deserted.

"Hello?" I called.

Nothing.

I was at a bit of a loss as to what to do next. Wait outside for Al? Settle myself on a stool and wait for someone to show up? Peer into the back of the building from where Tony had emerged that afternoon? I decided to peer. *I admit I'm not the world's most patient person.*

Beyond the bar was a short corridor, which led to the washrooms, then the kitchen. I pushed open a pair of swinging doors, stepped into a small but gleaming kitchen, and shouted, "Hello?" Still nothing. Now that *was* odd. Surely Tony wouldn't just leave the whole place completely unattended?

I walked farther into the kitchen. No one in sight. The humming of refrigeration units buzzed in the air, and a wonderful aroma of herbs, spices, and cooked meat filled my nostrils. My tummy grumbled. Nuts and fruit weren't able to hold me for long, it seemed. Covered containers of ingredients stood ready to be used, *mise en place*, and a couple of pots were bubbling on a gas range. *Definitely odd.*

There was a door in the far wall of the kitchen that I assumed led outside, so I opened it and stuck out my head. I immediately spotted the blue pickup truck that had roared past the crime scene just as Bud had been discovered. I wondered who it belonged to.

"Hello?" came a voice from inside the bar.

"In here," I called in response, as I allowed the back door to close again.

Al's head appeared through the swinging doors. "Where is everyone?"

"I don't know," I replied. "Is this normal, for there to be pots boiling and food prepped, but no one here?"

Al shrugged. "I don't know. It seems odd to me. Haven't you seen Tony? Callie? Anyone at all?"

"Not a soul," I replied.

Al drew his gun. It didn't make me feel any more comfortable about the situation. He gestured for me to walk toward him, while he approached me and whispered, "Have you looked out back?" I nodded. "Anyone there?"

"Not that I could see, but there's a blue truck there. Does that belong to Tony?" I tried to make my question about the truck sound innocent.

Al moved across the kitchen a lot more stealthily than I had done—*I'm not really built for stealth*—and pushed open the back door, peering outside.

"It's Juan's truck, the blue one. I'm surprised he's still here at the hacienda—it's well past his finishing time, and I thought he'd be pretty keen to get away after I gave him the news about his daughter. Tony's truck isn't out there," he whispered over his shoulder. "Nor is Callie's car. If it wasn't for the fact that the place is wide open, and there's food cooking on the stovetop, I'd say they'd left the property altogether. I'm going to check their apartment upstairs. You stay here."

He came inside, allowing the back door to close, and disappeared up a narrow staircase that led from the kitchen. I've watched enough movies in my time; I didn't follow him. Instead, I stood my ground, registering the news that Margarita's father's truck, at least, had been at the scene of her murder, within the right time frame. I ran through some possible reasons for why the place currently resembled a restaurant version of the *Marie Celeste*. Quite a few involved extraterrestrial or paranormal interventions, but none of those made any sense. Had Juan caused harm to the couple who ran the restaurant? Or was he just wandering his fields? Of course, if one of the Booths was responsible for Margarita's murder, then it *did* make perfect sense that they'd have done a runner—but the food on the stove was bizarre. If Tony, or Callie, or both of them had planned an escape from justice, why would they bother putting anything into a pot, let alone turn on the heat?

Standing there on my own, with steam and spices in the air, I realized I was literally dripping with sweat. It was running down my back. I walked across the kitchen and turned off the heat under the pots. My curiosity kicked in and I lifted their covers. Water. Boiling water. That was all. The words "curiouser and curiouser" popped into my head unbidden. Immediately I replaced the lids; I felt as though my nasal passages were on fire. My eyes were stinging, and I started sneezing. *Gas? Poison?* I grabbed a nearby roll of kitchen paper: what it lacked in absorption and softness, it more than made up for in proximity. I thought my head was going to explode. I had to get out, away from . . . what on earth was it? I knew that I recognized what I'd inhaled, but I couldn't fix on it.

I pushed open the back door to catch what little fresh air and breeze there might be. I fanned myself with my hand, did the best

I could with the kitchen roll, and gradually the sneezing subsided. But my eyes? They were a right mess. I must have looked as though I'd been crying my eyes out.

"Their stuff's all over the place upstairs, but there's no sign of them," announced Al, who was suddenly about three inches away from me. I nearly jumped out my skin.

He looked alarmed when I turned to face him. "What's wrong?" he asked sharply.

"There's boiling water in the pots," I replied, my voice thick with mucus. "And pepper." *That was it—pepper.*

"What? Pans full of pepper and water? I don't like this. It's weird. It doesn't feel right."

You're not kidding!

I managed to keep my mouth shut, but I nodded my agreement. "What do you suggest we do?" I asked.

"I'm going to get hold of the FOGTTs. They can decide what they want to do for themselves. Tony and Callie run this place on their behalf. Come into the bar with me and give me a few minutes to make some calls. Maybe you can grab a drink? You look like you could do with it. Let me check the washroom, then maybe you can take the chance to wash your face with some cool water. Pepper's nasty stuff."

"Yes, cool water, good idea," I replied, sniffling.

In the washroom I stood and looked in the mirror at the mess that was me. I wanted to cry. Instead, I had some choice words with myself, washed and wiped my face—mascara's overrated anyway— and then headed to the bar to grab a cool drink and catch up with Al's news.

I was surprised to find no Al, but instead a man I guessed was Dean, of the Dean and Jean pairing described to me by Ada. Seeing him now, I realized he was the African American guy I'd seen arrive on the crime scene. I guessed that his wife, Jean, would turn out to be the woman in the tennis outfit I'd seen rushing toward the flower shop. *Dean and Jean. Casa Nova. Oh dear.*

If I'd had any doubt about the man's identity, it didn't have a chance to linger. He came toward me, offering a massive hand and an equally large smile. I put him at about six feet five, around two hundred and fifty pounds, and somewhere between sixty and sixty-five. His head was shaved, or, at least, completely bald, and he was wearing the most lurid Hawaiian shirt you'd ever want to see. If my eyes hadn't been sore already, that shirt would have done the trick all on its own. His voice was a deep bass, and it resonated in the empty bar.

"You must be Cait Morgan. I'm Dean George. Dean is my name, not my occupation, you understand." He grinned. *I wonder how many times he's said that.* "Al's outside talking to the rest of the FOGTTs, or at least those he can reach on the phone. I just happened to be arriving. Gonna meet my child-bride here. You'll like her. Everyone does." He was still holding my hand, but now in both of his, and I was beginning to get a crick in my neck from looking up at him. It occurred to me that Punta de las Rocas seemed to be inhabited by very tall people: Ada was the only person I'd met who was of what *I* thought of as normal height.

"Oh my *goodness me*, honey-pie! What *on earth* is going on here today? Our little piece of paradise is quite out of sorts. First poor Margarita, dead! Now Tony and Callie, disappeared! What *is* the world coming to?" For a moment, I thought that Scarlett O'Hara had floated in.

The woman who was walking toward us was quite a vision, but there were no crinolines involved. Her hair was snowy white and cropped very close to her head. She was about five-two, weighed around ninety pounds, and, despite being close to sixty, didn't have a wrinkle on her face. There was almost nothing to her, except a waft of jasmine, a hint of coconut, and an aura of gracefulness and quietude that seemed to surround her. Dressed completely in white, she carried herself with a casual elegance. All you noticed were her eyes, and her voice. The rest was almost insubstantial, and certainly inconsequential.

She reached up to her husband's neck, which was just about as far as she *could* reach, and he bent his head, so she could kiss him on his bald pate. "Now don't you worry, honey-pie," she said, doing her best to look her husband in the eye, "Captain Al will get all this sorted out." She looked at me. Her expression changed. "Are you the woman who's *supposed* to be able to help him?"

Jean George's ethereal charm had evaporated. Her tone was dismissive, to say the least, and I was being treated to an expression that her husband couldn't see, which I suspected was the point. She had decided to be hateful toward me, that much was clear. *I wonder why.*

"Oh, come on now, honey," boomed Dean. "Al speaks very highly of Cait. He said she's known all around the world for her work. We're lucky to have her. You know we all want Al to crack the case before the Federales get here, don't we?"

Jean nodded and smiled coquettishly at her husband.

As she did so, it struck me that Dean had used almost the exact same words as Ada had done when speaking about the case. I guessed that was because they were friends, and co-investors, and they'd all been at the crime scene—so the topic must have come up at some point.

Al joined us. "Dorothea, Ada, and Frank are on their way. Greg's not back from PV yet, you guys are here, and, of course, Henry's not around at all. I'm taking Cait with me to the station, where we're going to get to work. You all are going to call anyone who knows either Tony or Callie to try to find out what's going on here, and you can all decide what to do with that food in the kitchen before it goes bad. I'll call you later to find out how you're doing, or you can call me if you locate Tony or Callie. I'm not going to hide the fact that I'm concerned. If we can't get wind of them, I'll set the wheels in motion for state-wide law enforcement to be on the lookout. But *we* need to find out where they are, if we can."

Dean and Jean nodded. "I always think it's best if folks do their own housekeeping, before they involve outside elements." Dean grinned. Directly at me. *Odd.*

Al addressed me. "Come on, Cait. This has been one hell of a day, and it doesn't look like it's going to get easier as it gets older. I'll show you our 'facilities.' I'm not bragging when I say I have the best-looking police station in all of Mexico. So let's go. You alright now?"

I nodded, and we headed toward the door. We got there just as Frank and Ada arrived.

"I've explained everything to Dean and Jean," said Al, as he propped the door open with his body. "I haven't the time to go through it all again. They can explain." With that he all but pulled me outside.

"Come on, Cait," he said abruptly, as he politely held open the passenger door of the dusty white police car for me to get in. *A bit different than when you shoved Bud in here,* ran through my mind, but I smiled and buckled up.

The tires spat gravel as we sped off down the hill in the gathering gloom. I wondered if it would ever be possible to get used to the way the sun just drops out of the sky at southern latitudes. For some reason, I've always found it deeply unsettling.

I checked my watch. It hadn't long turned 6:00 PM, but I was tired—feeling the stresses of the day, no doubt—*and* I was hungry. But at least the air was cooler now, and the wind that buffeted me through the open car window was *finally* refreshing. Al drove us back to the tarmac road, and we turned left, as though heading toward the Rocas Hermosas Resort, but before we arrived at the side road that Bud and I had headed down so joyfully that morning, he turned left again, onto another track that led up the other side of the hill we'd just descended.

By the time we parked, it was dark. That didn't really matter, because the building at which we'd arrived was floodlit and it was quite a sight. I even heard myself say "Wow!" when I first saw it. I noted that Al smiled. *Proudly.*

"What style of architecture is this? Does it have a name?" I asked, puzzled. The white adobe building had a traditionally Mexican tiled roof, but a square gray stone clock tower in the middle, just like something you'd see on a Welsh church of the Norman period. The stone was not local, that much was clear; the local hills were a reddish-gold. Mirrored wings of a two-storied structure jutted out at angles, like the top of a Y pointing toward us, with the body of the building extending straight behind the tower. On the top story, tall shuttered windows were surrounded by decorative iron railings, while below, the first-story windows were totally encased in decorative metal cages. All in all it seemed to be a mish-mash of ancient French and Spanish colonial, with a bit of local styling thrown in.

Al shrugged. "Punta de las Rocas special?" He smiled. "It was designed for a French family with pots of money and a wild imagination," he said enigmatically. "And it's my home." His voice conveyed a surprising amount of warmth.

I was puzzled. "You *live* here? I thought we were going to the police station."

"This *is* the police station, at this end," Al indicated the wing nearest to us, "*and* my home—the mayoral apartments are in the other wing—*and* the municipal hall, which is the main body of the building. Everything, all rolled up into one. The mayor, the intendente, didn't want to live in his official apartment, so they offered it as a perk for the top cop in the area. That would be me. Captain Al." He grinned. "Juan Martinez is the mayor. And Margarita's father."

"How did he take the news, by the way?" I asked gently. *Juan might be a suspect.*

Al let out a loud "Ha!" It surprised me. "In a day where everything is off, everything is wrong, that was one of the *most* wrong parts of it! I finally tracked down Juan wandering in his fields of agaves. I broke it to him as gently as I could, and all he said was, 'I see.' I'd just told him that his only daughter had been brutally murdered, but that at least we had the guy who'd done it, and that's *all* he said. No questions about who the guy was, or why he might have done it. He just walked away from me, and that was that. What do you make of it all, Cait? What does his reaction mean to you?"

I took a deep breath. I had decided to be honest and open with him whenever I could. I *assumed* that Al had been inside the bodega when the murder had taken place, because he'd emerged from there when Serena screamed, but I still wasn't one hundred percent sure about exactly when he, and his companion-cop, Miguel, had entered it, so, until I knew more, Al himself was still a possible killer.

"It could mean any of a number of things," I replied thoughtfully. "I heard it mentioned, earlier today, that Juan and Margarita didn't get along. It might be that there was such great enmity between them that he is truly glad she died. It would be unusual, but not unheard of, and it would reflect more on *his* personality than on the nature of the rift between them, I would suggest. It *could* be that you witnessed how that particular man deals with shocking news. I know that his wife and sons died in a house fire that scarred Margarita for life, so maybe, in dealing with that loss, he's built a wall about himself that keeps him safe from the worst blasts of tragedy and loss." *Or it could be that he killed her himself and was playing it cool,* I thought.

Al didn't answer for a moment. When he did, he surprised me. "You've learned a lot in a few hours, haven't you?" he said. "Is that one of your skills? Getting people to tell you secrets about others, or themselves?"

I pounced. "Well, if it is, why not tell me all your secrets now, and get it over with? You could start by telling me a bit about your background, and how you came to be Captain Al." I wanted to find out something about the man, because he seemed such an unlikely person to be holding his position.

"Sitting here, in the car, by the light of those giant lamps?" he asked.

"Why not? No time like the present. Then it's done. After all, you do seem to know a lot about *me*, so it's only fair."

Al nodded. "Okay then. Short version. You comfortable?"

"Am I allowed a cigarette?" I dared. I could tell by the smell of the car, and of Al himself, that he was a smoker.

He smiled. "Let's both smoke," he replied, "but come to the little table and chairs over there." He signaled toward the side of the building. "It'll be more comfortable than this—my mobile office."

As I hauled myself out of the police car, each of the one hundred and sixty-eight pounds that I carry around every day felt twice that heavy. I'd proudly managed to shed twelve pounds in the six weeks before our vacation, but it didn't seem to be helping at that moment. Tiredness will do that to you. We settled ourselves on the little plastic seats, lit up our cigarettes, and Al began.

"My ma was quite the woman. Still is. An artist. Loves pottery. She moved to Jalisco State to follow her muse, got pregnant by my dad in Guadalajara. He was a player in a mariachi band. Ma said he was good, but I was too young to ever be a good judge of his skills. She gave birth to me on her way to her family's home in South Carolina. Her name's Beselleu. Belle Beselleu. Old family. Money. Her parents threw her out when she showed up at their front door carrying a half-breed, a mestizo. So she left, went back to Guadalajara, and set up home with my father. She told me she married him. From what I can remember it was a pretty good childhood. But my dad died when I was fourteen, and although Ma managed to keep us going for a while, eventually we went back to her parents. By then they said I 'looked quite white.' Around here there's a lot of French blood. When the forces from the French Intervention reached Jalisco in 1865, they mixed up their blood with the locals, as fast as they could. They might not have been in the state for long, but they sure left an impression. My dad had the light hair, greenish eyes, and taller stature that you often see hereabouts. As did I. Still do, of course, and, with my ma's blood too, I could 'pass for white.' That was what my Gram Beselleu, my mother's mother, used to say. I didn't like her, but my ma needed to be there, so I did as I was told. As a teen in South Carolina, I was known as Al Beselleu. I stopped speaking Spanish. I even picked up the local accent and manners. And I got myself a good education. Went to university in South Carolina, where I was 'allowed' to take Latin American studies. By then, Gram's health was failing, so Ma got her way with her father. She sure could wrap that man around her pinkie finger." I caught the twang of his once adopted, but now absent, accent, and half expected him to add a quick "y'all." But he didn't.

Al pressed on, lighting another cigarette. I followed suit. "I graduated and decided to take some credits toward a master's degree at the University of Guadalajara. When I got there, everything felt so natural to me that I stayed. I felt as though I'd come home, which, of course, I had. But by then I'd become so 'American' I wasn't accepted by the locals, so I started using my full name, Alfredo Jesus Beselleu Torres."

"So did you study Latin American politics? Law?" I was interested in what had brought him to Punta de las Rocas as a cop.

"No. I prefer to understand the fascinating and bloody history of my country, the Estados Unidos Mexicanos, through the eyes of its writers and artists. I was an arts grad: art, literature, cultural aspects of the Latin American civilizations from pre-Columbian times to the present day. Whatever the name of the country, whoever might think they're in charge, those with artistic talent have reflected, and even shaped, the way that the people of this region of the world see and define themselves. That's what I wanted my post-graduate work to be about: how art can give a people its identity, even as the warring politicos argue about titles, names, ownership, and loot. Non-Mexicans seem to know nothing about our culture. They think it's all about painted pots and sombreros. But it's so much more than folk art—and even that's been dumbed down for the tourists. Sure, many people will have heard of Frida Kahlo and Diego Rivera, but who knows about José Joaquín Fernández de Lizardi, who wrote the first Latin American novel? Or about the poetry of Manuel Gutiérrez Nájera? There are so many artists who have helped us become who we are. Have given us the fire in our blood."

As he spoke, I could feel Al's passion for his topic, but I had to admit that I wasn't well informed when it came to Mexican culture. I made a note to do some internet surfing when I had a chance, because the point he was making was important: all my research over the years had been carried out with non-Latino cultural subjects. Of course, in the world of academic psychology, we read journal papers from all around the world. As far as I knew, there wasn't a great deal being done specifically with Latino groups. Given the way that the Latino population was growing in the US, I suspected that might change pretty soon, but for now, maybe gaining some insight into Margarita's cultural background would help me consider how the theories about human behavior with which I was familiar might play within this novel landscape. True, psychological theory is supposed to be "universal," but I don't believe for one minute that we psychologists know all there is to know about the human condition. Maybe artists *do* know more, in their own way.

"You're quite right, Al," I replied. "I came here knowing I wasn't well versed in Mexican culture, and hoping to have some time to dive into it. But, with this case to consider, maybe we could put that on the back burner for now?" I knew I had to get him back on track, or I'd never get ahead.

Al nodded. "I guess," he replied. "So, where was I?" Before I could respond, he'd picked up his life story. "Oh yes, I was at the university in Guadalajara. Even though Ma had a trust fund in the US, I didn't have much money at that time, so I lived in a pretty sketchy part of the city. It's a great city, but every place has them—the areas where you don't go out after dark unless you're making trouble, or at least expecting it."

I nodded. "Yes, every city has those areas. The Downtown Eastside in Vancouver, for all its creeping gentrification, is still a pretty wild place between dusk and dawn."

"So you know what I mean," he continued. "All around me I saw the results of poor education, low incomes, or no incomes, and the pervasive evil of drugs. Instead of sitting in an ivory tower, talking about art and society, I decided to get involved and help. I volunteered with youth groups. I mentored kids who wanted to get out but didn't know how. After a few years of getting to know the beat cops there, the ones who try to keep kids out of trouble instead of throwing them into the system so they come out ten times worse than they went in, I realized that I could do more good by becoming a professional rather than remaining a volunteer. I did my training, and this post came up. I did some research into the place, you know, its history, how it came to be what it is today, and I decided to apply for the post. They offered it, and I took it. And now, when I get my criminology degree as well, I think it's a career where I can progress and do even more good work as I move ahead." *Yes, definitely ambitious.*

"And are there many young people walking the tightrope between success and sad failure in Punta de las Rocas?" I asked. I couldn't imagine it.

"You'd be surprised," he said. "Serena? The one who found Margarita's body?"

I nodded.

"Serena has two younger sisters who were on their way down the wrong road. Now they're both back at school, and they help out at a local restaurant evenings and weekends. They wanted to run off to Guadalajara. Thought it was glamorous. Serena asked me to get involved. They hadn't broken the law, as such, but they found the young men with the new cars in PV exciting. They liked to dress up and hit the tourist bars along the coast. Serena saw the way they were heading. Maybe now they'll stay, settle, and not become a part of the flood of young people leaving our villages."

"Was Margarita ever a wild girl, do you know? Or was she one of the girls who followed the 'good path' to womanhood?" I asked.

Al smiled and looked up at the black, starry sky. "You see how that sky looks?" he asked. I nodded. "You can see in it whatever you want. Allow it to be a backdrop for your dreams. Margarita's nursery was like that to her. She saw the soil as her blank canvas: she worked it, planted all sorts of things, cut and arranged what she grew. She made beauty from the dirt. She wasn't outgoing or showy. Kept her head down and did her thing, and knew the right and the wrong roads. But what she traveled was her own road. Her scar, the one she got in the fire, very much molded who she was. She told me she was so badly bullied at school that she left earlier than she really wanted to, but she threw herself into learning about the land, plants, and nature in general. It meant she didn't have to mix with people too much. Then, when she turned eighteen, she inherited her mother's holdings just up the hill here, so she had her own home, and her own land to do with as she wanted."

I was beginning to get a picture of Margarita. I still couldn't see how her role as a plantswoman, however wonderful or knowledgeable she might have been, could have led to her murder.

"I'm sorry to ask, Al, but are you quite sure that everything Margarita grew was—well, legal?"

Al gave me a sad look. "You too? It's not all about drugs here, you know, Cait." He sounded disappointed.

"Hey, I had to ask, Al. Believe me, I understand what you're saying. After all, I'm from British Columbia, where our biggest export is that particularly potent weed-crop BC Bud, which they raise in grow ops in perfectly respectable suburban subdivisions all over the place, not to mention out on lonely hillsides set up for cultivation, where the conditions are perfect for fast growth and turnover."

Al stood. "You're right, of course. We have flybys around here. Well, not this area so much, because it's not such a big deal here, but across the state in general. They use heat-seeking equipment to detect the growth of a 'certain type of vegetation,' shall we say? So I happen to be one hundred percent certain that Margarita *was* only growing what she said she was growing."

"And what *did* she grow?" I asked. I was imagining all sorts of exotic specimens.

Al beamed a warm smile. "Roses were her thing. I'll drive you to her place in the morning. You'll get a kick out of it. Anyone would. For now, how about we go inside and I pour us a drink?"

"Well, I was rather hoping you could tell me some more about Margarita and the crime scene. I'd like to get a better idea of where it all happened." *I'd really like to know if there is a back entrance to Margarita's store, through which someone could have entered and exited without anyone, me included, seeing them from the street,* was what I wanted to say, but I couldn't, because Al "knew" that Bud had done it, so the logistics of the crime scene were of no interest to him, and weren't supposed to be of any interest to me.

"Okay, but let's go inside. I'm starting to get cold," replied Al.

Personally, I was relishing the still-warm evening and the chance to be comfortable and not sweaty. I reminded myself that the evening might feel delightful to me, but for someone who was used to much higher temperatures, it might feel a bit chilly.

"Okay," I agreed, and I walked in through the heavy wooden door at the police station end of the building that Al had pushed open for me.

As I peered into the gloom, I could only make out vague shapes. Al threw some switches and the whole building lit up. To my right, someone gasped, and I turned, startled.

There, inside a cage made from thick iron bars, was Bud, lying on the floor on a dirty mattress that looked as though it were made of straw.

"Oh, Bud . . ." was out before I could stop myself. *Damn and blast!* "Oh, but . . . is that *him*?" I added, as quickly as my heart was beating. *Will Al work out that I blurted out a name, or did I cover my mistake?*

"Yes, that's him alright," replied Al. "Nasty looking beggar. Could be from anywhere, couldn't he? What do *you* think?" His tone made me feel he hadn't noticed my blunder. *Phew!*

I looked across at the man I loved and hoped I was managing the micro-expressions on my face well enough that Al wouldn't be able to work out what was spiraling through my brain.

Bud was in long gray pants and a white, short-sleeved shirt: *that's a spare police uniform.* They must have stripped him to preserve forensic evidence. A metal plate and mug were on the floor: *they have fed him and given him something to drink.* He showed no signs of having been beaten—Al didn't strike me as that kind of cop, in any case. Bud seemed to have been cleaned of blood: *that's odd, but maybe with the heat, and the flies, it's best. They've probably got a load of photographs of the blood spatter that I saw covering him.*

He'd been lying in the dark, and I know him well enough to know that he'd actually dropped off—*he's got that look about him. That's a good sign.* Bud blinked in the light: *good, that's giving him a chance to hide his surprise at seeing me. Oh, poor Bud, I love you, and I'm here to do all I can to rescue you!*

"What do I think?" I said aloud, in response to Al's question. "I think you've got yourself a killer in a cage, and we'd better work out exactly who he is before you hand him over to the Federales the day after tomorrow. Of course, if I can work out why Margarita was killed, that'll give us the best chance of establishing who this fellow is. You didn't say whether you'd circulated a photo of him—have you?" Al shook his head. "Okay, let's keep it that way. If the Federales know who he is before you hand him over and tell them you've worked it out for yourself, it won't look as good for your career," I added.

Al nodded, then said quietly, "Come on. I don't know if he speaks English or not, but I don't want us to talk in front of him. Let's go to my office. Follow me." He spoke surprisingly sharply.

"Lead on," I said, risking a backward glance at Bud once Al had turned away. In that one look I tried to condense all the love, pity, hope, and determination that I felt. I had no idea whether Bud would pick up on such a complex message, in a flicker of an eye, but I'd done all I could to communicate the situation and my plan to him in a couple of sentences. I couldn't risk trying to tell him that I'd been in touch with Jack, or that Jack was sick. Maybe I'd find a way to do that too, eventually. I followed the jailer of my loved one to his office, and wondered how best to move my investigation forward. I looked at my watch. It had just passed 7:00 PM. I might be in for a long evening. I hoped it would be productive.

Margarita Time

IT FELT VERY STRANGE TO be so close to Bud, and yet for him to be so utterly beyond my reach. I followed Al into his office, but I didn't close the door on the off chance that Bud might be able to hear something comforting.

The office was neat and tidy, and each wall was lined with tall, old-fashioned wooden filing cabinets. It was a small room, but the ceiling was high. It had the same polished hardwood floors that the entire building seemed to have, as well as a similar ceiling. It was a bit oppressive. Not even the white walls helped. Al had turned on three fans, one in each of three corners, and the cross-draft they created pulled in some cool air from the open barred windows.

I sat in a worn leather-covered swivel seat. I tried to stop it spinning, but it seemed to have a mind of its own.

"It does that," said Al, pulling a folder from a drawer. "Miguel says it's a haunted chair."

"And why would 'Miguel' say that?" I asked.

Al picked up on my double query. "Miguel is my right-hand man. Well, he's my only man, actually. Just the two of us. And he works the short hours."

"Does he live here too?"

Al smiled. "No, he doesn't, thank heavens. I don't say that because I dislike him. Poor Miguel is a good man, but there isn't *just* him. He, his wife, his four daughters, his mother, *and* his brother all live together." Al sighed. "Poor guy, lost his eldest last year. It's been really tough for him."

"What happened?" He seemed to want to tell me.

Al looked at the file in his hand and laid it on his desk. He sighed again and rubbed his hands over his face. "It was November 1 last year, el Día de los Muertos. A big deal around here. The Day of the Dead. It's nothing like most foreigners think. It's nothing like Halloween. It's a family day, a day for remembering our ancestors. Miguel's eldest, Angélica Rosa, was supposed to be with her family that night, but she never arrived. I mentioned a local restaurant earlier, where Serena's sisters help out?" I nodded. "Well, Rutilio is Miguel's brother, and his restaurant is directly behind the crime scene—it's near the Rocas Hermosas Resort; the front side faces the sea. Miguel's daughter was helping at her uncle Rutilio's restaurant back then. At that time, Rutilio wasn't living with his brother. Angélica Rosa said she'd walk home after they closed up. It wasn't unusual. She was eighteen, and it was a busy evening, with people traveling to and from family gatherings, but she never made it to her father's house. Of course, Miguel was annoyed at first. He thought she'd gone off to have some fun with her friends instead of being with her family. We soon realized she wasn't with any of her friends, so we did what we could locally, but we also called it in to the Federales."

"Did they find her quickly?" I asked.

"It took them three days. She was laid out, wrapped in white sheeting, hands folded in prayer, on a bank near the edge of a side road about fifty miles from here. No interference, thank heavens. Miguel was still overwhelmed. And, if that wasn't bad enough, when he went to Guadalajara to identify her body, they kept him there. Locked him up. The questions went on for days. Terrible. It nearly broke him. By the time they worked out when she'd been killed, and that he probably couldn't have done it, because he really *was* with his family that night, he was a mess. They allowed him to come home to his family, but he needed weeks off work, and the Federales kept buzzing around Punta de las Rocas, asking questions about him. There was another killing. Same MO. Luckily for Miguel, he was well and truly out of the frame for that one because he had a watertight alibi. They were able to work out pretty much exactly when the second girl was dumped on the roadside, and they knew it would have been impossible for Miguel to have made it from the dump site in time to be on his knees in front of the altar at Our Lady of Guadalupe, in Puerto Vallarta, saying a Requiem Mass for his dead daughter. It was a big deal around here: he and his family carried out a simultaneous crucifix of Requiem Masses. Miguel's mother went to her old hometown in the south, his wife to hers in the north, and his brother, Rutilio, was here in Punta de las Rocas, to the west. That sort of thing doesn't happen too often. It's one of the old ways of this area. Everyone who lives here went to one of the services; most stayed in Punta de las Rocas with Rutilio, but I know that Margarita went with Miguel to PV. So the heat was off him, at last, and he recovered enough to return to work."

"It sounds awful to say, but he was lucky there was a second killing, in a way," I said.

A wry smile crossed Al's face. "I know what you mean. And what you say is sad, but true. There's been another murder, by the same killer, every month since. Not *exactly* every month, just over the four-week mark each time, it seems. In fact, if the 'Rose Killer' keeps to his schedule, there'll be another dead teenager within the next few days."

"The *Rose Killer*?"

"Miguel's daughter's name was Angélica Rosa, and the serial killer, because that's what we now know him to be, puts two red roses in his victims' hands, between their praying palms. Seven of them to date. State-wide. Gone." He shook his head. "But enough of this. It's not a case that I can do anything about. The Federales are the ones charged with finding this monster who somehow convinces girls not known to be off the rails in any way to drink themselves to death, before he lays them out on the side of the road, far, far away from their homes and their distraught families."

"They die from alcohol poisoning?" I was puzzled. "That's *very* unusual. You have to drink a great deal of the stuff to die from it, and, even then, it's hardly what you'd call a dependable way of killing someone."

"You're not wrong," said Al. "Unusual, horrible, and depressing. The theory is that, although there's no sexual involvement, he likes to watch them get drunk and then die. They found some evidence in the case of the second girl that the killer had force-fed her the alcohol, bringing her round out of unconsciousness several times, making her drink, then waiting until she could drink more, and that he drugged her too. Evil. I only know about the first two cases because, as I said, after that there was no reason for any information to be given to Miguel, and there was *never* any reason for me to be informed. I only knew what I did from my grieving colleague. Like I said, poor Miguel. It struck so close to home. Just as close as Margarita's death. Here's the file, Cait. I can't see any reason why you can't have a look at it. After all, we're on the same side. Right?"

"Absolutely," I said and reached for the folder.

"How about I get us a cold beer from the official intendente's refrigerator, in my apartment, while you settle down with that?"

I nodded, and he was gone. I flicked through the file to see what it contained: some notes, crime scene photographs, that was it. No autopsy report. Not much. I looked at the photographs—the ones showing Bud, covered with blood, were the hardest to take. The ones of Margarita with her throat clearly cut from ear to ear weren't pleasant to see either, of course, but they were more informative. The notes were in Spanish. I could only just about read them, not because my Spanish abilities were lacking, but because Al's handwriting was appalling. As Al entered the room again, I had to make a big decision. I did.

"How are you doing?" he asked, putting a well-chilled bottle of

Pacifico on the table in front of me. I couldn't resist and took several big gulps. By the time I relinquished my grip on the bottle, there was only about a quarter of the beer left.

"Thirsty?" asked Al, smiling and still holding his full bottle.

I smiled back. "Just a bit! These notes—are they written by you? It's hard for me to tell."

"Spanish not up to it?" he asked.

"I *could* do with some help," I replied truthfully. *I didn't go so far as to lie by saying I couldn't understand Spanish. He inferred it. Not my fault.*

"Most of my notes are about the crime scene, Margarita, and the suspect, as you'd expect. Pass them over and I'll go through them." He held out his hand and took back the folder.

I sat back in my rickety chair and sipped my remaining beer as he spoke.

"Margarita Rosa García Martinez, age thirty-three, height five feet three inches, weight approximately one hundred and ten pounds, of Hacienda García, Punta de las Rocas, Nayarit. Found expired at her flower shop, Margarita Flores, Rocas Hermosas Resort, Punta de las Rocas. Throat slashed, displaying a deep, ear-to-ear wound. Suspect found on site, with hands around the victim's throat. Suspect's name, not known; country of origin, not known. Body and suspect found in situ by Serena Marquez García, of Spa Serena. The suspect had been encountered by Roberto and Maria Guitterez, owners of Bob's Bodega, when he went into their store to purchase supplies. He spoke a little Spanish to them and paid in cash. They directed him to Margarita Flores as a place where he could purchase roses." Al paused and looked up at me. "I wondered why he wanted to buy roses. Maybe it was just a ruse, to have an excuse to enter the flower shop? What do you think?"

I gave some careful thought to my reply. "Yes, that's interesting. Why didn't he just buy flowers at the bodega?"

Al smiled. "That's easy. I know that Margarita had often told Roberto that she promised to not sell beer if he promised to not sell flowers. It was their little joke." The smile faded on his face. "She didn't like it that Rutilio literally gives them away at his place of course . . ."

I interrupted, puzzled. "I thought you said Rutilio had a restaurant?"

"Yes, but he always has cheap roses in plastic collars that he gives to the ladies at their table when the check is being paid. You know the sort of thing? It gives him a chance to speak to all the women."

"Ladies' man?" I asked. I was guessing that Rutilio was the chef in the red shirt I'd seen standing in the lane behind the crime scene that morning, but I hadn't met the chap yet.

"You could say that," replied Al enigmatically. "Likes himself, and, to be fair, he's a pretty handsome guy. But a 'ladies' man'? I believe that's what he'd like to think—but he's not known for having lots of girlfriends, locally. Though what he and the tourists get up to, I don't know. No complaints on that front, though. I've had some problems with his restaurant sign annoying the locals. It's a giant fluorescent portrait of his face, and it shines out in the night. The local fishermen say it frightens their catch away from the shore, and the folks who live close to the restaurant have complained ever since he erected it about a year ago. I think I've managed to calm things down, and now he's promised to turn it off at 1:00 AM each night."

"So, flowers?" I pressed on. "I don't have a suggestion as to why the killer wanted flowers."

Al sat forward in his seat. "I thought he might not be alone here. I thought it might suggest he had a woman with him." Al's words made my heart beat faster. I sipped at my beer bottle, but it was empty. I looked at the bottle and made a sad face. Luckily, Al bit.

"Another?" he asked. *As I suspected, the perfect host.*

I smiled. "Thanks. I'm more thirsty than I thought." He got up and left the room. *Phew!*

When Al returned with my second beer, he looked grim. "I've been thinking," he said. *Damn and blast! How can I stop him doing that?* "If the perpetrator did have a woman with him, maybe they were staying somewhere local." He sat at his desk and picked up a pad and pen. "I'll check it out in the morning," he said as he wrote.

"As you see best," I replied. "I think it's more likely that the killer sought out the flower shop with a purpose. He was simply giving himself a cover story, as you suggested, not expecting to be found on the scene. By the way, am I correct in understanding that Serena went to Margarita's store because she'd offered to take photographs of the storekeepers' wedding anniversary celebration? And that's also why you and Miguel were on the spot, in dress uniforms?"

Al smiled and looked at me. "Like I said, you're good at finding things out, Cait. Yes, that's all true. Serena had made the arrangements. We were all to meet at the bodega; she'd baked and decorated a surprise cake, and Margarita was to record the event for posterity."

"So you and Miguel were inside the bodega when the suspect was in the flower shop?"

Al nodded. "We were a little late, but the best shade for parking down there is near the spa, at the opposite end of the building to the bodega. We thought we might catch Serena at the spa before she left, but she was already out in the street when we arrived. She'd bumped into Frank Taylor and was trying to get him to join in, so we ended up beating her to the bodega. Miguel and I went in just before the killer left. He held the door open for Serena and Frank to enter. Yes, I was *that* close to a good friend when she was murdered, *and* to the man who did it, but I could do nothing to save her. I couldn't stop him." He took a deep drink from his bottle. His frustration was palpable.

My mind was racing. Roberto and Maria at the bodega, Serena and Frank, Miguel and Al—none of them could have killed

Margarita, because they'd all been in the company of others when the poor woman's throat was slashed. Allowing for the time it would have taken her to bleed out, she must have been attacked about two or three minutes before Bud entered her store. *That* was a real problem. At that time, not only had Serena been in the street with Frank, but two cops had also been there. No one could have left the flower shop without being seen within the critical time frame. *Wonderful!*

"If Margarita was a wonderful plantswoman, with a spotless reputation and a quiet personality, who lived the sort of life that didn't bring her into contact with anyone who might wish to do her harm, then this is an unsolvable puzzle," I said. Aloud as it turned out.

"As you say," said Al thoughtfully.

"What else can you tell me about the victim?" I asked. *You're a victim profiler, Cait. Get on it!* "She wasn't *just* a woman with a fabulously green thumb; she was also a photographer. If she was out and about with her camera, she might have photographed something she shouldn't have," I suggested. It was an avenue worth exploring.

Al thought for a moment, then said quietly, "Margarita and I knew each other quite well. I think it might be because we both felt we didn't fit in too well with other people. Her scar, my mixed background. I can't say we were close, but I did know her better than most. Maybe not as well as Callie Booth knew her, but I knew her in a different way. Birds, landscapes, and plants were Margarita's favorite things to photograph. She did weddings and social functions for the money, but her cameras were almost a part of her. She was always ready to shoot, so, yes, you have a point. Maybe she did, inadvertently, photograph something she shouldn't have." He sucked on the end of a pen. *Yuk! You'll put anything in your mouth!*

"Where did she go, Al? How did she live her life? Where might she have been, on a regular basis, to spot something out of the ordinary?"

Al sat back. "Her life was pretty simple, but it was dictated by what she was doing on a particular day. She might be out gathering flowers at her own hacienda early in the morning, before their blooms opened in the sun, then she'd jump onto her bicycle and take them directly to her store. If she'd ordered flowers that she didn't grow herself, for a function or a wedding, she'd cycle to the store, collect her little van, and get to the big flower market in PV very early, then do all the arranging back at her store. On days when she didn't have a special occasion, she'd fulfill her contractual agreements with the Rocas Hermosas Resort, tending to their gardens and plants, or delivering displays she'd made to other locations. Her store was open to the public from 10:00 AM until noon, then from 3:00 PM until 6:00 PM each day. She never took a siesta, she worked. Out in the heat of the sun, or in the torrential downpours we have here in the summer months. If she didn't have contract work, she'd cycle back to her place when the store was shut to work on her plants there. When she closed up, she might drive to some final places with arrangements. I know she did that for the Amigos del Tequila deliveries, because it meant she was less likely to run into her father. He works at the Hacienda Soleado all day, tending the agave there, but he is finished by 4:00 PM, so she'd only go there when he had gone home. Then she'd drop the van back at the store and cycle home. She cycled most places because she loved it, and because it was cheaper than putting gas in her van. People around here have to be careful with money because there's not much of it and their income can be highly seasonal. I swear, she loved her bicycle more than any person. Especially her father."

I jumped in. "So what's the story there? Do you know the cause of the rift between Juan and his daughter?"

Al drew closer, becoming more conspiratorial. "Honestly, I don't think either of them came to terms with the loss of Margarita's mother and brothers: she and her father were distant from that point on. He hardly visited her when she was in hospital recovering from her burns. At least, that's what she told me. He's never spoken of it. Juan being both the mayor of the municipality *and* the one responsible for the agave crop at the Friends of Good Tequila Trust property meant that he and Margarita were at loggerheads over the past year or so. You see, as mayor, Juan has a responsibility to the whole community for certain aspects of municipal life, one of those being the water supply. Our water comes from a collection of 'public' springs up on the hillside, springs that were designated by one of our far-sighted forefathers, Juan Carlos García García, as being essential to the public good. But, as the man also responsible for ensuring a good crop of agave at the Hacienda Soleado, Juan is employed by one of the biggest water users in the municipality. Agave don't need much water to survive and thrive, but making tequila uses a *lot* of water, and Margarita accused him of putting the interests of his employers, the FOGTT, ahead of the interests of the local community. She was also very angry that Juan had sold off such a large portion of his land to the developers who built the Rocas Hermosas, a resort down on the seafront, then went and sold off even *more* to the FOGTT."

I was pretty sure I was missing something. "Hang on a minute. Are you telling me that Juan owned the land where the Rocas Hermosas Resort is built?" Al nodded. "*And* he owned the land where the Hacienda Soleado is now?" More nodding. "*And* he's the mayor? *And* the jimador at the FOGTT property?" He nodded again. "How come? I know this is a small place, but one man seems to own a lot, or *have owned* a lot, *and* has a lot of power. How does that happen?" Scenarios featuring rampant corruption were racing through my mind, so I thought it best to ask.

"Ha!" cried Al. It seemed it was quite his thing! "Of course. You don't know. A quick history lesson will explain . . ."

As I thought to myself, *oh yes, please let it be quick*, my tummy rumbled, agreeing with my brain that I needed to do something other than suck on a beer, so I put down the bottle, almost untouched.

"Okay, here are the facts: the French arrived, they married, and they bred. General Phillipe Dubois was a very well-connected French general, and he married the daughter of the most powerful family in this area. It was a good political match. When the French were defeated, Dubois was allowed to stay, with all of his lands intact, because of the influence of his wife's family. He dropped his 'Dubois' name and adopted her family's 'García.' There are a lot of people in Punta de las Rocas with García somewhere in their name because Dubois, aka the husband García, and his wife, García, had six sons and five daughters, all of whom stayed and were granted land of their own from within the family's huge holdings. Most of *them* also married and had children, who also stayed. We Spanish adopt both the name of our father's and of our mother's families. Around here, it's possible to run into a few people whose name contains García twice. It can become confusing. The eldest son of the original couple, Juan Carlos García García, never married and never had children of his own. He traveled a great deal, especially in the southern states of America, and he was recognized as a talented negotiator and diplomat, involved in both local and international politics. He kept the family's fortune in one piece through revolutions and wars, and by the mid-twentieth century he was in a position to grant that the lands held at that time by the children of the García family would become their own property, which they could then dispose of as they wished. Juan García Martinez, in other words Juan Martinez, our mayor, has inherited land from at least five deceased family members. You see, back then people had more children than they do now, so, as there have been fewer offspring to inherit, and as siblings die, the land is now becoming consolidated into fewer hands. Margarita inherited *her* land from her mother's side of the family when she reached the age of eighteen. It was, at one time, three parcels of land, which all happened to abut each other, which isn't always the case."

I was beginning to get a hint of something that might have caused problems in the locality. "Are people now angry with each other if they inherit a parcel of land they can't access because they have to cross another person's land to get to theirs?"

"Very perceptive," replied Al. "When it was all about brothers and sisters I guess it could get a *bit* heated, but now we have people who haven't been closely related for a couple of generations needing to work together to make the land viable. Access is just one issue. The other is water."

"Water?" I was surprised.

Al nodded. "It's all well and good attracting the tourists, but they use so much water it's alarming. I swear they just sit in those condos on the front and leave the taps running all day. Within the last few months, before the rains started, it became a real hot-button issue hereabouts. You see, it's been dryer than usual for the last couple of years, so those with one of the dozens of hillside springs on their property are doing much better than those who rely on the rains or the communal springs. It's been tough for a lot of people, and Juan hasn't helped at all, some say, because he hasn't tackled the subject of a sustainable water supply for all."

"His daughter thought he should put the needs of the community ahead of his personal finances? That selling his land to developers just put greater pressure on the local water supply?"

Al nodded. "I'm in law enforcement, so I'm not supposed to have an opinion. If I were pressed . . ." He raised his eyebrows, and I nodded. "I'd say that our mayor, the estimable Señor Juan Martinez, doesn't care about anyone but himself. He'll sell every square inch of land he owns one day very soon, then disappear into the sunset with a well-padded bank account."

"Will he inherit Margarita's property?"

Al nodded. "As far as folks hereabouts know, he's Margarita's only living relative. Certainly her closest, so I believe he'll get her hacienda and with it one of the most productive and reliable springs on the hill. Margarita also owned two large waterfront parcels, handed down from her mother's side of the family. She wanted them to stay natural, to remain wild and accessible to all. She loved them very much, and I know she'd go there often, hiding in the sand dunes, or behind huge rocks, photographing birds, plants, and, sometimes, the fish that come close to the shore. Back in the old days everyone wanted hillsides where they could raise agave and animals. Only the ones who wanted to fish were interested in the beaches. Now, of course, it's a different story. Look along the coastline. It's not just the beaches that are golden, it's the land itself. It's the new gold rush."

I gave it some thought. There was a clear motive for Juan to kill his daughter: land. *A lot of it.* He hadn't seemed overly upset when Al told him she was dead. Was it that dreadful, and that simple—a man had killed his child for the cash he could make? And where *exactly* had Juan Martinez been when his daughter was killed? Had he been the one driving his truck past the crime scene that morning?

"I don't think Juan would have hired a killer to get Margarita out of the way," said Al, thumping his desk, making me jump.

"Why not?"

"If he'd wanted her dead he'd have probably just slit her throat himself. I think he's got it in him." Al made the statement wearing a grim expression. I was quite taken aback. "But he didn't. That guy in there did it." He sucked his pen again. He'd sounded almost disappointed.

My tummy gave an almighty growl, and I blushed.

Al grinned. "I've got an idea. Why don't I take you for something to eat at Rutilio's? It's Sunday, which is Grill Night, when all he does is salsas, salads, and meat and vegetables on the grill. He reckons the smell of the meat attracts the tourists staying at the Rocas Hermosas Resort, and that when they see how wonderful his place is they'll keep going back all week. I don't know, but it's a good night to go. Meat's not cheap, but he makes it go a long way. You up for it? We could keep talking about Margarita, if you like. Or you could even have one to drink." He smiled wistfully. "She couldn't stand them. Margaritas. Margarita didn't like margaritas."

"Yes, I get it," I said softly. "Okay, I'm game, and I am pretty famished. Let's go." I tried to sound cheery. It meant I could meet Rutilio, and maybe get a look into the alley behind the flower shop, to check out if the store had a back entrance, which was the only way I could imagine that this otherwise impossible murder had taken place.

I pulled my purse onto my shoulder. "Will we have to pass . . . ?" I nodded in Bud's direction.

"No, let's not," replied Al. "We can go through the back and around to the car that way. The trip won't take long; it's only about ten minutes away."

Yes, I know, I thought. Al flicked the light switches and I imagined Bud being plunged into darkness again. My heart ached for him, but I knew that the only way I could help him was to press on with my investigation. We set off in Al's car once more and made our way toward the blackness of the sea. In the distance I could see the lights along the Malecón in Puerto Vallarta, glittering like a diamond necklace set in a jet velvet case, and all I wanted to do was take Bud by the hand and enjoy the night air.

Time to Dine

UPON OUR ARRIVAL AT RUTILIO'S Restaurant, the first thing I noticed about our host was his wide, white, and worrying smile. The folds in his tall chef hat looked like an elongated version of his teeth.

"Alfredo!" called the chef to Al, as we entered. Having only seen Rutilio from a distance that morning, this was my first chance to get a close look at him. What I had thought was a red shirt was, in fact, a red chef jacket. His black pants were snug, and I could see the flash of a heavy gold chain that hung about his neck, nestled in dark hair. I understood what Al had meant about Rutilio being good-looking, but to me, he was just a bit . . . *too much.* His facial hair, which I hadn't noticed at all from my perch in the condo, was of the type that suggests a man has little else to do with his time than stand in front of the bathroom mirror and painstakingly carve tiny little rims of beard along the contours of his face. He sported a mustache across his top lip that couldn't have been more than four hairs wide, and it looked as though someone had used a Sharpie to draw a line around his jawline. It gave a very unsettling impression. As he held out a welcoming hand all I could notice was how hairy his arms were. *I hope none of those hairs make it into the food I'm about to eat,* was my less than charitable thought, and I immediately visualized his back as being chimp-like. *Way to go, Cait, there's no unimagining that one!*

"Pleased to meet you, I am Rutilio," said the grinning chef, shaking my hand.

"Hello. Likewise, I'm sure. I'm Cait," I replied, smiling politely. I told myself that his hands were soft and slippery because he'd been working with food.

"And what are you doing, Alfredo, bringing an older woman to dinner?" Rutilio asked Al in Spanish. He'd obviously decided I couldn't possibly speak his language, and I made sure that my expression didn't give away the fact that I understood every word he'd said. I wasn't pleased about being referred to as an "older woman." Okay, I *was* older than the two men talking about me, but honestly—if forty-eight got me that title, what on earth would I be called when I reached my sixties?

Al glanced at me sideways, then replied in Spanish, "She's going to help me find out who that guy is who killed Margarita." It was odd—this was the first time I'd heard Al speak Spanish, and he more than changed his language, he changed his voice. It dropped at least half an octave and took on a harder edge. *Interesting.*

"Ah-ha!" exclaimed Rutilio, adding, in English, "You are the Canadian. You speak oddly, but you will help make Alfredo's career take off!"

It seemed that the entire population of Punta de las Rocas had Al's career progression in mind. *Very odd.* And what did Rutilio mean by "speak oddly"? *I don't speak oddly.*

"That's one way of putting it," I replied, quite tartly, "but I don't know what you mean about how I speak." *Oh shut up, sit down, and eat something, Cait!*

Al and Rutilio had the good grace to exchange embarrassed glances. The chef flung his hands in the air and beamed even wider—*I hadn't thought that possible.*

"Come. Sit. Eat. I will bring drinks," declaimed the chef. Since none of the other diners paid any heed to us, I assumed he must treat all his guests the same way. "Tonight we grill. We grill everything. Chicken, beef, pork. Everything. Even the vegetables we grill tonight. But the salad? No. We do not grill the salad!" He laughed loudly at his own joke. He was the only one who did.

Al and I sat at a small table inside the restaurant. The place surprised me. I'd expected something more . . . authentic. Instead, the walls were bedecked with Mexican blankets—which also served as under-cloths on the tables, on top of which were paper covers, with patterns cut into them. The walls displayed sad sombreros and even a few plastic lobsters. Tealight candles danced inside colored jars on each table, and the background music was elevator-style mariachi. I cast my eyes over the giant plastic-covered menu, which offered a dizzying array of burritos, tacos, fajitas, salsas, margaritas, and tequilas—among other traditional Mexican fare. Despite their presence on the walls, there were no lobster dishes on offer. I couldn't help but longingly recall the much more appealing menu at Amigos del Tequila. Rutilio's prices seemed fair enough, but the small sheet that was attached for Grill Night displayed one, much higher, set price for the evening's offerings. I decided what I wanted in about thirty seconds, then raised my head and looked around. I noted that all the tables outside were occupied by pale-skinned tourists like myself, and that there was only one other table being used inside. The couple sitting at it waved to Al, and he waved back.

"Friends?" I asked, knowing full well who they were.

"It's Roberto and Maria. They own the bodega. It is their wedding anniversary. For them to come here is very unusual. It's very expensive, by local standards."

I dared to wave as well, hoping they'd come to speak to us. I was thinking they might give me more insight about Margarita, from a local perspective. I was in luck. The man spoke hurriedly to his wife and came toward our table, smiling. Upon his arrival he nodded at Al, grinned at me, and held out his hand.

"I am very pleased to meet you, Doctor Cait," he said in delightfully formed English. I stood and shook his hand. I guessed his English must be good, given the location of his store and the fact that pretty much all of his customers must be English-speaking, probably with little Spanish.

"Would you like to join us?" I asked. "Your wife too, of course. I understand it is a very important day for you both, and maybe we can send you on your way with a celebratory drink?" It was clear to me that they'd finished their meal and were almost ready to leave.

"We do not drink, thank you very much," replied Bob. "My wife would like the chance to greet you." He turned to his wife, nodded, and gestured to her to join us, which she did.

"I am pleased to meet you, Doctor Cait," said Maria, smiling. She almost curtsied. *Bless her.*

As Al brought two more chairs to our table, I noted that Bob and Maria were a well-matched couple, at least physically. Both were about my height and about my girth, *short and plump*, and they both had kind, gentle eyes. The folds in their faces had been formed by smiling, not frowning, and their hands moved automatically toward each other's, as though they were joined by a force that kept them close. Maria was a giggler, that was evident within moments. Bob whispered something to her, and she couldn't stop herself from tittering after that. I wished I could have heard what it was that he'd said, because I could have done with a smile myself. I suspected it was one of those "couple-y" comments that makes no sense to an outsider, but builds bonds in a relationship and keeps it fresh.

Rutilio arrived with coffee for our guests, as well as chips, salsa, and water. He took our orders and set off to prepare our food on the grill and the margarita that Al insisted I needed. It seemed as though an impromptu little party was about to break out, and, although I felt sorry for the anniversary couple, I couldn't let that happen. I had to steer the conversation toward Margarita, to find out as much more about her as I could.

"It's a delight to meet you both," I said honestly. "I am guessing you already know that I'm going to be working with Al to try to find out who the guy in his cells might be?"

They nodded. Bob spoke, "Yes, we know this. News travels very quickly around here, as Alfredo knows." I noted that the Mexicans tended to call Al "Alfredo," whereas the imported residents seemed happier to refer to him as "Al." As he'd said, he was a man partially accepted by both groups.

I continued, "So, if it's okay with you, I'd like to take this chance to ask a few questions about Margarita. I'm trying to understand her life, you see?"

Bob nodded. "Yes, we all would like Alfredo to be able to show the Federales he is clever," said Bob. *What is it with this community? Why are they all so supportive of Al?*

"Great," I said, "so what sort of a person would you say Margarita was?"

Bob and Maria looked at each other and spoke very rapidly in Spanish, their voices low, their heads close. I found it difficult to catch every word, but I understood enough.

"She was wicked. Very wicked," said Bob. Having already picked up on what they were saying, I feigned shock. Al looked genuinely horrified.

"You can't mean that," said Al sharply. "She was a very gentle woman. She was kind and thoughtful." He sounded wounded.

"That was what she wanted people to think. Since she was a child, she has been mean. Spiteful, and keeping secrets. She does not like people. She has no husband, no children. She said she did not like children, even. *And* she did not say Mass." That seemed to seal it for the short, portly couple with the smiling faces.

Al looked less concerned. I suspected that, like me, he was registering the dislike this couple had for the dead woman as more a reflection of their own values than of Margarita's. I decided to probe a little further.

"What do you mean, she kept secrets?" *This could be fertile territory.*

Again the couple chattered to each other. Half sentences, not needing to finish them.

This time Maria spoke, more gently than her husband. "It is difficult to say. But she always looked like a woman who knew something that she was not going to share. A look in her eyes that said 'I know,' but she did not say what she knew." *Interesting.*

"Can you give me an example of what you mean?" I needed to know if Maria had really seen Margarita say, or do, something that might have given someone cause to be afraid of her knowledge.

This time the couple didn't confer; they said "Si" simultaneously, then laughed. Bob gestured that his wife should speak first.

"One day last week she was inside our bodega when Greg arrived. You know Greg?" she asked.

"I haven't met him yet, but I know of him," I replied quickly.

She nodded her understanding. "He arrived at the bodega in a hurry. He needed some snacks for people who were coming to his house, and he came to us. He likes that we have a very good supplier of nuts, and, having been a nut farmer for most of his life, he is very fussy." I could feel myself wondering where this story would go. "He was paying Bob, and he said that it was a good thing that he could come to us to provide supplies he could rely on for good quality, and Margarita said she knew how important good, reliable quality was to him. But she said it in a way that I didn't think she meant snacks. Her eyes, her expression. She was saying something she was not saying. This is what I mean." *Very interesting.*

Bob spoke up. "It was the same one day when we were outside the store closing the doors at night. She had come back to her place for something and asked if she could get some milk. Of course we opened the door and gave her the milk. As we were locking the door again, Dorothea walked by, on the way to her car, I think, and Margarita held the milk to the sky and said, very loudly, 'Milk from the local animals, you cannot do better. The best quality, very fresh. Local milk, local cow.' Dorothea laughed a funny laugh and went on her way. Margarita had a face that was sly when she spoke this way. She was mean. She kept secrets. *And* she did not go to church except when Miguel's daughter died. She attended the Requiem Mass with Miguel that day, but it was unusual for her."

Al looked puzzled and silently chewed on the end of the straw that poked out of his glass of water.

"And you say that she'd been spiteful since she was a child?" I asked. I had to keep going.

A quick conference resulted in Bob replying, "Yes, but maybe this is understandable. It was very sad when her mother and her brothers died. When she went back to school, the children were very mean to her. One of our boys was in school at the same time. He was older than Margarita, and he tried to stand up for her when some of the others made fun of her scar. But she beat our boy, who was helping her, then told him he was to leave her alone. He tried to help her again, another time, but again she turned against him. We spoke to him about it, but our boy said she did not want to be helped. So it went her whole life. Margarita never asked anyone for help. She did everything for herself, by herself. That is not good. In life you need family and friends. She needed a husband. It was sad, but she was a very lonely person because she chose plants, not people."

It appeared that Al could be silent no longer. "She had *some* friends, Roberto. I think that Margarita and I were friendly, and Callie and she were good friends." I didn't dare frown at him. If it had been Bud butting in, I would have done.

Maria smiled. "Ah, Callie Booth. She is a nice girl. Very young, very modern. She is from America, where they do not lead very religious lives. Maybe this is why they were close."

I could see that the couple was getting a bit restive, and I suspected that running the bodega meant that their days began early. Also, Rutilio was sending our food from the grill, but I wanted to ask one more question.

"This has all been most helpful," I said, "but I have one more question. If your name is Roberto, why is your store called Bob's Bodega?"

The couple giggled in unison. Maria covered her face and slapped her husband on the arm.

Bob raised his hands in mock submission. "Ah, that is me." He grinned. "It costs less to have the man paint 'Bob' rather than 'Roberto' on the sign. We saved a little money," he leaned toward me and whispered, ". . . and it makes the foreigners feel happier to come into the store, I think. They like that I am 'Bob.'"

As our food arrived, the little couple took their cue to leave. Al insisted that their coffee was to be our treat, and they happily went on their way as I tucked into my mixed grill, which, in Rutilio's Restaurant, comprised a chicken breast, a pork chop, a small steak, a skewer of grilled peppers and mushrooms, and a couple of pieces of grilled sweet corn. *I was really hungry!*

Eating didn't allow much chance to talk, and it was clear that Al was as famished as I was. We both sat there, eating quickly and silently, nodding and smiling occasionally as the food on our plates disappeared, and I gradually began to feel more human. After about fifteen minutes, both our plates were empty, and a young girl wearing a full red skirt and a white, peasant-style blouse whisked them away. I realized I'd hardly touched my margarita, and I could see that the ice had almost completely melted. The guests at the outside tables were starting to drift away. It was gone ten o'clock.

"Let's take our drinks outside and smoke," suggested Al.

"We have to smoke *outside*?" I shouldn't have been surprised. I don't think there's anywhere left on the planet where you can smoke *inside* a restaurant.

Al smiled. "We only have to move to the next table."

He rose, and I followed. He offered me a chair, which I accepted. I sipped my drink. It was still cold enough for me, because I'm not a big lover of icy drinks—my European upbringing is to blame for that—but it was strong. *Too strong.* And sharp. A lime margarita would not have been my choice.

"Good, right?" asked Al.

I decided to be honest. "It's a bit acidic for me, and it's *very* strong."

Al grinned. "I guess Rutilio was a bit heavy-handed with the tequila because you're such a special guest."

"Is yours as strong?" I asked. Al had already knocked back two drinks that looked to be the same as the one I was sipping at.

Again Al smiled his slightly lopsided grin. "I might be of mixed race, but when it comes to tequila, I am Mexican through and through. It might sound terrible, but I was drinking tequila when I was very young. I would slip off with my father to the bars where he played his guitar   I told you he was a mariachi player of some note, and that is how my mother met him. Did you know that mariachi was invented in Jalisco State?" I nodded that I had known that little nugget. "When we were in the bars I would drink tequila with water. Just the young tequila, not the very strong stuff, of course, because I was just a child. My father and mother would argue about it. It stood me in good stead when I went to university." As he reminisced, he drew deeply on his cigarette and smiled warmly. "The number of drinking games I won, the number of times I beat someone at a game of pool because the other guy was so drunk—it made me some money, my ability to drink tequila. Maybe you think that's very bad of me?" His eyes twinkled.

"Not really," I replied. "I'm Welsh. The Scots have Scotch, the Irish have Guinness, the English have bitter, but the Welsh don't really have a national drink, which, I think, is because we'll drink anything and everything, so long as there's a lot of it. The Welsh tend to drink quite a lot, Al, we just don't make a song and dance of it. Well," I corrected myself, "maybe we do make a bit of a song of it, because hymns and rugby anthems are likely to be sung when enough has been drunk, but that's about it." I decided that knocking back the margarita was the only graceful way I was going to get myself a more pleasant drink. As I did just that, Rutilio appeared at our table.

"Good meal?" he asked. Al and I praised his abilities at the grill, as he drew up a chair and made himself comfortable. He waved as patrons left their tables, and two young girls cleared around us, obviously used to their tasks. I suspected they were the previously wayward sisters of Serena the Screamer, as I found myself thinking of her. It made me smile.

Rutilio called to one of the girls in Spanish, "Bring the bottles." She did. The tray she bore looked alarming: a dozen empty shot glasses and four of the stubby, dimpled bottles I'd seen at Tony's restaurant earlier in the day.

Rutilio opened one of the bottles with clear liquid in it. "And now, as my guest, Cait Morgan, you will learn about tequila," he said. "We will begin with this, the youngest. I am guessing, like most visitors, you know nothing about tequila?" It seemed he was keen to teach me, and I felt my heart sink. *I don't need this; I need to get my head around what I'm learning about Margarita.*

As Rutilio filled three glasses from the bottle, Al's cellphone rang. He answered, listened, said "Si" a few times, finally clamped it shut, and popped it back into its little holster. He stood and said, "I must go. It is Tony and Callie. They have been found. They are back at their apartment. Callie had a minor accident in her car, and Tony went to collect her. She is not hurt, which is good. She was upset by the news about Margarita and lost control on the highway. It sounds as though her car is in bad shape. She wants to talk to me. About something Margarita said to her. Tony says she is getting herself cleaned up. I must go. Do you want to come, Cait?"

The words "pope" and "Catholic" flew across my mind, but I managed to edit that and said aloud, "Absolutely! Sorry, Rutilio, maybe I can come back some other time to learn about tequila?"

Rutilio leaped to his feet and bowed with mock gallantry. "Anytime you like. But I have poured these glasses now, so raise them with me, and here's to a safe journey and a good meeting." He picked up one shot glass, Al picked up another, and I felt I had no choice but to pick up the remaining one. The two men didn't knock back their drinks, but, instead, took down the liquid in two savoring mouthfuls. I did likewise, my lips burning, then my tongue, then my throat. *Tequila's really not my thing.*

I forced a smile as I thanked Rutilio for a wonderful meal. Al insisted upon settling up, and as he paid, he winked at Rutilio and asked in Spanish, "What, no flower for the lady?"

Rutilio shrugged and replied gruffly, in his mother tongue, "It is the summer. The season when the tourists are looking for a bargain, so they do not spend much money. That means I have to save every peso I can, so no flowers for the women until October when the rains stop, and the people with the money come back again."

Al shrugged in response. As we left, he whistled a tune that had been playing on the loudspeakers at the restaurant, and lit a cigarette. I wasn't at all convinced that he was in the best shape to drive, and I thought I'd be doing myself two favors if I could talk him into letting me see the crime scene. I decided to give it a go.

"Since we're so close to Margarita's store, is there any chance I could just take a quick look inside? I was thinking that I might gain some insights by seeing her place of work. I wouldn't need long."

I dared a sweet smile, and Al hesitated. "Just five minutes. That's all I'll need. Or don't you have the authority to open up the crime scene?" *That should do it.*

"Of course I have the authority," replied Al huffily, "*and* I have the keys with me. I don't have to hand them over to the Federales until they take the prisoner, so, yes, let's go. I think it would be good for you to see Margarita's store." He strode off toward the building that housed the crime scene. *Hurrah for ambition and pride!*

Time to Smell the Roses

IT SURPRISED ME THAT THERE was no tape across the door to Margarita's flower shop, but I was completely shocked when Al opened the door and turned on the lights. I'd expected a pool of blood to cover the floor, as I'd seen at the time of Bud's discovery, but there was almost none.

"Where's all the blood?" I asked. It seemed a reasonable question.

"Ah, yes," replied Al, clearing his throat. "That was Miguel. After the photographers left, and Margarita's body was gone, he collected the knife, which we found next to her, then, it seems, he decided to mop the floor. His brother brought him a bucket and brush. He thought it would prevent the flies from congregating. Miguel *has* been trained in crime scene preservation, but he found the blood . . . upsetting."

I could tell by Al's expression that he was feeling a mixture of emotions—embarrassment and anger were clearly uppermost, but I could also sense pity. It was clear that he indulged Miguel, to a certain extent, and I was pretty sure it was because of the man's own recent tragic loss of a daughter. It's an aspect of murder that I've become too familiar with—the way it completely changes the lives of all those left behind, *and* how they are treated by others. Right now the main reaction in the local community was shock, but I knew very well that once I managed to work out who had really killed Margarita, there would be more ramifications.

I allowed my eyes to adjust to the light. Margarita had installed low-energy directional lamps, the type that take time to reach full luminosity. When they do, they replicate daylight, without giving off too much heat, which is ideal for a floral store where color and temperature are critical elements. *Obviously a woman for whom detail was important.* The store was very small, and the whole room had been whitewashed. To the right was a workbench, allowing space to build arrangements; to the left was a small counter with a cash register. The rest of the room was almost entirely full of flowers in layered rows of buckets, all painted white, leaving very little floor space. My heart sank as I realized that there was no back door. The entire back wall housed a refrigerated unit with sliding double doors—the sort that holds drinks in grocery stores but, in this case, held more buckets, a few of which contained flowers. *Damn and blast—I was counting on a back entrance!*

The store was cool, but the smell was almost overpowering—a mixture of floral fragrances, which was to be expected, but there was an undertone of chemicals.

"Did Miguel use bleach when he cleaned?" I asked.

Al looked puzzled. "He didn't say he did, but who knows?" He sounded exasperated.

"If he did, he'll have compromised any blood forensics," I said.

Al sighed. "I know, but that doesn't matter, right? I *have* the guy." He sounded testy. *Careful, Cait.* "What does this place tell you about Margarita?" I could tell that Al was beginning to get impatient with me, so I decided to "do my thing"—just a little bit.

"Okay, let's see . . . her attention to detail is everywhere: the lighting, the temperature, the layout allowing her to see and access her entire stock, the white décor to allow the colors of the flowers to stand out, as well as her cleared workspace and her super storage ideas—see how she's stacked photographic equipment underneath her workbench?" Al nodded as I pointed to the neatly piled black plastic cases. "She's got schedules pasted to the wall: the planner shows she's well organized and plans ahead, but it also shows that she has no personal time—the hours where work tasks are allocated run from 6:00 AM until 7:00 PM, and she has 'home work' planned in for the evenings. Margarita clearly lived to work, rather than working to live. One thing—I can see she had a wedding planned for the day after tomorrow at the Rocas Hermosas Resort, the name is Sullivan, and they ordered '24 rosas rojas con gyp,' which I believe is red roses with gypsophila, or baby's breath. Maybe you could get hold of the family and tell them they'll need to make new plans?"

Al nodded and took out his notebook. "That's thoughtful, good point," he said, scribbling down the details and glancing at the wall planner.

"There is nothing personal here. *Everything* is related to the plants, the flowers, the business, and her professions as a plantswoman and photographer. There are no photographs of her, or of her family members—dead or alive—and there isn't even a mirror. This place is all business. *She* is all business. Her plants are her life. In fact, I get no sense of Margarita the person in this store, just Margarita the businesswoman."

I took the five steps needed to get to the refrigerated units at the back of the shop and peered in. "Are these the type of roses that Margarita grew, or would she have ordered these at the market?" I nodded toward the two buckets of red, and one bucket of yellow, long-stemmed roses that were accompanied by a huge bucket full of baby's breath.

Al smiled. "She didn't grow those." He looked around and spotted a photograph on the neat cork noticeboard. He pointed. "These are Margarita's roses," he said proudly.

The photograph showed pink, shrubby roses, with full, slightly nodding heads. Some canes were trained onto arches. It was as though I could smell them—a true rose scent.

"Constance Spry," I said.

"Pardon?"

"It's the name of the rose. Constance Spry, named after the famous English flower arranger. She was quite the woman in her day and really popularized the concept of floral arrangement as an art. How wonderful! Obviously Margarita knew her field: it was Constance Spry who changed how people thought about floral arrangements. She introduced unusual materials, containers, and shapes. She herself was very involved in the cultivation of old English roses, and when David Austin introduced his first English Rose in 1961, he named it after her. This is *that* rose: classic, a true rose pink, with a true rose scent. Beautiful."

Al looked surprised. "You seem to know a great deal about roses, and those who arrange them," he said quietly.

I have no idea what came over me. Maybe it was the stress of the day, maybe it was the tequila, but I could feel myself fill up with tears. *Not now, Cait!* "It's because of my mum. Her wedding bouquet was arranged by a woman who trained under Constance Spry herself, at her Flower School in London, England. The woman who made my mum's bouquet, back in the 1950s, was known throughout South Wales, and my mum and dad had to drive into the wilds of the Welsh Valleys to collect the bouquet the day before their wedding. It was quite an undertaking, they said."

"They told you this?" Al seemed intrigued.

I sighed. "Yes. My mum spoke of it often. They didn't have much when they married—nothing, in fact, especially by today's standards. But that was one thing she spent money on. I remember she had a pressed rosebud from her wedding bouquet that she would show me when I was a child."

"Are your parents . . . passed?" asked Al awkwardly.

I smiled. "Yes, they are. They died quite a few years ago. A stupid, tragic accident. They were driving . . . oh, it doesn't matter where they were going. All that matters is that I didn't have a chance to say goodbye . . ."

"I know how that feels," said Al with obvious emotion. It seemed that my very personal revelations were allowing him to open up to me. *Of course!*

"You and Margarita. You had feelings for her?" I knew the answer before I asked the question.

"She was a very private person, as I have said. She didn't have much room in her life for personal relationships, but I enjoyed her company, when I was able to share it. I had . . . maybe 'hope' is too strong a word, but I hoped for hope. Do you understand?"

Al looked very vulnerable at that moment. His anger upon finding Bud kneeling over Margarita's dead body made more sense. In fact, considering that he believed Bud to be the man who killed the woman for whom he clearly felt affection, Al had behaved in a very honorable manner toward Bud, clothing and feeding him in the jail as he had.

"I'm sorry, Al. Loss is very difficult, and I know for a fact that there's nothing I can say right now to help you deal with it. But I *can* try to help you work through your emotions by being proactive, and trying to solve this mystery."

"Yes," said Al gently. "It will help me if I can find out who he is, and understand why he did this."

We were both silent for a moment. I didn't look at Al—he deserved a little privacy. Instead, I took in all that I could about Margarita's store. There was literally nowhere for anyone to hide. There was no way in or out, except by the front door. So how on earth had someone managed to get into the store, kill her, and get out again, unseen, within a three minute window, when there were two cops, and at least two other people, in the street outside the door? It was *impossible*!

I noted that Margarita must have had a lot of money tied up in stock: the most valuable, and delicate, blooms were in the refrigerated unit at the back of the store. I noted the still-plump heads of the almost two dozen red and dozen yellow roses. Then I noticed something glinting between the dark green leaves.

"What's that?" I said, pointing at the shiny object and bobbing my head about to try to make it out.

Al drew himself from his reverie and stepped forward. He slid open the floor-to-ceiling door of the refrigerated unit and moved one of the buckets of roses. There was a chrome handle in the back wall. He pulled it, and the wall swung out. *A door! Yay!*

"It's a *door*!" I tried to sound surprised rather than jubilant.

Al stepped into the refrigerator, then right out through the narrow opening. It was tight, but it was clearly big enough for most people to fit through. Once he'd stepped out over the foot-high lip, he looked around. "It's the lane. Her van is here. I guess this is where she loaded in her chilled stock," he said. "I had no idea. I've driven along the lane many times, and it's quite obvious that the spa, the bodega, and the restaurant all have rear entrances that lead out onto it, but I wasn't aware that this existed. Not that it matters except . . ." he stepped back into the refrigerator, shut the door, then joined me in the store again, sliding the glass door shut, "that it means the murderer didn't know about the way out." He smiled. "That's useful to know, right?"

"I certainly think we've learned something very useful in the past few moments," I replied truthfully, though, for me, the discovery of a way to access the crime scene that avoided the street meant I now had a way forward. I had to stop myself from getting overexcited. I took a deep breath, then one last long look around. I like gardens, but I'm not a big fan of cut flowers. The idea that Bud was coming to this store to buy flowers for me meant a great deal. It's the *idea* of flowers that's lovely, rather than having them. I hate to think of them dying, little by little, in the vase. As I looked about, I saw death all around me. There must have been hundreds and hundreds of dollars' worth of flowers, all about to wilt, then rot. What a shame. Like Margarita herself. A terrible waste.

As though he'd picked up on my feelings, Al said, "If you're done, let's go. I'd like to find out what it was that Margarita said to Callie. It might be nothing, but it could be something."

"Hoping for hope?" I said.

He nodded. "We can *at least* do that," he replied, and we left the store as we'd found it, full of death, decay, and silence.

Too Late

AL PARKED THE CAR AT the open back door of Amigos del Tequila. The kitchen was deserted, and there were no aromas of food—which was just as well because I was still feeling quite full.

"Hello?" called Al.

Footsteps descended the staircase in the corner of the kitchen, and Tony appeared, shh-ing us as he did so. "She's asleep." He nodded toward the apartment upstairs. "Let's go into the bar," he added, heading off through the swinging doors. We followed. Tony flicked switches, and the lighting behind the rows of bottles that stood in front of the mirrored bar came on. "Drink?" he asked us. "I'm having one, so, please, let me get one for you guys too."

"Pacifico," said Al and I in unison. We all smiled.

As Tony poured the beers, I could see that he seemed to have aged since I'd met him earlier in the day. *Shock will do that.*

"How is your wife?" I asked.

Tony smiled. "She's fine, physically. They checked her out at the roadside, but she wouldn't let them take her to the clinic. She hasn't got a scratch on her, which is a miracle, but mentally, she's a mess. She said she'd been crying as she was driving and just misjudged things a bit. She came off the road and crunched the car up. She called me when it happened and I just ran out of the place. I don't even remember driving there. I saw her on the far side of the highway, but I had to pass her, because of the median, then drive back again. It was awful. I was so close to her, and yet she was out of reach." *I know that feeling.*

"You said she wanted to speak to me?" asked Al.

"Yes. When we got back here, everyone was sitting around eating.

Dean told me that, in my absence, they'd raided the kitchen and decided to eat. Which was fine, of course. But then Callie started crying all over again. I guess she felt relieved to be home at last, but she started blubbing that Margarita had told her something, and she needed to speak to you. Ada Taylor managed to calm her, and she and Jean took her upstairs. Dorothea went off to her house and came back with some sleeping pills. I wasn't very keen on Callie taking them, but Dorothea insisted. She can be very . . . overwhelming. To be fair, I think she means well, but you'd think she'd have learned her lesson by now. I heard that she talked a lot of her friends who shared the gated community where she lived in Florida into investing with some guy she knew. Everybody lost everything. So she sold up, moved all the way over here, and sunk every cent she had into this place. But *still* she tries to bend everyone to her will. Callie finally agreed that taking something would help her relax, and she's in a very deep sleep now, which I'm sure is a good thing. Would you mind dropping by in the morning, Al? I've got to go to the market, and I thought I'd go visit Callie's car and give it a good looking over. I got them to tow it into Bucerias. I think it might be a lost cause. It was old and battered anyway. I don't know what we'll do without it. The insurance won't buy us a replacement. Oh well, Callie's safe. That's all that matters."

"I'm glad she's okay," said Al, draining his bottle.

"Another?" asked Tony. Al nodded; I declined. I glanced at my watch. Almost midnight. That meant I'd already had a twenty-hour day, and I could feel myself flagging. It must have shown on my face as I drained my beer. Rutilio's grill had made me thirsty.

"How about I walk Cait to Casa LaLa, then come back and have that beer with you, Tony? You okay with that?"

"Sure, go ahead. I'm not going anywhere, and I need to wind down before I hit the sack." He, too, looked at his watch, then added, "I've gotta be out of here at 6:30, but I've got an hour in me yet."

I didn't want to impose. "I'm sure I can remember the way; I can get there on my own, Al. You stay here. Tony, when we were in your kitchen earlier today, there were two pots full of boiling water and, I think, pepper. Why was that?" I hoped to solve at least one of the day's mysteries.

Tony smiled. "Don't laugh—it's a thing I do." He looked embarrassed. "I'm not really a superstitious person, not in the way that some of the older generation can be around here. The things they get up to with their ancient sayings, habits, and beliefs. They seem to mix it in with Catholicism and it's all accepted by the church. But I do have a few little things that I like to do, and one of them is to season new pots with white pepper. A Mexican guy I worked with in a kitchen years ago said it makes the pot 'sweet'; in other words, everything it cooks will taste the best it can. You don't want to get too near the pots when they're boiling, though, 'cause the pepper in the steam can really do some damage."

So that was it. Instead of explaining that I'd learned that lesson for myself, I asked, "Do you have a flashlight I could borrow to help me on the track back to Casa LaLa?"

Tony grinned. "I have a supply out back. Just a sec," he said, leaving Al and me alone for a moment.

"Could I meet you here in the morning, to find out what Margarita told Callie?" I asked. I was desperate to know.

Al gave it some thought. When Tony reappeared, handing me a heavy flashlight, Al asked him if it was alright.

"I don't see why not. I suggest you give her a call around eight, or nine, and check? She should be awake by then, so if she's okay with it, you guys can come over to talk to her."

Al and I nodded our agreement. We all said goodnight, and I made my way out into the night.

Everything looks different by flashlight, so it took me about fifteen minutes to get back to Henry's place. I got inside, turned off, then reset the alarm, and headed straight for the washroom. The bed looked very appealing as I changed, but I ignored the temptation to just slip between the sheets and sleep. I picked up the pad of paper I'd made notes on earlier in the day and curled up on the sofa. It was comfy. *Too comfy.* I got up, canceled the alarm again, and pulled open the doors to the patio and pool. I managed to find a dimmer switch for the lights and set them at just the right level to be able to sit and write. The metal chair wasn't as comfortable as the sofa, but I needed to be alert—as alert as I could be. *Come on, Cait—Bud needs you!*

I'm good with lists. They help me organize my thoughts. So that's how I began. Having established that there was a rear entrance to Margarita's store, I decided to begin with a list of those I believed had the opportunity to gain access to the flower shop undetected, in the few minutes before Bud had entered it.

SUSPECTS WITH OPPORTUNITY

Unknown persons: killer MUST have been on scene in the three/ five minutes around time Bud entered flower shop, so MUST have been visible to me, or hidden from sight in roaring blue truck. Stick with the people I know were there.

Ada and Dorothea: both were at the spa, but not in sight of each other. Spa has back door onto lane. Time and opportunity to change blood-spattered clothes inside the spa before they entered the street. (Note: Door from the refrigerated unit to the lane would be a very tight squeeze for Dorothea. Possible?)

Dean and Jean: both appeared after the crime scene was discovered. Where had they been? Arrived from opposite ends of the building at different times. Had they been together, or not? Where would they have changed their clothes? FIND OUT!

Rutilio: was in the lane behind the crime scene around the time of the crime. (Note: Did he see anyone in the lane at the time? Did

Al even ask this? CHECK!) He could have changed his clothes inside the restaurant kitchen.

"Truck driver": the driver of the blue pickup truck that sped away just as Bud was discovered could have been Tony, Callie, Juan, or Greg. (Ada said Greg was in PV, might not have been.) Any one of these would have had the chance to clean themselves up before they were in public view. Also could have been total stranger in truck.

OTHERS

Bob and Maria: in the bodega at the time of the murder.

I paused. I questioned my assumption. All I knew for sure was that both Bob and Maria had been in the bodega when Al and Miguel had entered. I didn't *know* that they had both been there when Bud was buying our supplies. Either one of them could be providing an alibi for the other. I put a question mark beside their names. *They* had told me that Margarita was not the good person Al had thought her to be. Did their dislike of her run so deep that they might have wanted her dead? Had she "said something she was not saying" to them? Did *they*, or *one* of them, have something to hide that Margarita had found out about? Was there somewhere inside the bodega where they'd have had the opportunity to change out of blood-stained clothing before Al and Miguel saw them?

Serena (the Screamer) and Frank Taylor: with each other in the street at the time.

Al and Miguel: with each other at the time.

Okay, that was opportunity sorted, and the field was narrowed a little. Now, what about motives for those *with* the opportunity?

MOTIVES

Bob and Maria: disliked Margarita's lack of religious devotion, lack of a family life. They might have had secrets she knew about.

Juan: probably inherits his daughter's land. He and his daughter were already estranged. At loggerheads over his roles and responsibilities. LAND. WATER.

Greg: what did Margarita mean when she said to him that he knew the value of a "reliable, good-quality supply?"

Dorothea: what did Margarita mean when she mentioned "local milk from local cows" to her? Why did Dorothea lie about the time the crime took place?

Ada, Dean, Jean, Tony, Callie, Rutilio: any one of them might have a secret that Margarita had found out about, maybe because of her photography, and she might have obliquely mentioned her knowledge to them. This applies to possible outsiders, too.

Clearly I had more work to do in this area. Finally I addressed the question of the way in which Margarita had been killed. She was a small woman, but probably strong. That accepted, any one of my possible suspects could have slit her throat from behind, when she wasn't expecting it.

But who *would*?

It was such a violent way to kill someone that it suggested the hand of a man, rather than that of a woman. That didn't rule out a woman as her killer—the right woman, with the right motivation, *could* do it. Easily. It is a method that requires surprisingly little force, just accuracy and determination. So it didn't eliminate anyone. The knife was found at the scene, but, because of the presumption of Bud's guilt, Al wasn't going to follow that as a line of inquiry. Even if it was plastered with the killer's fingerprints, that wouldn't be discovered until long after Bud had been transferred to a jail in Guadalajara full of vengeful drug dealers. Too late to save him, in other words. Without having seen it, I had to assume there was nothing particularly unusual about the knife itself or

Al would have mentioned it. Anyone can get hold of a knife, and it's easy enough to conceal one in a pocket or a purse. I paused again and remembered I had two chefs in the frame. Chefs work at knife skills and are possibly less squeamish than others when it comes to slicing into flesh. Maybe the weapon pointed to Tony or Rutilio. Or Callie, who helped her husband in Amigos del Tequila's kitchen, as well as doing people's accounts. Ada was the daughter of a butcher. Juan worked with blades in the fields all day. And maybe Jean's liking for tae kwon do suggested a violent streak. Dean might have retired from a boring government job, but in his spare time, he might be an avid hunter or fisherman, or he might pursue any number of hobbies that would allow him to sublimate anger, while developing good knife skills.

I stood up, stretched my neck, and looked at my watch. It was one in the morning. I was exhausted and I was aware that I wasn't thinking as clearly as I might. I pushed the glass doors closed, locked them, and headed for the bed. I could do a better job for Bud if I slept. I just hoped he was managing to get some rest himself.

Thinking of Bud made me think of Jack. I sat up with a start: who was Jack's contact? I hadn't given that any thought. Who could be the "operative" with "good cover" that Jack had referred to? Someone I'd met already, or someone completely unknown to me? Was it important that I worked that out as well? Another thought occurred to me. Why on earth would there be an operative of any sort in the area? My mind was racing—in circles, as it turned out. *Cait—rest!*

As I lay there on my back, looking at the inside of my eyelids, I felt hot tears start to trickle toward my ears. For the first time since I'd dragged myself out of my own bed in my little house on Burnaby Mountain back in beautiful British Columbia at 4:00 AM that morning, I felt as though I was living in the real world. It had taken that many hours of seeming unreality for me to get here: *the worst possible place.*

Wake-up Call

WHEN I WOKE THE NEXT morning I was immediately aware of a couple of things: a bus must have run over me as I slept because my entire body was aching, and someone had entered my room since I'd gone to bed. The first realization told me I needed to head for the painkillers. The second, that I should take stock of my surroundings before I stirred at all. *Stay very still, Cait.* From where I lay, I could see that my hairbrush was now very close to the taps on the basin surround, and not on the outside edge of the bathroom sink where I'd left it. My shoes were still next to the bed, but they were the right way around, different from how I'd left them.

Why would someone come into my room and rearrange my shoes?
Lie very still, Cait. There might still be someone here.

I strained my ears. Beyond the heavily glazed windows I could hear birdsong. I also identified the faint hum of the refrigerator in the open-plan kitchen, beyond the bedroom. I'd left the bedroom door ajar the night before. Now it was half open. My heart thumped. I could sense a slight wheezing in my breath. Minutes passed. I lay there listening. Eventually it all seemed too ridiculous. I pushed back the bedclothes and sprinted to the washroom. When I emerged, I was wrapped in my robe and carrying a can of hairspray as a potential weapon—it was the only thing with heft that wasn't attached to a wall.

I crept toward the bedroom door. If there was someone there, they would already know I was up and about. I slipped the hairspray into the pocket of my robe and strode out of the room, ready for anything. But there was nothing. No one lurking about to bash me on the head. I checked the front door. It wasn't locked, and the alarm was not set. Recalling the previous night, I was certain I'd locked the door when I came in, but I knew I'd turned off the alarm to be able to go out onto the patio. I must have been more tired than I'd thought, because I'd clearly forgotten to reset it. *How convenient for the person wanting to break in.* I opened the front door and checked the lock. There were no scratch marks, no scuff marks. It didn't look as though the lock had been picked. Maybe someone had a key? I remembered that Tony had said that the pool boy had a key for the place. Who among the FOGTTs might also have access to one?

I shut the door, turned the lock, and paid attention to the inside of the house. Yes, someone had moved a few bits and pieces—but only things that belonged to me. I hadn't left my cigarettes and lighter in that exact spot, and when I went back into the bedroom, I could see that Bud's suitcase had been moved inside the closet. It was obvious to me that someone had searched the place while I was asleep. It was also clear that they had done it so quietly, and professionally, that I had slept through it all. My watch told me it was almost half past seven, so I decided to make myself some coffee. The Taylors had kindly brought me a small jar of instant. As I watched the kettle boil, I gave some thought to what it was my "visitor" might have been looking for, and what they might have found. The notes I'd made about my suspicions were my main concern, along with my purse and its contents. I'd left them all dumped on the patio table the night before. I pulled open the concertina glass doors and saw that everything was exactly where I'd left it. *Of course, the garden is completely enclosed by walls, and the intruder didn't dare open these heavy, noisy doors.* Thank goodness—no one had read my notes, nor had they found Bud's bits and pieces, which could identify him, in my purse.

I took my coffee to the patio, lit a cigarette, coughed a fair bit, told myself I'd be fine, and reread my notes. I picked up the pen I'd also left out all night and added a comment: "Why does everyone seem so keen to help Al with his career?" I wasn't sure of the significance of that question, but I knew it needed to be answered at some point.

I decided to get myself showered and ready for the day before the water boy arrived at eight o'clock. But he didn't show up. Luckily I still had enough bottled water to make another coffee, and I decided to check my email once more, hoping against hope that there might be something there that could help Bud. There wasn't. *Damn and blast!*

While I was online, I did a little surfing: I trawled through some lists of South Carolina families—*who knew there were so many French family and place names there?*—and found Al's. It was easy to discover that his mother's father had inherited a fortune from his forebears and had gone on to make a pile more for himself. Her mother, the Gram Beselleu to whom Al had referred, had come from another French line, being a Dubois, and had brought her own money to the match. *Why on earth would a scion of such a wealthy family be working at all?* I checked out Frank Taylor's old brewery and found that it had a significant online footprint and was, as he had said, doing very nicely indeed. I found nothing about Dean or Jean George, or Dorothea Simmonds or Greg Hollins. Tony Booth's Facebook page was interesting, and he obviously kept in touch with folks who'd known him at his previous restaurants. *A very social group, by the looks of it.* There was a wedding photograph of him and Callie. They made the perfect beach-wedding couple—he was casual in a white linen shirt and pants; she looked delightful in her flowing white dress, with flowers in her hair. Fit, bronzed, healthy, and muscular, they certainly looked happy, but then, who wouldn't on their wedding day? I took a few minutes to check out the place where I was staying, and the tequila it produced. I wandered around a few general websites that allowed me to find out more than I'd ever thought I'd want to know about making tequila. It was clear from their own website that the FOGTTs had invested in the most modern equipment, including autoclaves that shortened the cooking time for the *piñas*, the hearts of the agave plants used to make tequila. They produced the four most popular types of tequila: *blanco*, the youngest, and therefore the quickest to produce, which is clear; *reposado*, which the Mexican government decrees must rest in the barrel for at least two months; *añejo*, or aged, which must be in a barrel for at least a year; and, finally, *extra añejo*, which must be in the barrel for at least two years. This last categorization had only been introduced half a dozen years earlier. The FOGTTs didn't make *oro* tequila, which is the type that's young and colored with caramel to make it smoother. The Tequila Soleado brand for all four types of tequila seemed to be well reviewed by aficionados. Triple-distilled and naturally fermented, its smooth, complex flavors and reliable quality, as well as the excellence of the extra añejo, aged in French white oak barrels, were often commented upon, especially in the US, which is, apparently, the fastest grow-ing market for tequila. It seemed that the FOGTTs had invested in the right plants, the right equipment, and the right people to make good tequila.

A few more clicks took me to the website for Jalisco's newspaper, *El Informador,* where I checked on news about the Rose Killer. It seemed that most of the information about the Rose Killer's deeds centered on the first and second victims, which was not unusual in terms of a serial killer. The police often use the media when they are hunting the killer of one person, but when they realize they might have a serial killer on their hands, they become more circumspect. Often, by the time there's a third victim, the official number of known kills to designate a killer *serial*, the details dry up. Miguel's daughter had been killed immediately after she went missing. Her time of death had been estimated by analyzing her stomach con-tents, due to the length of time that had passed between her death and her discovery. The second victim, however, had been found much more quickly, and there seemed to be a question of when she had died, exactly. The autopsy seemed to suggest she'd been dead before she even disappeared. *Odd!* I read on.

The second victim, a nineteen-year-old girl from a good home, with no boyfriend, attending her local college to study as a beautician, had disappeared at 3:00 PM. At least, she'd been seen by friends about ten minutes before that, when she'd set off to walk home from a friend's house. When she was found, very early the next morning about forty miles away, her estimated time of death was put at 2:00 PM on the day of her disappearance. It was a puzzle that consumed the Federales for quite a while, and one that put her friends in the frame as certain liars, if not murderers. The cops had then further ascertained that her body must have been dumped sometime after 6:00 PM that day, because a police car had driven along the road where she was found at that time and the body hadn't been there yet. The article went so far as to mention that it was this fact that had led the Federales to no longer believe that Miguel Juan-Carlos García Perez, the father of the first victim, Angélica Rosa, was responsible for killing his daughter. *If Miguel hadn't been seen by dozens of people saying a Requiem Mass for his daughter at 7:00 PM in Puerto Vallarta, he might not have been so lucky.*

I moved on to the most recent article, which dealt with all the killings to date. By the time the piece had been written, the coverage simply stated the facts and warned young women that they should not walk alone. Approximately every four weeks a young woman had been found on a remote roadside, swathed in a white sheet, her hands closed as if in prayer, with two red roses clasped between them. It was also clear that each victim, except the second one, had been abducted at night, and that they were all small young women, most no more than five feet and around ninety pounds. Every serial killer has their type, and the Rose Killer was no exception it seemed. Angélica Rosa was the only one who had died of simple alcohol poisoning. *All* the others had been found to have ingested large amounts of diphenhydramine, a strong antihistamine that is a common ingredient in many sleeping pills, which is widely available and, the report helpfully stated, found in about sixty percent of all homes. *Maybe the killer wasn't as patient with his later victims?* There were photographs of families dazed with grief, and snaps of the victims, all of whom smiled from the webpage on the TV screen in wide-eyed innocence. *All dead.* Terrible. I haven't done a lot of work on serial killers, but I have studied many of the so-called "classic cases" as a part of my master's program, the deviant psychological factors being of interest to any criminal psychologist.

I closed everything down and once again settled into my little corner of the garden. It seemed odd that this place already felt so familiar. I felt strangely peaceful, given my circumstances, and those of poor Bud. I was acutely aware that all I could do while waiting for Al to call was think. I've spent decades studying people, and, although it would be generally accepted that I have accumulated a great deal of knowledge about why humans do what they do and how they signal their true thoughts rather than their intended ones, I am more than ready to face the fact that I know only a fraction of what I wish I did. Bud? He's a different matter. Until yesterday morning I had *thought* I knew him well. *Stop it, Cait!* I'd made a decision to not dwell on the things he had chosen to keep secret from me, but the hurt was creeping up on me again.

"You're looking thoughtful." It was Al. A few feet away. I jumped. "I knocked, but you didn't answer. I hope it was okay for me to come in?" He spotted the alarm on my face and looked concerned. *I locked that door, I know I did!*

I'd already decided to not mention the break-in to him. What was the point? Nothing had been taken. I hadn't been murdered in my sleep. And, although we were working together, I didn't want him to focus on me.

"You just startled me. I didn't sleep too well. Nor nearly long enough. It was quite a day yesterday." I waved toward a chair as an invitation for him to sit, but Al preferred to stand.

"If you'd rather not pursue this any further, Cait, we'd all understand . . ." His words hung on the morning air. I sensed something different in his attitude. He seemed to be on edge. *Cross? What had I done?*

I stood. "We're on a mission, Al. You and me—we're going to find out who this guy is, and why he killed Margarita. Right?" Al nodded. "Tell me, has he said anything this morning?" I was desperate for an update on Bud's condition.

"He ate his breakfast, drank his water, but not a word. When I got back there last night, he was fast asleep. Like a baby. Not a care in the world. How can that *be*? How can a man kill and not feel remorse?" Al was angry. All I could think about was the fact that, *thank goodness*, Bud seemed fine—for now.

I wanted to get going. "Well, we're not achieving anything by hanging around here. I'm not going to wait for the water boy. Can we go to see Callie now?"

"That's why I came. I thought we could go over together. I haven't been able to get an answer on the phone at the apartment, so she might still be asleep. I don't like the idea that she took pills prescribed for Dorothea—she's a much bigger woman than Callie."

"I'll just pop to the—you know . . ." I said and did just that. A glance in the bathroom mirror told me that I didn't look too bad. In fact, since I'd packed the clothes I thought I'd be wearing to wander Mexican beaches, holding hands with the man I love, I looked very relaxed, which was not at all how I felt. At least the pale crushed-tomato hue of my lightweight tunic gave me the illusion of having some color, and the bit of sunburn I'd managed to get on my nose while sitting at the airport the day before had, thankfully, turned from red to brown. My white capris were roomy, and summery, and the long white scarf I'd tied in a bow around my ponytail topped off the look—literally. *Bud would be proud to be seen with me.*

Finally ready to leave, I shoved my notes, pad, and pen into my purse and shut up the house, then Al and I walked down the little hill to Amigos del Tequila.

I wasn't at all surprised to find that the door to the kitchen was wide open, and there was no one about. It seemed to be the normal state of affairs for the place!

Al sighed. "I'm supposed to get it through to people that crime often happens because of an opportunity presenting itself. Why do people not lock their doors?" He shook his head as we entered.

"Hello?" he called. There was no answer. He turned to me. "Let's check upstairs." I nodded, and we climbed the steep, narrow staircase with me following Al. At the top we emerged into what was obviously the scene of a disturbance: clothes and decorative items were scattered about the furniture and the floor. The room was in total disarray. I gasped. Al turned and said sharply, "What's the matter?"

"It looks like the place has been ransacked," I said.

Al grinned. "I've been here before. This is how they live."

As we stood surrounded by discarded clothes, books, papers, files, soda cans, drink bottles, dirty mugs, and plates, I wondered how anyone could find anything in such a mess. I know that my home's not pristine, but even *I* am tidier than these two. I spotted a laptop and a tablet, so I believed Al's assertion that this was normal, because any thief would have made off with such items. That knowledge didn't make the mess any prettier to look at.

In front of the tiny kitchen was a breakfast bar, which was completely covered in piles of paperwork. I noticed that at least this seemed to be in an orderly arrangement, and I spotted accounts, receipts, and records for Amigos del Tequila, Serena Spa, and the FOGTT. Tony had mentioned that Callie did accountancy work for people—at least it looked as though her work had some order about it.

"Would you check in the bedroom?" asked Al. "The bathroom is silent. Callie might still be asleep."

I nodded and knocked on what was obviously the bedroom door. There was no response, so I opened it a crack and peered in. There were two mounds in the bed.

"I think they're *both* still in bed," I whispered to Al over my shoulder. "What do you want me to do?"

Al shrugged.

I knocked again and said, "Hello." Nothing. I went in, saying loudly, "Come on then, rise and shine. Time to get going." But neither lump stirred. At all. Panic gripped my sadly empty tummy as I approached. My instincts kicked in and I reached for the pulse point on Callie's neck. I couldn't feel anything, but she wasn't cold. *Good sign!*

"Al, come here and check for Tony's pulse," I called.

There were no obvious signs of a struggle in the surprisingly tidy bedroom, and there were no signs of blood. I pulled Callie's arm free of the bedclothes and held her wrist. Finding a pulse is a lot harder than you might think. It's especially difficult when your own heart is pounding. Luckily, I noticed Callie's eyelids flutter.

"She's alive!" I said triumphantly. "I'm worried that she is so deeply asleep, though. How's Tony?"

"The same," said a very grim Al. "I know that Callie took Dorothea's pills, but what about Tony? He and I had a few more drinks after you left, but this is no hangover."

I scanned the room. No sign of pills or a pill bottle. "We don't know if Dorothea brought Callie one or two pills, or a whole bottle."

Al pulled out his cellphone. "I'm calling an ambulance first. These guys need to be checked out. Then I'll call Dorothea and find out exactly what she gave Callie."

Al left the room to make his calls. Once again, I turned my attention to the Booths' bedroom. There was a glass on Callie's nightstand. I peered at it. I scrabbled in my purse for my reading-cheats, shoved them onto my nose, and took another look. *White crystals.*

Tony's side of the bed didn't have a nightstand. Without touching anything I bent down and peered under the bed. A beer glass lay on its side on the floor. I pulled a pen out of my purse, stuck it into the glass, and rolled it out from under the bed. *White crystals.*

Maybe neither of them liked to swallow pills and both had chosen to grind them into a drink? *Unlikely.*

Al stuck his head through the doorway, and I told him about finding white crystals in the two glasses. "An ambulance is on its way, and Dorothea says she gave Callie a container of her sleeping pills, which have a Z in their name. She can't remember what they are called. She buys them at a pharmacy in PV, where they know what she takes. She thinks there were about forty pills in the bottle."

"Sleeping pills are all benzodiazepine receptor agonists, often referred to as Z-drugs, so we can at least tell them that."

As he walked into the bedroom, Al looked puzzled. "You seem to know a lot about sleeping pills. Why's that?"

I sighed. "You'd be surprised how many medicine cabinets I've been through on cases where I've been working for the local cops as a victim profiler. Checking out a person's medications can tell you a great deal about them physically, their lifestyle and sometimes even their psychological makeup. Different sleeping pills are prescribed for different types of sleeping disorders, so I've researched which are which so that I can assess victims more accurately. The Z-drugs are used to treat people who cannot get off to sleep easily, rather than those who wake during the night. They are available under a variety of brand names that differ from country to country, or, sometimes, as a generic—that's because the patents on some of the earlier formulations have expired. If Dorothea was getting her pills here, in Mexico, she might have been getting a generic. Whichever case it is, they are not the sort of pills that should ever be mixed with alcohol, and it's possible to overdose on them quite easily. That said, we can't even be sure that it was Dorothea's pills that they were dosed with. So it really would be best if these guys were shipped off to a place where their vital signs can be monitored."

"The ambulance shouldn't be long. It helps that it was me who called it in. Sometimes my position here helps in practical ways." Al looked proud, but I was feeling totally useless.

"Let's go back into the main room," I suggested. "We can still see and hear the Booths from there, but I won't feel as though I'm intruding so much."

Al agreed. I was tempted to tidy their living room—*odd for me*—but I resisted. Instead, I stood in the middle of the mess and looked around, carefully noting what I saw. There was a tiny desk against one wall, and upon it sat the base unit for the handset telephone, but no handset, and a jotter. I picked my way across the room and peered through my glasses at the last notes made—by whom, I didn't know. "M. mileage? S. wax? FOGTTs barrels vs. bottles?" The "M" and "S" notes had been crossed through. The "FOGTT" note hadn't been. Not terribly helpful, as notes went, but they must have meant something, or at least enough, to whoever made them.

I returned to study the only area of order in the room: the piles of accounts arranged relatively neatly on the breakfast bar. I spotted a yellow sticky note poking out of the pile that related to Serena Spa. The word "WAX" had been written in a green highlighting pen with a question mark next to it. I looked at the sheet it was stuck to: lists of expenditures, all for consumable supplies. Someone—presumably Callie Booth—had highlighted the line for wax in green pen, and I could see why. The amount spent on wax supplies at the spa had been pretty steady for five months, then had dipped down to about half the usual cost. Clearly Callie had needed to ask Serena about this fact. That explained one cryptic note on the telephone pad.

I turned my attention to the other piles. Nothing jumped out at me. There were no yellow notes on the FOGTT papers, but there were a couple of sheets with calculations—not so unusual for financial paperwork. One was largely covered in multiplications and divisions—it looked as though Callie Booth preferred to use her brain rather than a calculator. I looked at the figures for a few moments but couldn't fathom their significance. All I could see was that both the multiplication and division seemed to be using the same base figures. *Odd—was she just checking her own work?*

As I replaced the FOGTT pile, I spotted something out of the corner of my eye, under a plate that still bore signs of a partially consumed fried egg! It was another relatively neat pile of papers. I very carefully moved the plate and found that this mound related to Margarita Flores. Again, I couldn't see any sticky notes, yellow or otherwise. Undaunted I picked up the papers and started to flick through them, hoping to spot something that Callie had highlighted. If S was Serena Spa, then M could be Margarita Flores.

Sure enough, Callie had run a green highlight through a list of gas costs. She'd scribbled a big question mark across the whole page. I read through the figures. I couldn't understand why Callie had highlighted that particular page. It looked as though Margarita made fairly regular trips to one specific gas station with a Bucerias address, and an occasional visit to another in Puerto Vallarta. Her overall mileage figures were at the top of the page, and a quick calculation told me that she was getting great gas mileage. I wondered what she drove. Margarita's van, whatever type it was, was getting her better mileage than I got. *That is weird, unless she drove a hybrid.*

Al's cell phone rang. He listened, scribbled something in his notebook, thanked whoever it was, and tucked his phone away. "Dorothea says Zaleplon is the name of her pills. She's certain there were forty-seven capsules in the bottle. Now at least we can tell the paramedics." He seemed relieved.

I shook my head. "Zaleplon is traditionally blue. The residue I saw in the glasses was white."

I finally heard a siren in the distance.

Al brightened. "Here they come! You stay here, I'll go show them the way." *Great!*

He couldn't get down the stairs quick enough. After he'd gone, I grappled with my conscience for about two seconds, before I ripped the page from the notepad beside the phone and took the sheet of gas expenses from the pile of accounts for Margarita Flores. I stuffed everything into my purse, put the papers and the plate back where I had found them, then practiced looking innocent. I wasn't sure what it all meant, but I felt it was important. If Callie had been speaking to Margarita about her gas expenses and mileage figures, might Margarita have told her something that had put her in danger? *How on earth could information about gas costs and mileage be life threatening?*

The next thirty minutes came as close to watching a real-life farce as anything I've ever seen in my life. The arrival of the ambulance brought all the FOGTTs running, panicked and worried. They all assumed that Callie had taken ill as a result of her accident the previous evening, and were then aghast when Al and I told them of the state in which we'd found both Tony and Callie. Dorothea was first to arrive, and she was in full flight. If she'd had something to flagellate herself with, she'd have done it. She kept reminding everyone, very loudly, that she'd told Callie to take just one pill, and not to drink. She wailed that she'd never forgive herself if they died because of this. Ada Taylor managed to calm her a little, and Al suggested that rather than hang around the ambulance, and possibly get in the way, it might be better if everyone stepped into the bar.

The poor paramedics had a terrible time getting the stretchers down the steep narrow staircase. The shouting and gesticulating that accompanied the whole thing was priceless. I thought it best to join the FOGTTs in the bar, where their final member had arrived. Greg. It was my first chance to meet him.

He was about Bud's height, but slimmer, and had an air about him that reminded me of Peter O'Toole at his most lugubrious. He had a deep tan, wore leather flip-flops and a rumpled white linen shirt with matching pants, and held a panama hat in one hand, a stub of a fat cigar clenched between the fingers of his other hand. He must have been seventy years old if he was a day, or else he was in his sixties and had lived a hard life.

"The illustrious Cait Morgan," he said. His strong Australian accent was immediately recognizable, and a surprise. If, as Ada Taylor had told me, Greg hadn't lived in his native country for many years, I'd have expected his accent to at least have toned down a little. There again, I'm always being told that my Welsh accent is still strong, despite more than a decade of living in Canada. However thick his accent, his voice crackled as he spoke, suggesting years of cigars and, I suspected, hard liquor. The twinkle in his eye was unmistakable. He looked at me in a knowing way, and his grip on my hand didn't waver as he said, "I find it hard to believe that a woman as beautiful and, if I may say, curvaceous as yourself is still single." His eyes wandered to my bust and dwelt there just a little too long for comfort. *The curse of an ample bosom!*

"You're single too, I hear," I said. My reply was stunningly polite, given his leering.

He released my hand, stood to attention, and saluted. "At present, ma'am, but possibly not for long." He winked.

My internal slime-o-meter hit new heights. Suddenly he didn't remind me of Peter O'Toole at all. Greg Hollins was an aging lothario, with skin like dried tobacco leaves and a scent to match. I told myself that he was a possible suspect, so I had to take my chance to find out all about him. It seemed he was keen to help me out on that score.

"Let me pour you a drink," he offered. I noticed that Dorothea, Ada, and Jean were each having a glass of Baileys over ice. I heard Dorothea utter the words "for the shock," which seemed like a good enough excuse for everyone else to start helping themselves to Tony's bar supplies.

"Thanks, I'll have a bottle of water," I replied.

"Your wish is my command," said Greg greasily, as he slunk off to the bar and returned a moment later with a bottle and a glass. As he poured he said, "You were the talk of the place last night, my dear. Dorothea googled you before she arrived for the evening, so she was able, as usual, to be the font of all wisdom for our little group." I took the glass from him, barely managing to avoid his hand touching mine as I did so. *Yuk!* "You're quite the woman, I hear. Bright—a Mensan, no less—and famous for changing the way the criminology community thinks about victims. No mean feat, I'm sure. Though I've never been a victim of anything in my life—except wounds to my heart, suffered at the hands of many, many beautiful women." *Double yuk!*

I braced myself and set off on my journey of discovery. "I'm sure you're just as fascinating," I said, as coquettishly as I could.

"I'm nuts!" he said, smiling. He waited for me to bite. I didn't. He pressed on, undaunted. "Well, I used to be but I've retired from it now. Nuts. Macadamia nuts, to be exact. Started on my own land in Australia, ended up with holdings in Guatemala, South Africa, Kenya, and Hawaii. Got fed up with nuts, so I sold up, and here I am. Now I get to smoke my cigars wherever I want and drink my own tequila. What could be better?"

Greg's strong Australian accent was matched by a full-on

Australian attitude. I was just waiting for him to say "Strewth!" But he didn't.

"You're Welsh, I hear. Loads of Welsh in my family, way back. Quite a number of your lot got shipped over to Oz to 'serve at Her Majesty's pleasure,' right? Stealing sheep, I wouldn't be surprised." He laughed and nudged me. Too hard. "No need to go chasing sheep when the women look like you, though, right?" He winked again. I smiled, as graciously as possible.

"You were in PV yesterday, when Margarita was killed?" I asked. *Go for it, Cait.*

He nodded. "Terrible. Very sad. Not that I knew the woman myself, you know. But it's always sad."

"Where were you?" I asked. *Blunt might be the only thing that works with this guy.*

"Here and there, you know. Dropping in on friends, checking out the beaches, taking in the views." *Bikinis and binoculars, I bet.* "But Al's got the guy. I don't need an alibi, right?" He grinned and held up his hands in mock surrender, but his micro-expressions told a different story. *He is worried about something and trying to hide it.* He would stay on my list of possibles for now.

"Breakfast, Cait?" Once again Al had managed to get within feet of me without my noticing him. *How does he do that?*

I was delighted. "Yes, please. I'm absolutely starving," I said, possibly with too much enthusiasm. Unbelievably, it was still only 10:00 AM. "Where shall we go?" It was clear that no food would be served at Amigos del Tequila that day.

Dorothea piped up. "You should go into Bucerias. Don't go down to Rutilio's, he'll rip you off. They shouldn't be allowed to get away with it. And he's the worst of the lot!"

I stood, pulled my purse onto my shoulder, and was ready to leave with Al, when a short, withered old man in filthy clothes entered the room from the kitchen. He held a large battered straw hat rolled up in his hands, which looked as though they were made from coarse leather. His face was a mask of dark, folded, weathered skin. His sunken jet eyes glittered, his head was covered with a slick of black hair, and, as he spoke, I noticed he had almost no teeth at all.

"Margarita," he said gravely.

No one moved. I noticed that the general emotion displayed was embarrassment.

"Oh, Juan, you poor thing! Let me hug you!" called Dorothea, throwing her arms in the air and rushing toward the tiny man.

Juan? Juan the intendente, the jimador, the dead woman's father? *Not what I'd expected at all!*

Seconds In

AS I STARED AT JUAN, I wondered about him. Could this man be a murderer? Even Al had said Juan was capable of such a deed. His clothes hung off his tiny frame. They'd seen many hours in the fields that day already. Unless he never washed them. My online research had told me what a jimador did—his job was to cut the leaves from the agave plant at exactly the right time, so that the sugars in the remaining heart of the agave, the piña, were at their best for making tequila. It seemed to be extremely skilled, yet physically exhausting, work, the piñas often weighing up to seventy pounds each and needing to be cut from their roots and pulled out of the narrow rows of plants by hand. A jimador might cut and move eighty to one hundred piñas each day. I'd seen acres and acres of the spiky blue-gray plants growing in neat rows up the hillsides and on the high, flat plains, as Bud and I had driven from the airport just a day earlier. We'd laughed about visiting a tequila tasting room together. Now, here I was, sitting in just such a place, with a group of murder suspects and a clock ticking in my head. *A lot can happen in a day!*

After Dorothea had finished hugging Juan, a process during which I thought he was going to suffocate, she released him into Al's care. The men spoke quietly in Spanish, and I realized that we were about to leave.

Al came to my side and almost whispered, "Our trip to Margarita's hacienda will have to wait, Cait. I'm going to take Juan to the mortuary, where he can see his daughter's body. On our way, I'll drop you at Rutilio's Restaurant, and I'll call Miguel and get him to meet you there. I prefer that you are with him or me all the time. You need to eat, and you can talk to Miguel and Rutilio about

Margarita. I'm . . . I'm not sure how long I'll be gone, but I'll meet you there. You'll be okay, yes?"

I nodded my agreement, though I was annoyed that Al seemed to think I needed to be accompanied at all times. We exited through the main door, leaving behind the FOGTTs, who were buzzing about the latest emergency to strike their little community and trying to work out a plan of action for opening the tasting room that afternoon and the restaurant that evening.

Given that it was still relatively early in the day, the heat outside was a shock, and I hunted for my sunglasses in my purse. The police car was no more than two minutes away, but even in that short time I started to sweat, and the humidity made it hard for me to breathe. I sat in the back of the car, as did Juan, and Al took off, with us looking like two people he'd arrested. *This is where poor Bud sat yesterday, covered in blood,* I thought.

"I am sorry that we are meeting under such sad circumstances," I said to Juan, as gently and plainly as I could.

The man's expression didn't alter, and he paid me no heed at all. *Maybe he speaks no English?*

"If we could have met at a different time, I'd have been eager to ask you about your work as a jimador. I understand it takes many years of practice to gain the skills you need?" I hoped that a question would draw some response.

"I am the most excellent jimador in this State," said Juan harshly, and with pride. *Not too grief-stricken to be boastful. Good.*

"It must bring you great satisfaction to know that your plants are making such well-spoken-of tequila. I understand that the Extra Añejo Tequila Soleado is doing very well indeed, and this is just its first year on sale."

Juan turned himself in his seat to look at me with his raisin eyes. The folds in his face made it difficult to read him: few micro-expressions were visible, except around his eyes, and even there it was difficult to tell if he was smiling, squinting, or sneering. It took him a long time to speak, or so it seemed to me. I wasn't feeling very patient, and my tummy was rumbling.

Eventually, he spoke. His voice was graveled with age. "It is good if they make money. It is better if they make a lot of money. Then they can pay me more. I am very good. I work very hard. I deserve more than I get."

I tried to not be too judgmental. Bud's always accusing me of it, and I've been working on it. Being a criminal psychologist rather presupposes making judgments. As I looked at Juan, I saw a selfish, greedy, but clearly hard-working man, who'd probably had to scrape by his whole life without much of anything at all, eventually learning not to *expect* much of anything at all. He struck me as a very angry man, and I didn't get the impression that was because of his daughter's death. It might have been a mantle he'd assumed when he'd lost his wife and sons.

Although I was pretty sure of the answer, I wanted to study his reaction to my next question very closely. "Did you see your daughter the day she died?"

Juan licked his thin, dry lips. Then he smiled. It was a difficult smile for me to read because the contours of his face were impacted by his lack of teeth. One thing I was certain of, it was not a kind smile. In fact, it gave me quite a chill. He wiped his rheumy eyes with the back of a desiccated hand. "No. Not yesterday," he replied.

I reacted as naturally as I could. "I expect you were at church; it was Sunday, after all."

Juan seemed to chew over his answer, quite literally: his jaw moved up and down, and he finally said, "I said Mass early. I walked home. Then I went to be with my plants. Margarita, she was not the only one who loved plants. I love them just as much. But my agave are not pretty like her roses." He gave that creepy smile again, then added, "My plants make more money than hers ever could." *Smug. Self-centered. Dismissive of his dead daughter. What a delight!*

Al pulled up in front of Margarita's store. "Do you want to go inside?" he asked Juan in Spanish. Juan's gruff dismissal needed no translation.

"I'll pick you up here later," said Al, as I hauled myself out of the car. I nodded and waved, then headed for Bob's Bodega. I pulled open the glass door and walked in. Bob was behind the counter, and Maria was arranging bottles of sunscreen on a shelf. They greeted me like an old friend.

I cast my eyes about. There was a wooden double door in the back wall of the store. One side had stacks of boxes in front of it; the other was clearly kept free for access to the back lane. The entire store was open to the public, so nowhere for either of them to change out of blood-soaked clothing, unless they'd done it in the lane behind the store, which Rutilio would have seen from his vantage point. It was what I was afraid of, but, in a way, I was pleased. I didn't want either of these warm, round little people to be on my list of possible suspects anymore, and now they weren't. I explained that I'd just popped in to say hello because I was going to have something to eat at Rutilio's, and they waved me happily on my way.

As I rounded the end of the building, I decided to walk along the lane. I had no reason to creep, but I did. Margarita's van was parked where she'd left it. It certainly wasn't a hybrid, but it *was* a curious shape. Walking closer I realized it had a refrigeration unit on the roof. *Of course, she'd want to transport her precious flowers in a chilled environment.* I examined the door at the back of her store. It sat flush within the wall, its edges a bit dented, and a few black scuff marks bore testament to its use. There was no lock, or handle, so there was no way of opening the door from the outside. It was clear that Margarita would have had to open it from inside the refrigerated unit, which meant it didn't present a security risk, but also meant that it didn't offer a viable entry point for the killer. Unless the victim herself had opened this door from inside the store for her killer to enter by—which seemed very unlikely to me—they *must* have gone in through the front door. But no one did! *Damn!*

The little door was set into the wall about a foot off the ground, and was itself about four feet tall. As I'd observed the night before, it was narrow, no more than eighteen inches wide. Al had needed to duck *and* turn sideways to get through it. I guessed it was just about right to load in flowers in buckets without allowing too much cold air to escape, hence the step at the bottom—that's where all the cold air goes when you open a fridge door: it literally falls out onto the floor. *Again, Margarita's attention to detail at work; she must have had the unit specially designed.*

I walked toward Serena Spa. The back door was wedged wide open, and the rear entrance was covered with a beaded curtain, which swayed in the ocean breeze. I peeped inside. The spa smelled awful: a mixture of potent aromas, none of which were pleasant. I could see through to the front of the store and could hear Serena singing to herself. To the left, against the back wall of the building, there was a small room with a massage table inside. I guessed that was where Dorothea had been at the time of the murder, though I wondered how the relatively small table had coped with her size. A narrow corridor led to the front, and I supposed that was where Ada had been. Either of them could have left without the other one knowing if the door to the massage room had been closed, which I reasoned it would be when in use.

Finally, I turned toward the sea, heading for the front of Rutilio's Restaurant, and I was rewarded with a waft of ocean air that cooled and refreshed me. Even my eyelids were sweating, so I took off my sunglasses and wiped them dry. I was glad I hadn't bothered with makeup that morning. *What was the point?*

It was a beautiful view. Seagulls swooped in the luminous blue sky, the surf made its siren call as it caressed the shoreline about twenty feet away, and I could feel the healing and rejuvenating power of the ozone in the air. *I should be sharing this with Bud!*

"Ah, Cait Morgan! Cait Morgan?"

I wiped my eyes again, but this time not because they were sweating. I pushed my sunglasses on and observed the man who was hurrying toward me. Miguel was shorter than me, and fatter. He puffed as he rushed. He was holding out his hand in greeting and smiling broadly. Although he was a heavy man, his gun belt was buckled at the tightest hole, his pants were way too big for him, and the collar and shoulders of his shirt were loose. *You've lost a fair bit of weight since you started wearing that uniform.*

"Hello, hello, I am Officer Miguel," he said, shaking my hand with both of his. "Come, come. Captain Alfredo said you would be hungry. My brother will feed us." He waved me toward a seat at a table that was just outside the now fully-opened glass front of the restaurant, beneath the shade of a jolly red parasol. I sat facing the glittering sea, delighting in the breeze and noticing, as yesterday, that clouds were gathering on the horizon.

The gaily striped tablecloths, the painted wooden chairs, even the plastic lobsters on the walls looked so much better in the sunlight. The piped mariachi music was the same as the night before, but it seemed more tuneful by day, less dissonant and mournful.

"You have returned! How wonderful!" It was Rutilio.

Seeing the two brothers together merely highlighted that there can be huge differences in terms of what can come out of one gene pool.

"This is my brother, you know. My little brother," announced Miguel proudly. "He is so handsome, so clever with food. He is a great businessman. He is the best little brother in the world." He beamed with genuine affection at Rutilio, who puffed out his chest and basked in the compliments. The expression on Rutilio's face exactly matched that of the huge neon sign that stood at the end of the building. The sign, which was a giant version of the chef's face, was as tall as the man himself, and it showed him beaming with pride. They'd even done a pretty good job with the teeth, though I imagined that the local fishermen might have a point when they said that the giant fluorescent face frightened the fish after dark.

For the second time I looked at Rutilio's huge menu. I was so hungry I felt I could eat everything listed, but I settled for a snapper salad, which seemed to be the only item that didn't feature some sort of wrap, shell, or tortilla chip. I didn't want to fill myself up with that stuff. I also declined beer in favor of bottled water. *Clear head, Cait!*

Miguel offered me one of the local cigarettes, which I declined as politely as I could. He eagerly accepted one of mine, which he found extraordinary: he'd never seen the super-slims that I favor. He dragged hard and smoked almost half the thing in two puffs. He smiled politely, but it was clear that he thought I was mad to smoke them, especially when I explained that they cost the same as regular cigarettes. He had clearly expected them to be only half as much, since they are just half the size of normal cigarettes.

I was keen to get past the chit-chat and find out what Miguel knew about Margarita, but it seemed he was desperate to tell me about the *devil* that he and Al had arrested for her killing. Miguel had apparently been charged with keeping an eye on Bud earlier that morning, and he took great delight in describing how he'd stared Bud down. *Yes, right!*

I had to get him to talk about what I wanted to know, and I thought that the arrival of the food would give me the chance. What I hadn't counted on was that Rutilio didn't just bring the food—he decided to take a break and sit with us, munching on a giant burrito as he did so.

We ate in silence for a few moments, then I said to Rutilio, "Al told me you were in the lane behind the flower shop yesterday,

Rutilio. I expect you were glad that your brother was on the scene too, or you might have had to get involved yourself."

Rutilio wiped his lips with his napkin and smiled. Unfortunately, the refried beans from his burrito were still smeared across his huge teeth. "Yes, my brother captured the man. He is a hero. Me? I was here, in my kitchen, my other home. I could hear screaming, so I ran. What could I do? I would have done more, but my brother had done it all. By the time I arrived, he had the man. And we are all grateful for him. Our mother kissed him last night."

"Yes, she did," chimed in Miguel. "Usually she only kisses Rutilio, because he is the baby, but last night she kissed me too. It was as though *I* was the pretty baby." He laughed and slapped his leg. *Interesting.*

"So you didn't see anything, before you heard the screams?" I directed my question at Rutilio, but it was Miguel who answered.

"What would he see? The devil was in the bodega, then he went to kill her. He was never behind her store, only in the front."

"Yes, this is true," said Rutilio. "Why do you ask?"

I shrugged it off. "Oh, I'm just trying to get the full picture, you know, who saw what, who was where when it happened."

"But why?" asked Rutilio.

"Because I wondered if the killer might have said something to someone that might explain his actions."

"He said 'No police' to Serena," said Miguel.

"He did?" Rutilio and I spoke in unison. We each sounded as surprised as the other.

Miguel nodded. "Yes, this is what she told me when I helped her. She told me he looked at her with his evil eyes and threatened her. 'No police,' he hissed. That's what she told me."

"So he speaks English?" asked Rutilio.

"At least that much," replied Miguel. "I told this to Captain Alfredo this morning when I remembered it, but he does not think that is much to go on, though he believes the man might understand enough English that we always speak in Spanish in front of him, if we have to speak at all."

"He might speak Spanish too," I said. Miguel and Rutilio both smiled. "Why are you smiling?" I asked.

"Not many non-Mexicans speak Spanish," said Rutilio. He shook his head. I decided to let his comment pass.

"So no one saw, or heard, anything that might suggest why this man killed Margarita?" I said, then sipped my water. Both men shook their heads. *Nothing.*

"So what about Margarita herself? What can you tell me about her?"

"She was a good woman," said Rutilio.

Miguel nodded. "She was a hard worker," he added.

They applied themselves to their food, shaking their head in disbelief at the loss of a woman they clearly had hardly known at all.

Timing Is Everything

I DECIDED THAT I'D ALLOW the brothers their chance to enjoy their food, but my mind was whirring as I nibbled my fish and leaves. The fish was well cooked, and the dressing on the salad was heavy, but tasty. I took a moment to observe the other patrons and noted that the fare of wrapped, rolled, fried, and crunchy dishes was being eaten with gusto all around me. The same two girls who'd been serving the night before were chatting and bringing food to the tables. I wondered who was preparing the food, given that Chef Rutilio was sitting right in front of me.

"Do you have an assistant?" I asked. I thought it was an innocent enough question, and I certainly didn't expect the reaction it drew from the brothers.

Rutilio stood up, pushing back his chair so hard that it fell over, causing quite a stir among his customers. Miguel buried his face in his hands and started shaking his head. I was confused.

"An assistant? You think I need an *assistant* to run my business?" Rutilio waved his arm around his domain. He seemed incensed. He'd gone from cheery and chatty to incandescently angry in a heartbeat. *Wow!* "I need no help! I am Rutilio. I make the menu. I make the food. I *am* this restaurant!" I half expected him to start beating his chest.

Customers began to look as alarmed as I felt. The two serving girls giggled nervously and started to attend to their tables, fussing and calming their patrons. Miguel motioned to his brother to sit and be quiet. I glugged my water. *What was all that about?*

Rutilio picked up his chair and sat with us again. He nodded at his brother, then said to me, "I am sorry, Cait. It is not your fault. You did not know what you said." He wasn't wrong.

Miguel continued in this calming, conciliatory vein as he whispered, "My brother is finding the business difficult at the moment. It will pass. He is an excellent chef. The bank—they think he should close the place. Or else have somebody buy into the business with him. But he is a hard-working man, my baby brother—" he smiled at his sibling indulgently, "and he has a plan. He is open here now for more hours than before, so he has more customers. The business, it is looking better, but our mother, she worries about him. He works so much, she thinks he needs help. Not just the girls to serve, but a helper in the kitchen. She has been . . . talking about it to him for a while, but he says he can do this alone. Mothers worry; this is their job. And our mother has always worried so much about Rutilio. All his jobs in the past have not worked out well. People did not understand that he needed to have authority, and to be creative, as he is here with his food, so they made life difficult for him. But now he has found his place. Of course, we have helped him all we can, and we understand that it takes time for a restaurant to work out. But the bank? They are not family. So now he must work even harder. My poor brother only managed to get to bed a couple of hours before he had to return here this morning. We all know how hard he is trying, but it has been very difficult for us all since my sweet Angélica Rosa was taken."

Throughout Miguel's loving testimonial to his brother's work ethic, Rutilio munched and nodded his head sadly. I detected the smell of burning martyrs wafting across the table, and wondered about the extent to which the family had supported this much-loved son, who was, apparently, sadly misunderstood by all. I also wondered why he hadn't gotten to his bed earlier the night before. All he'd had to do after Al and I left was brush down the grill, which couldn't have taken *that* long. I suspected that Rutilio was not quite the man his brother thought him to be.

Our little group became silent, and the rest of the customers settled down again. It seemed that the normal balance had returned.

Rutilio finished his food, rose, took his leave, then returned with his a tray of tequila bottles and glasses. *You're kidding!*

"Last night, you were tired, and you had to rush off with Alfredo; it is understandable that you could not drink with me. But today? Today you are the Canadian on vacation again. Let us drink!"

Obviously Rutilio thought that being hospitable toward me and pouring tequila down my throat were synonymous. I couldn't do it. Bud was depending on me. I looked at my watch and stood up. Miguel looked confused.

"I'm sorry, Rutilio, you are very kind to offer, but I have to go to Margarita's store, and then to the police station. Until we discover who this evil murderer is I cannot rest."

Although he looked disappointed, Rutilio deflated with grace. "But of course. I know this is important to Alfredo. We can drink and celebrate when he has handed this devil to the Federales." He gave a little bow and took his tray of bottles back to the bar.

"There will be nothing to pay," said Miguel, as I hovered, uncertain what to do next.

"But I *must* pay," I said. I didn't want to be in debt to Rutilio for anything.

"He is my brother, you are my guest. It is normal. Do not question him about this." Miguel was being as firm as I could imagine it was possible for him to be. *No wonder Rutilio's not making any money.* "You said you wanted to go to Margarita's store?" Miguel asked. I nodded. "Let us go. Then I will take you to the office, where you can meet up with Captain Alfredo."

I knew very well that Al had said he'd meet me at Rutilio's place, but I needed to get away from the man and his attempts to get me to drink, so I gathered my bits and pieces, shoved everything into my purse, and strode off toward Margarita's store once more. I was glad to move. The shade of the red parasol under which we'd been eating had been helpful, but the humidity was beginning to build, and the sea breezes seemed to have died down. I felt less than fresh, and walking at least allowed me to move through the air, cooling me down a little.

It was only once we were standing in front of the door to the flower shop that it occurred to me to ask Miguel if he had a key. He looked hurt that I'd asked, but I thought it a reasonable question. He pulled open the door and stepped aside to allow me to walk in. As soon as I did so, I knew something was wrong. Even without the benefit of man-made lighting, I could see that the little shop, so neat and tidy the night before when I'd visited with Al, had been completely trashed. I gasped, which made Miguel panic.

When he switched on the lights, and we both stood where Margarita had lain, the destruction was painfully obvious. Flowers, buckets of water, and unrolled spools of colored ribbon and tape were all strewn about the place. A neat row of albums that had been sitting on a shelf above Margarita's workbench had also been flung on the floor. The dead woman's photographs were now all puddled with water, stomped on, curled and ruined. A copy of a local newspaper with the headline "Beware Girls," warning of the next Rose Killer cycle, was crumpled in a corner, soaked and, ironically, strewn with roses.

"Who would do this?" asked Miguel plaintively.

"I'm guessing whoever wanted Margarita's photographic equipment," I replied. I nodded toward the empty space beneath the workbench. "She had a lot of black cases and containers stored under there. I saw them when I was here with Al last night. Now they're all gone." *Interesting.*

"I must tell Captain Alfredo," said Miguel, sounding alarmed. "He will know what to make of this."

"Maybe you could also check if Bob and Maria heard anything?" I said, as Miguel pulled out his phone. He nodded, looking grim.

I wondered what Al *would* make of this. He believed he had

Margarita's killer in a cell at his police station. I wondered who he might think had drugged the Booths and stolen Margarita's cameras. I added the search that had been made of my temporary digs to that list of mysteries, but I couldn't tell Al about that. Not now. The only time to tell him would have been when he collected me that morning, and that ship had sailed. As Miguel stepped outside to make his call, I took my chance to survey the damage in more detail. I didn't want to interfere with the crime scene, but so long as I didn't touch anything, and I tiptoed between bits of debris, I didn't think there was much I could do to spoil this one.

The moment I had seen the space where the cameras used to be, it seemed to confirm the possibility that Margarita had seen and photographed something that had put her in danger. It made sense. If someone had been seen in any sort of a compromising situation—with someone they shouldn't have been with, or at a place they shouldn't have been—they might have discovered that Margarita had found out and photographed them. Who knows, maybe she was even blackmailing them? Considering the scene again, it looked as though someone had been checking through Margarita's photographs, discarding them as their search turned up empty. The photos on the floor were clearly not going to contain any incriminating images, because they'd been left behind by the searcher. As I looked at the images she'd captured, it was clear that Margarita favored nature over humanity: none of the photos showed any people, just seascapes, landscapes, the odd bird, bunches of flowers, and grasses bending in the breeze. Had the intruder taken the photographic equipment to access anything that Margarita had not yet printed out? That had to be it. It seemed more likely than ever that Margarita had some photo that someone wanted to get their hands on. I returned to the question of blackmail.

Bob and Maria had been quite convincing when they described how Margarita would say odd things to people. Maybe that was the florist's way of telling them she had something over them? Or maybe they already knew that, and she was being spiteful, pushing them as far as she could in public. The tragic loss of her family, estrangement from her father, terrible scarring, being bullied at school, and, if Bob and Maria were to be believed, an angry streak could all point to the sort of psychopathy that might lead a loner with a camera to become a voyeur with a fat bank balance. Margarita, indeed, bore all the hallmarks of a woman who could, quite easily, turn to blackmail. Or maybe she wasn't in it for the money; maybe power was her motivating force.

Without the opportunity to check through all the photo albums, or take the cameras, at the time of the murder, last night would have been the killer's first chance to get the evidence out of the shop. I wondered where those cameras were at that moment. Possibly being pored over by a person desperate to make sure they had, indeed, collected all the evidence against them, or maybe at the bottom of the sea, having been tossed off a cliff somewhere along the coast.

I told myself I was running away with the theory that Margarita was a malicious person maybe a little too far, and too fast. I had little real evidence to support it, other than the psychological picture I'd built up of the woman. A woman driven to succeed in order to fill the void she'd created in her own life by not trusting people, or giving them a chance to really get to know her. *Hmm . . .*

"Don't touch anything!" Miguel was back.

"I haven't," I replied. *I wouldn't,* was on the tip of my tongue.

"Captain Alfredo says we are to lock up the store, and I am to take you back to your house," he added officiously.

"But I wanted to . . ." *quick, think, Cait,* ". . . take another look at his crime scene photographs, back at the station." I was desperate to see Bud again.

Miguel hesitated. "But Captain Alfredo said . . ."

I smiled. Beamed, in fact, and gently touched Miguel on the arm. "I'm sure that Al won't mind. He let me look through the case file last night, and even read me his notes. He won't mind me taking another look, I'm sure. I can wait there for him, at his office. It will save you the trouble of driving me all the way out to the Hacienda Soleado. I'm guessing he wants you to go back to the station to check on the prisoner, right?"

Again Miguel hesitated. "You are right. I have to go to give the prisoner some food, and to make sure that he is still secure." He puffed out his chest. It was obvious that he was proud that Al put such trust in him. "If it was alright for you to see the file last night, I am sure it will be alright today. He has added nothing to it." *He will soon!*

Having managed to get Miguel to agree to take me to the police station, I didn't want to waste any time, or give him the chance to change his mind. I stepped out into the dazzling sunlight once more, so he could lock the door behind us—for all the good that seemed to do.

We walked toward the spa, which seemed empty, and there was Miguel's car. Not a police car, but his own personal vehicle. At least, I assumed that was what it was. I must have looked puzzled.

Miguel smiled. "It is a good undercover car, yes?"

I smiled and nodded. If you could call a battered, aging, pale blue Honda Civic that. I certainly never would have guessed it was being driven by a cop. Miguel pulled open the back door, reached inside, shut the door again, and slapped a magnetic decal onto the passenger door. "Now, it is not undercover anymore," he said, grinning like a magician who has just performed a spectacular trick. The badge matched the one on Al's white sedan, and Miguel seemed very proud of it. "This way we save money," he explained. "Captain Alfredo allows me to claim expenses for the miles I do when the badge is on, when I am on official business, but I take the badge off and I can drive to collect my daughters from school in Bucerias from wherever I might be."

I got into Miguel's car. He carefully shut the door for me, then took his own seat, and we set off for the police station. He proudly pointed out the blue flashing light that he could put onto the roof of his vehicle if he had to drive to an emergency, but he explained that didn't happen very often. He was a careful driver, taking more time than Al would have done to deliver us to our destination, but I was glad for that little delay because it allowed me to observe Miguel alone, without his brother's presence dominating him. His car was full of symbols of his Catholicism. A rosary hung from the rear-view mirror, a little prayer card was taped to the dashboard, and a plastic model of the Madonna wobbled precariously above the glove box on the passenger side.

"You're a man of faith," I said gently.

Miguel nodded. "It is my faith that sustains me. In difficult times, in happier times. I named my firstborn for the angels and the roses, and now she sleeps with the angels, and every week her mother and I place roses on her grave. She is with her God. She was a good girl, an innocent girl; I know she is with Him." His faith might have been firm, but his voice shook with emotion as he spoke.

"Al told me that you revived a local custom and held a crucifix of Requiem Masses in her memory. That speaks highly of your dedication."

"This is true," said Miguel gravely. "We held them on December 7, the day before the Feast of the Immaculate Conception. Poor Margarita, she helped us a great deal. She made the floral arrangements for the church here in Punta de las Rocas, and she came with me to the Church of Our Lady of Guadalupe in Puerto Vallarta to make her displays there. They were beautiful. Roses, of course. White ones, for the purity of my poor daughter. In all four churches. She sent the flowers with my wife and daughters for them to arrange in the church where they worshipped, and when my other brother, *not Rutilio*, came to collect our mother, to drive her to her home village, they had bunches of flowers to take with them." I felt the man's anguish.

"It must have been a very sad day for you all, Miguel."

"It was sad, though not as sad as the day we knew we had lost her. It was a day to allow us all to remember her and celebrate that she was at peace with God. I, and all my family, discuss this often: my baby is at one with her Master. We should be happy for her. So it was also a happy day, in a way. Everyone in Punta de las Rocas attended one of the two local services. It was wonderful to know. Margarita closed her store to be able to help me in Puerto Vallarta, and Rutilio even closed his restaurant for the day. He was so sad. So angry with whoever had killed my baby. He lost interest in his business at that time. It is why he is still struggling now. It is why he had to give up his apartment in Bucerias and move in with my family. We love to have him, of course. Our mother is pleased to have her baby with her. When God closes a door, He opens a window. It is always this way. We must pray to see His plan for us. If we pray enough, His Will becomes clear."

The poor man.

Upon our arrival at the unusual municipal building that served three purposes, Miguel let us in through the rear entrance to the police office, thereby avoiding the cells where Bud was housed. I was grateful for that because I didn't want Miguel to see Bud and I meet face to face—it had been difficult enough to mask my emotions in front of Al; I didn't want to have to go through that whole performance again. I asked for directions to the washroom and found it to be clean and well decorated with dried flowers. I wondered if the arrangements had been supplied by Margarita.

Refreshed, I rejoined Miguel in Al's office and sat down, picking up the case folder from Al's desk, as though to study it.

"If you need to get on with other duties, like feeding the prisoner, don't let me stop you," I said, quite casually.

Miguel thanked me, nodded, then went off in the direction Al had taken when he'd gone to his apartment the night before. When he returned, some time later, he looked at me and said, "I do not know why I am feeding that dog. He does not deserve it."

I pushed my internal edit button and managed to say, "You must look after him properly, or the Federales will want to know why you didn't."

Miguel laughed. "The Federales? They will show him a thing or two. He won't be silent with them, as he is with us, for long. They have ways of ensuring they get the truth." His ominous words stung my heart. He might have been a religious man, but Miguel didn't seem to carry charitable feelings toward Bud. Maybe he was more the eye for an eye type of Christian than the turn the other cheek kind.

"There was a phone call that I answered," I lied. "I don't know who it was, or what they said exactly, but I heard the words 'niño enfermo' and 'escuela.' Does that mean something to you?"

Miguel looked panic-stricken. "My girls. The school. There must be a problem. I must go. You will come with me."

"Oh, no, Miguel, I'll stay here and work on this case file. You go and attend to your girls." He didn't seem keen to leave me. I smiled warmly. "I'll be fine. I'll just stay here and, if necessary, I know where the washroom is. I'll wait here for Al and tell him where you are when he comes to collect me. Don't give me another thought." I hated to trick him and cause him to worry about his daughters, but it was my only chance to get to see Bud.

It was clear that the poor man was desperate to get away, and I all but steered him to the door. As soon as I saw him disappear in his car down the track toward the road, I tried the handle of the door that led to the area where the cells were located. It was open. I pulled at it, peered inside, and saw Bud, sitting on his straw mattress on the floor, eating bread. It was the most wonderful sight!

I rushed in. Bud looked up and dropped his bread. "It's okay, we're alone," I shouted, as I flung myself against the metal cage. Bud didn't move. He looked behind me, all around, and motioned that I should be quiet. We both listened. As I strained my ears, I noticed that he looked gaunter than he had the day before. His silvery beard had grown in a little, and he looked older. I know it's not possible to acquire prison pallor in a day, but I could have sworn he was paler than when we'd flown in to Puerto Vallarta.

"Are you sure?" he mouthed.

"Yes," I replied quietly. "Are you okay?" *Stupid question, Cait!*

"I'm fine," he replied very softly, pushing himself upright as he spoke. "You?" *Oh Bud!*

I reached through the bars to touch him, and we held each other as best we could, just for a moment.

"You've been smoking," he said.

I pulled away. *What?* "You're here, locked up in a Mexican prison, accused of a murder you didn't commit, about to be carted off to Guadalajara, where the cells are full of drug dealers who'd love nothing more than to see you dead in a matter of hours, and all you can say is that I've been smoking? *Are you nuts?*" I was beside myself.

"You promised you'd stop, Cait. I need you to be healthy, to be alive, to live with me. I *need* you, Cait Morgan. That's what I'm saying. I've . . . I've been thinking about us, about life, a lot in here, Cait. It didn't come out right. I *love* you." He smiled. I smiled back. I could feel the tears welling, but I refused to lose control.

"Bud, I don't know how long we've got, so I have to tell you a lot of stuff—ready?" He nodded.

I filled him in. He nodded as he listened.

When I finished he asked, "So nothing by way of a name from Jack about who he might have gotten in touch with?" I shook my head. "And no one's approached you to make themselves known to you as someone who is working with CSIS, or the FBI, or the Canadian

Gang Task Force?" Again I shook my head. He cursed under his breath. "What do they know, or think they know, about me?"

"You speak enough English to be able to say 'No police,' and you're possibly a hit man working on behalf of someone else. That's it. By the way, why did you say 'No police' to Serena?"

"If you mean that woman who started screaming fit to burst, what I said was, 'No. Police.' I meant I *was* the police, but she didn't get that, I guess. I thought it best to follow protocol and go silent. It keeps it out of the official channels that way, so thanks for getting hold of Jack, even though that might not have helped. Tell Sheila to tell him I say get well soon." He looked thoughtful.

"I'm doing my best to work out who did it, Bud. I've got a lot of leads, but, I don't know, there's something weird about this place. It's lovely, and it's got the normal tensions you find when there's a rich immigrant population rubbing along with a poorer indigenous one, but there's something under the surface. Something's not *right*. It reminds me of *Alice in Wonderland*, or *Through the Looking-Glass*, where nothing is as it should be, or what it seems. At least, that's what it feels like at the Hacienda Soleado. It's all *off*. Everyone seems so *keen* to help Al identify you before the Federales show up. He's a nice enough guy: bright, diligent, ambitious, but I cannot fathom what it is about him that makes everyone want him to succeed in front of the Federales. Like I said, *weird*."

We both sighed. I looked at poor Bud. "Bud, what can I do? I have to get you out of here. Are you sure you shouldn't talk? What about when Al ships you off to the Federales? What if I haven't been able to solve it by then? It could be terribly dangerous for you." My heart was pounding.

"As long as no one knows who I am, I'll be as safe as the next guy," replied Bud. I suspected stoicism and heard a slight tremor in his voice. "You're doing a great job, Cait, and I know it isn't something I should ask you to do, but I know you'll do it anyway, so if you're digging, dig carefully. You're dealing with a killer. Have you got something you could carry as a weapon?"

I pulled the flashlight that Tony had given me the night before out of my purse. "It's heavier than my hairspray," I said. I hadn't mentioned the break-in at the place where I was staying, because I didn't want Bud to worry. "I'll use it if I have to," I added, looking as fierce as possible.

Bud smiled sadly. "Cait, please be careful. *I need you.* Not just now, when I'm in trouble; I need you forever . . ."

"Hey—I told you there's to be no talk of marriage until September at the earliest, a year from when you first mentioned it. So don't start with it now. This isn't the time, or the place." I grinned the best I could. "What's that?" I'd caught the sound of tires on gravel. It suggested Al's parking technique. "Gotta go. Love you." I took one last look, dashed out of the door I'd entered through, and hung a right, which brought me to the community hall area of the building. I looked around, desperate to find a reason for being there, and stood in front of a large, framed piece of parchment that bore a huge red wax, beribboned seal. It was at eye level, so I gave it my attention and read it through.

A moment later, Al was at my shoulder. I jumped. "I didn't hear you arrive," I said, feigning shock. "You seem to enjoy making a habit of startling me." I grinned.

Al smiled back. "You like it?" he asked, nodding at the framed parchment.

"The lettering is very beautiful, and it looks old," I replied.

"It is our charter from the Dubois García family, or, as you can see," he pointed at a portion of the writing, "the García García family. They were quite wonderful, and we have to thank them for all that Punta de las Rocas is today."

I looked at the spot he was indicating and nodded. As he spoke I pretended to listen, but I allowed my eyes to play over the delightful piece of history, which spoke of land ownership, of the unusual idea of property passing from woman to woman as well as from man to man, and of how all García García offspring were to be treated equally. Clearly, as Al was telling me, the family had been well intentioned and farsighted in their plans for their municipality.

"Did you find what you were looking for?" he finally asked.

"How do you mean?" *Careful, Cait.*

"At Rutilio's, or at Margarita's, or here, in my office?" He seemed angry for some reason.

I considered my reply. "I think I'm beginning to understand Margarita a little better, and I think that the theft of the photographic equipment from her store is significant." Knowing that Al had had feelings for her made it impossible for me to get an objective answer from him about whether the woman might have been capable of blackmail, so there was no point asking.

"We had some luck on that aspect," he said.

"Really? What? Have you found something?"

"I think so," said Al. He put his hand into his pocket and pulled out a digital memory card, the type used in cameras. "I was on my way back from the hospital when Miguel phoned me about the theft. Tony and Callie are still in a dangerous state, the doctors say, and Juan asked me to leave him with Margarita—which I don't understand, but I am not a father. I drove to Margarita's store, saw the damage, and had a thought: if someone stole the photographic equipment, maybe they just made the rest of the mess to make it appear as though they didn't know exactly what they wanted. I also knew that Margarita always kept some photographic supplies in her van. I got the keys and found this in the glove box. Would you like to see what's on it?"

"Absolutely! Do you want to put it in my camera to look at her photos?"

"Good idea," replied Al. "Let's do it back in my office. It's cozier there, and the light is better."

I agreed, and moments later we were head to head, looking at expertly composed photographs of birds at rest, wild flowers on the cliffs, waves crashing against rocks. The pictures were beautiful, but none of them showed an illicit embrace, a drug deal going down, or an illegal, or even worrisome, act of any sort. In fact there were hardly any photographs with humans in them at all. Clearly Margarita had loved sunrise, and sunset. Most of the shots were taken at that time. In a few, she'd used her bicycle wheels to frame an otherwise plain subject. With some it was the contrast of blurred images in the foreground with sharp ones in the distance that made a shot work, with others it was the reverse. She was a good photographer. As I clicked through her work, I could tell it was a difficult process for Al, but I kept going.

"Oh look, someone's got a van just like Margarita's," I said, as I clicked through three or four shots that had clearly been taken in rapid succession. The shots showed the waves, touched by the first light of day, crashing against the huge formation of reddish rocks that sat off the shore, forming a point, which had inspired the naming of the area. In the background of the shot was the winding coastal road, upon which there was a little white van, just like the one that Margarita drove. "It's a shame it got in the way," I added. Clearly the photographer had thought the same thing because she had taken at least half a dozen more shots even after it had driven out of sight, the light on the water different in each one.

"She was so good at this, but there's nothing out of the ordinary here," said Al sadly, as we realized we were looking at the first photographs we'd seen for the second time. "I had thought that maybe she'd seen something or someone she shouldn't have . . ." He struck his desk with his fist in frustration. "If only that man would talk!"

Clearly he'd given *some* thought to the possibility that Margarita had known something, or photographed something, that might have led to her murder. But, equally clearly, he also still firmly believed that Bud was the one who had killed her.

If I am going to help Bud, I need to think!

"Al, could you do me a favor, please?" I sighed. "I know this is a difficult time for you, and I really want to help with your inquiries all I can, but I could really do with some quiet time. Is there any chance I could just take half an hour, in a comfy chair, in your apartment? It would save me the trouble of going all the way back to Henry's place. I just need to think. I need to consider what the drugging of Tony and Callie and the break-in at the store might mean. Would that be okay?"

"You mean you have to work out who might have done those things, when that man is still locked up in there?" he asked grimly.

I nodded.

"Sure, let me show you through. I'll set you up with a beer, and you can have some thinking space."

"No, no beer, thanks, but a couple of bottles of water would be great. I'm finding that all this humidity, and the perspiring that goes with it, is making me thirsty, and I don't want to let you down by drinking beer and not being at my best."

A few minutes later I was settled in a corner chair, which was obviously where Al sat to read at night, given its proximity to a small table that was covered with books and papers and held a reading lamp. He opened the windows and turned on a ceiling fan, as well as a fan that sat on a table, and another that stood in the corner of the room. I had a cold bottle of water in one hand, a head full of information, an aching desire to work out what on earth was going on in Punta de las Rocas, and an excellent place to do just that.

"I'll give you a shout if I get any news from the hospital. I'm hoping that maybe Callie or Tony can shed some light on who might have drugged them, and, of course, I'll let you know if my prisoner talks. You go ahead, Cait Morgan. I have read everything you have ever written, so I know that some of your methods are unusual. Give it your best. Come up with an explanation, and then come tell me what it is. Okay?" He half-smiled, but concern played around his eyes.

"Okay, I'll do my best," I replied.

As he pulled the door closed, he said in Spanish, "It had better be good." *Odd.*

Tea Time

I WOKE WITH A START when Al touched my shoulder. "You were tired. I let you sleep," he said quietly.

"What time is it?" I asked, then I looked at my watch. It was gone 5:00 PM. "Never mind," I continued. "What happened? I've been asleep for over an hour! I didn't mean to fall asleep. Oh no!" I was panicking. Bud didn't have time for me to sleep. I'd meant to do some deep thinking, to let my mind float in a technique I'd used before called "wakeful dreaming." My body had let me down. It had let Bud down. I'd achieved nothing at all, and his time in the relative safety of Al's cells was ticking down.

I jumped up, immediately regretted moving so quickly, and gave my body a moment to uncurl properly. I made noises like my mother used to make in her later years. My mouth was parched. I needed water. I drank from the bottle Al had given me earlier. It was warm, but at least it was wet.

Somewhere on the edge of my consciousness was a sliver of a thought. A remembrance from a dream. What was it? It was a question I had to ask ... who? *Think, Cait!*

"I'm sorry, Al, I've let you down. I didn't mean to sleep. I've wasted time. I need to talk to the people from the Hacienda Soleado who were on the spot at the crime scene, and to Bob and Maria too. But I have no way of getting to either place. Could you help me out? Oh—and is there any news from the Booths? What have I missed while I've been asleep?"

Al looked at me and shook his head heavily. He looked tired, haggard even. "The doctor at the American hospital says that Callie Booth has woken but has no idea what happened. She took

Dorothea's sleeping pill, and from half an hour after that, everything was a sleepy blur. That is the good news. The sad news is that Tony has died. He never regained consciousness. I am partly to blame." I noted that his red eyes were probably the result of weeping. "Last night, when you left to walk to Casa LaLa, I stayed with Tony and we had a few drinks together. The doctor says it is because he had alcohol in his system that he died. Callie had not drunk anything, so she survived. Though she does not see that as good fortune now, having just been told that her husband has died, on top of her best friend being murdered."

"You must blame the person who doped them both." Al nodded, then looked away from me. "Is there anything else?" I hardly dared to ask.

"The doctor at the other hospital, the Mexican hospital, where I left Juan this afternoon, has called me to tell me that Juan had to be ejected from the mortuary because he would not leave his daughter's body. Which, given that he did not speak to her in life, and I know that this hurt Margarita a great deal, has puzzled me greatly. I will also admit it has made me angry." He looked it.

"Miguel has telephoned me from his girls' school to tell me that they are all quite well, and to thank you for passing on the message, but to say you must have misunderstood, because the school did not call the police station."

Al let that sink in for a moment. He obviously suspected something fishy.

"Other than all of that, as if it wasn't enough, I have been in my office attending to my normal duties, one of which, sadly, means I have to go out shortly. I need to visit a local family. A niece of theirs, who lives about fifty miles from here, has just been found dead. She ran away from home a few days ago, after an argument with her father. Her parents thought she would go to stay with a friend, then come home. The Federales found her this morning, but they do not know exactly when she died. Maybe a day before she was found. It looks like she was the latest victim of the Rose Killer. The news of the killing has broken, but they have not revealed the identity of the girl to the public yet. I must speak with her aunt and uncle. I think that someone in their family will have told them already, but, although this is a case for the Federales, I can perform my community duties and visit them, to show them respect. The family lives in the village near the Rocas Hermosas Resort. I will take you to Rutilio's. I know that many of the people from the Hacienda Soleado will be there to eat. Of course, Amigos del Tequila cannot open tonight without Tony, but it seems that the FOGTTs choose to eat outside their homes most days, so they have arranged to eat at Rutilio's tonight. Miguel says Rutilio is very excited because this group of people doesn't usually eat at his place. He has called his brother to say he's going to take his chance to impress them all." Al rolled his eyes. "Is that a good plan for you?" His voice was flat, which wasn't surprising, but there was anger beneath the sadness. His movements were short, sharp, staccato. He was frustrated and angry. But I couldn't be sure why.

I agreed to his plan for me. Once again, we sped off toward the sea. This time it was still light, and there was a strange greenish glow in the sky. The clouds that had been bubbling on the horizon when I'd eaten brunch at Rutilio's now filled the sky. Layer passed across layer, some the palest of grays, some thunderous black, the fading sun streaming through fleeting gaps. The humidity signaled a probable storm, and I could almost feel the electricity building in the air. When we reached the resort, Al pulled over in front of Bob's Bodega, and I got out of the car. As he pulled away, I walked to Rutilio's Restaurant, where, sure enough, the full complement of FOGTTs was all present and correct. It was as though they operated like a flock. *Of crows.*

My arrival brought mild interest but no cheer to the group,

intent as it was upon discussing the terrible tragedies that had befallen the locality. Rutilio had pulled tables into a grouping so everyone could sit together, and there was a spare seat for me—between Greg and Frank. *Oh joy!*

I accepted the seat and found that Ada was pouring me a cup of greenish tea. It seemed incongruous, to say the least. I thanked her for her thoughtfulness, sipped at the tea, which was as disgusting as I had expected, and asked Rutilio for a bottle of water.

Poor guy's knocking himself out for this lot, I thought to myself. He was red in the face and shouting at the two girls, who seemed to work the same hours he did. They all appeared to be rushing about without achieving a thing.

With tea finally giving way to cocktails, served alongside chips and salsa, I accepted a chilled Pacifico from Rutilio, declined a glass, and sipped from the bottle. Jean didn't seem impressed, but impressing Jean George wasn't on my to-do list that evening—in fact, given the stinky look she'd shot at me when we first met, it wasn't ever likely to be. I still had no idea why she'd been so snotty. Everyone else, after all, had been quite welcoming.

The conversations ebbed and flowed, as they always do within a group. Shock, disgust, sadness, worries about how Amigos del Tequila could continue without a chef—these were the expected topics. I managed to remain noncommittal, nodding when required, but not really participating. Frankly, I was impressed that these people, who obviously spent a great deal of time in one another's company, still had so much to talk about. And, boy, could they talk. The dynamics were interesting. The six of them chatted, and I let it all wash over me, while I smoked a cigarette, sipped my beer—*my first of the day, delicious!*—and gathered my thoughts. At the farthest end of the table, I caught Dorothea expounding on how terrible it was that the man in prison had rushed in and killed Margarita without even taking the time to talk to her—*stupid woman.* Then I thought about what she'd said in a different way. *Context, Cait.* Of course—that's not how it happened!

I'd been grappling with who could have entered the flower shop while I'd been observing it. I'd become completely caught up in the idea that the whole incident had begun when Bud had left the apartment, because for me that's when it *had* begun. My thinking about the event lacked *true* context—a context that included more variables than Bud's part in it. It *could* have begun ten, twenty minutes earlier. There was no real reason to suppose that the killer had entered the store and killed Margarita *immediately*. Yes, her throat must have been slashed just a few moments before Bud entered her store, but the killer could have been in there with her for some time. My first visit to Margarita's store had presented me with a picture of an attack without much of a struggle. Margarita had either not seen the knife coming, because it came from behind, or, if she'd been facing her killer, she must not have suspected that they meant her harm. I'd been looking at the whole thing within the wrong time frame. I had to reconsider the whole series of events leading up to Bud's discovery of Margarita's body from much earlier than just a few minutes beforehand.

I felt compelled to remove Callie and Tony Booth from my list of possible suspects, but that still left a lot of folks in the running, including anyone, resident or visitor, who might have wanted Margarita dead, for whatever reason, and had simply walked into her store, killed her, and managed to get away unseen.

Looking around the table I realized that maybe someone who'd been on the spot had seen something useful after all. They just hadn't been asked the right questions, about the right time frame.

Purely by chance there was a lull in the conversations when I asked, "I don't suppose any of you saw anyone in the street, or going into Margarita's store, within the half an hour before she was killed, did you? And I mean anyone, even someone you didn't know or recognize." I heard Jean gasp. I turned in her direction.

Jean George glanced at her husband. "Dean and I had been walking on the beach together for at least an hour before we arrived at the flower shop, hadn't we, honey-pie? So we couldn't have seen anyone go inside the store at all."

Dean nodded, but no one else answered, because, at just that moment, Al arrived. I almost coughed up a lung when he appeared beside me. When I'd stopped choking, I managed to splutter, "You're going to give me a heart attack if you keep doing that."

I was annoyed that Al's arrival meant everyone had an excuse to not answer my question, as seats were rearranged to accommodate him, and then the food appeared. We all sampled different items from the large platters that Rutilio had decided to serve to us family style. It wasn't bad food; it just seemed as though it was all made from roughly the same ingredients encased in different things. To be fair, despite the fact that I was rethinking the entire case, I enjoyed everything I tasted, and some of it was very good indeed. Maybe Miguel had a point when he said that his brother prepared good food. Though I suspected that Rutilio had taken the decision to cater to the tourist palate just a bit too far, and we were missing out on many wonderful local flavors, sauces, and exciting dishes.

As I ate and thought about the people I was sharing my meal with, I caught a snippet of something that Dorothea was hissing at Greg in a whisper. ". . . color looks great in the bottle . . . never know," she said. My mouth was full of chicken fajita when it came to me in a flash. *Of course, maybe that's what you're up to . . . bottles versus barrels. Callie's notes . . . the calculations.*

"I'd like to make a toast," said Al, breaking across my train of thought. He was standing at what had now, de facto, become the head of the table. He cleared his throat. "This isn't going to be a normal sort of toast, but I think you'll understand why I'm doing this if you'll give me a moment." There were shufflings, and a couple of nods and smiles. "When I first met Professor

Cait Morgan, I spoke very highly of her." Smiles and nods were directed at me. "I was delighted when she said she'd help me look into the identity of Margarita's killer, because I have developed an admiration for her work as a part of my studies. I have read everything that she has published, and she is an excellent thinker and researcher." I was beginning to feel a bit embarrassed. "As some of you know, it was I who recognized her for who she is, because I had seen her photograph on her university's website." Nobody, myself included, seemed to have any idea what Al was rambling on about, and I wished he'd get to the point. "I visited that same website when I was in my office earlier today, and it was then I found out that at the end of the last academic year Professor Morgan was elected to her university's Roll of Honor for a second time."

I had no idea what was coming next, but I was squirming in any case because I hate being praised in public.

Al continued, undaunted. *His* expression was complex: a mixture of determination, anger, and . . . sadness. *Odd.* "To mark this, she was invited to a luncheon, which was followed by a ceremony where she was presented with a framed commemoration of her achievement." He pulled a roll of paper from his pocket, smoothed it out, and held it up for us to see. It was a color print of a photograph of me being presented with the item he'd just described. He turned the photograph so that everyone had a chance to look at it, which they did, most smiling at me afterwards and trying to look gracious.

"I've also made an enlargement of a figure standing behind Cait Morgan." As he said the words, my heart sank.

He unrolled the second photograph and held it up. I didn't need my glasses. I knew what it would show. There was Bud, smiling proudly and clapping, as I beamed into the camera.

"That's *him*!" shouted Frank. "The killer. In that photograph."

He was speaking on behalf of the entire group, and all eyes turned to me. I could feel my whole body shaking. I'd only ever felt that way once before in my life—when the cops dragged me out of my home, as the corpse of my ex-boyfriend lay on my bathroom floor.

I wanted to stand. I wanted to run away. I knew there was no point trying to hide my terror. I was rooted to the spot.

"Cait Morgan, you *know* the man in that cell, the one who killed Margarita. You have known his identity all along." Al's voice was as deep as when he'd been speaking Spanish. He was very angry. It was clear to everyone that he was trying to control himself. "That man asked for flowers in the bodega—roses, no less. You have inserted yourself into this case with the sole purpose of preventing us from discovering the identity of your murderous partner. I accuse you of drugging Tony and Callie Booth when you were at their home with me last night and, thereby, of killing Tony Booth. I accuse *you* of stealing Margarita's photographic equipment, which you spotted when you insisted upon visiting the crime scene with me last night. And I accuse *you* of doing all this to cover up your partner's vicious slaying of Margarita Rosa García Martinez because she could identify him as the Rose Killer." There was a table-wide gasp. "You have used me, and you have used and abused the friendship you have been shown by this community, to shield a merciless serial killer from the law. Please stand. I will now take you into custody, and you will be turned over to the Federales when they arrive tomorrow to collect your partner."

I still couldn't move. My brain was struggling to process what he'd said. He'd made the leap from truth to untruth without effort. I could understand his reasoning, up to a point, but why would he think that Bud was the Rose Killer? Why would he think I would defend such a person?

People at the table were moving away from me so fast you'd have been forgiven for thinking I'd developed a highly contagious form of leprosy. Within a moment, I was the only person still seated.

Unfortunately, there was enough truth in what Al had said that it might be impossible for me to prove the untruths. I was trapped. Literally, and figuratively.

There was only one thing I could do. I stood, picked up my purse, and said, "All I can say is that you are wrong, Al. *Very wrong*. About *so many* things. I won't say more than that for now."

As he led me to his car, I knew it would be a very different journey to the police station for me this time, and I wasn't at all sure what would happen when we got there.

Doing Time

AL DROVE US FROM RUTILIO'S to the police station in record time. He didn't speak, nor did I. He was fuming and I was terrified. The atmosphere was strained, to say the least. The silence continued when we arrived. Upon this viewing, the floodlit building looked forbidding rather than whimsical, and I wondered where Al would put me—the only cells I'd seen were where Bud was incarcerated, so I dared to hope I might at least be close to him. This thought sustained me as Al unlocked the doors into the main part of the police station.

Bud was up on his feet as soon as he saw us. His face conveyed almost nothing when he spotted my handcuffs. One blink that lasted twice as long as it should have done betrayed his feelings to my trained eye.

"There's no way any charges will stick," I said loudly, as Al pushed me forward. "This man is *not* the Rose Killer, and you cannot prove otherwise. He did *not* kill Margarita, and he certainly didn't kill eight innocent young women over the last eight months. I know for a fact this is the first time he's been on Mexican soil for many years." *Since he visited Playa del Carmen with his late wife, early in their marriage. That's why we're on the west coast, not the east,* I could have added, but it didn't seem to be the time or the place.

Al stopped pushing me. He looked me up and down and did the same to Bud. "I understand that you are trying to communicate a plan of action to your partner in crime, Professor Morgan. Once we leave this room, I will make sure to put you somewhere that will not allow you to confer and develop your cover story. So stop talking *now*!" His voice was rough with anger. "You have been very clever to encourage me to work out who this man is alone, without involving the Federales, and I have achieved that. You do not realize that I have friends I can call upon. Others who, like me, are using their time to study to be able to better their careers. I have a friend who works in airport security who will one day have the qualifications that will allow him to advance. In the meantime, he's prepared to help a fellow student. I sent him this man's photograph—the one I found on your university's website. He is able to look at old information on the system, and he has found several photographs of this man. My friend has informed me that your partner has visited Mexico almost every month for the last year, using several different names and traveling on several different passports. Why would a man do this? It can't be for a good reason. I believe he's come here to kill, and kill again. He is the Rose Killer. That is why he asked about roses at the bodega. I am even beginning to wonder if poor Angélica Rosa *was* his first victim, or whether he killed in other states before he began to visit ours. So there you have it, Cait Morgan. I *know* he's been in and out of Mexico. As for what he's told *you*, or why you are with him on this trip, covering for him and committing crimes on his behalf, I do not know. You can take that information to your cell with you, and make of it what you will, while you sit and wait to be taken to Guadalajara tomorrow afternoon. That's when they'll be coming for you *both*."

I didn't reply, because I was so shocked. Not just because of what Al had said, but because of Bud's reactions when he'd said it. Bud had dropped his shoulders. It doesn't sound like much, but it told me he was feeling defeated. *It's all true—Bud's been secretly traveling to Mexico on a regular basis!*

Al sensed my moment of weakness and took his chance to push me toward the main hall. Once we were there, he slammed the door between Bud and me. It was a horrible sound. *So final.* I suspected that the next time I saw him we'd both be in shackles and being hauled off by the Federales to the dubious, and dangerous, delights of a jail in Guadalajara. Meanwhile, I was in the comparative safety, and relative pleasantness, of the municipal hall of Punta de las Rocas. Al locked me in a little room that looked more like a large confessional than a jail cell. Its wooden construction didn't suggest it would be impossible to escape, and the door had a metal grille in it, meaning I could look out into the great hall. Inside my cell, a long cushioned bench ran along the outside wall, beneath a window, which I could tell was covered outside by a decorative iron cage. A table and chair stood against another wall. There was a large plain wooden crucifix on the wall above the table. That was it. When Al had secured the door, he spoke to me through the grille. "I will bring you water later on. You'll be able to use the bathroom in my apartment, but I will accompany you and stand outside the door. There is no way to get out of my bathroom. I will treat you well while you are in my care. You're not going to have anything to complain about to the Federales. They'll be here at 2:00 PM tomorrow. I suggest you get some sleep." He was addressing me more formally than he had done since we'd met, and his anger was not subsiding.

"What is this place? This room I'm in?" I asked. Despite my circumstances, I couldn't help but be curious.

Al turned. "When he returned from his travels in America, when he was still quite a young man, this was the place where Juan Carlos García García lived, the eldest son of the Dubois García family, the man who granted lands to his family and made sure the community was well served. The true father of Punta de las Rocas. He was a simple man. This was all he needed." *How strange that he's so passionate about this man, even at a time like this.*

Al walked away, turning off lights as he went, until I was completely alone in the dark. I gave my eyes some time to adjust: there was no moonlight coming through the window, so it took a few minutes. I peered at my watch, but it was just a blur. I didn't have my glasses, because they were in my purse, which Al had taken from me. I told myself that it didn't really matter what the time was. I wasn't going anywhere. Not until the following afternoon.

I was wide awake, adrenalin pumping around my system, and I couldn't do a single thing to help Bud, or myself. How had this happened? I gave it some thought. I *could* understand why Al, after discovering that Bud had been entering Mexico on a regular basis using pseudonyms, would suspect him of being involved in something illegal. But why had Al decided that Bud was the Rose Killer? What was it about those cases that made him jump to that conclusion? Maybe the dates when Bud had been in the country tallied with the dates of the murders? Would that be all it would take? Not that it was an insignificant factor.

I sat myself at the little desk, held my chin in my hands, and recalled the online reading I'd done about the Rose Killer case. I closed my eyes a little and hummed. In my mind's eye I reread the newspaper articles, and I quickly realized that the times of death, as well as the dates of death in some cases, had been set within pretty wide parameters. It hadn't occurred to me when I'd first read it, but, in this day and age of advanced forensic pathology, that was odd. I didn't know much about the Mexican system of coroners, pathologists, or medical examiners, *or* about the sophistication of their techniques or equipment, but I assumed that once it had been established that they were dealing with a serial killer, they'd have put their very best people and resources on the case. Ascertaining time of death is one of the most basic requirements of most autopsies. I gave some thought to the factors that can adversely affect estimating an accurate time of death. I might not care much for forensics, but I've studied enough to know the basics. And that was the point: this was basic stuff!

If I'd had a pen and paper, I'd have made a list. But I didn't have those luxuries, so I made mental notes instead.

There are many ways of working out time of death. Body temperature is one. The human body cools at a constant and predictable rate after death—1.5 degrees per hour—until it reaches the temperature of its surroundings. That's why a rectal or liver temperature is taken as soon as possible after a body is found. Factors like ambient temperature will impact the calculations made. If a body is left for too long, its temperature becomes less informative because it's just the same as its surroundings. That's when the reference point of rigor mortis is used. Rigor also works in a pretty predictable manner, affecting different parts of the body at different times. Unfortunately, hot conditions, or cold ones, influence the onset of rigor, as does the amount or type of activity undertaken by the victim immediately prior to death. Also, rigor is of little use after thirty-six to forty-eight hours, because by then it's worn off. That's why they'd had to use stomach contents to work out when poor Angélica Rosa had died. It was their only reference point, and it showed that she'd died shortly after eating, which, according to her uncle Rutilio, had been about half an hour before she'd set off to walk home after work. In the case of the second victim, they'd been able to use rigor mortis to work out when she'd died, but they had come up with a very confusing result: the girl appeared to have died earlier than the last multiple sightings of her.

I paused. Why on earth was I worrying about the time of death of these girls? *Because you need to prove Bud didn't kill them, and when they died might be critical.* Unfortunately, critical or not, the newspaper articles that dealt with victims three and onward didn't reveal time of death at all, only the presumed date of death. If Bud had so much as been in the country on those dates, then Al had a point—Bud had the opportunity to kill those girls. That's why the first two were so important: they were the only murders where I had access to more detailed information.

Angélica Rosa had been killed on November 1 and found

on November 4. The second victim had been killed on Friday, December 7, the day of Miguel's family's crucifix of Requiem Masses. My heart leaped! Bud and I had been at my School of Criminology Christmas party in downtown Vancouver that night. I'd taken photographs. I could prove to Al that Bud couldn't have been killing a girl in Mexico, because he'd been sipping warm beer in BC. I allowed myself a small internal cheer.

The dates of the other murders had all been very general, which took me back to the issue surrounding times of death. I had to concentrate on getting Al to understand that Bud hadn't killed Margarita, and that meant working out who had.

I had to make the most of what I already knew. I could eliminate some people from being in the frame for Margarita's murder, but now I also had to consider whether Tony's killing had anything to do with Margarita's death, or if it was to do with the barrels and bottles issue, which I'd worked out in Rutilio's Restaurant. It was confusing, to say the least. I needed a smoke. But I didn't have my purse. I strained to make out the time on my watch by what little light came through the barred window, but it was no use. If I was going to make the most of my time, it would be a good idea to first use Al's washroom, then settle in for the night. I called out to my jailer, hoping he would hear me.

"Hello, Al? Could I use the washroom, please?" Nothing. I waited. And waited. Having decided to go, I *needed* to go. "Al? Can you hear me? I need the washroom, please." Still nothing. *Damn and blast!* I told my bladder to be patient—*because that always works!* Eventually, I heard some clattering off in the darkness of the municipal hall. "Is that you, Al?"

"Yes, who else would it be? What do you want?" Al sounded angry.

"I could do with using your washroom," I replied, sounding as desperate as I felt. "I called and called, but you didn't answer."

Clicks in the distance led to the hall being illuminated, then Al was outside my door. "I was speaking to the Federales. It was an important call. I'm here now." He placed the big, old iron key into the lock of the door. It squealed as it turned. "I will accompany you to my bathroom. Don't even think of trying to run away—the whole building is locked. You have nowhere to run. Just follow me." He pulled the door open, and I rushed out.

"I really need to get there quickly," I pleaded. Al picked up on my genuine distress and marched quickly to the bathroom, flung open the door, and ushered me in. As I ran the water to wash my hands, I looked around the room for anything that might be of use to me, or Bud. This being Al's own bathroom, not just a public washroom, I dared to peep inside his medicine cabinet. Caffeine pills—possibly to help with late nights spent studying; a fair stock of Band-Aids—it looked as though he was as clumsy as me; and a couple of bottles of over-the-counter antihistamine pills were all that was there. I closed the medicine cabinet and took stock of myself in the mirror on its door. I was pretty much a blur; my face lacked definition and color. I was a pasty blob, with little eyes. *Cait Morgan, you've got work to do. Stop thinking that you're living in a looking-glass world and make some sense of all this stuff.* I turned off the water and opened the door. Al was right outside.

"Use enough water?" he asked acidly.

I blushed, recalling his point about how all we visitors use too much of the precious resource. And that gave me a thought.

"The water supply for the Hacienda Soleado tequila-making plant, where does it come from? Who runs the manufacturing, or I suppose it's the distillation, operation? Is it Greg?"

Al glared at me. "He oversees it, with Juan, though it's none of your business." Any sense that Al and I were on the same side had clearly evaporated. I needed to make the most of the short walk back to my cell.

"Al, I know you're angry with me, but all I can do is ask that you believe me when I tell you that neither I nor the man you have incarcerated had anything to do with Margarita's death, let alone the Rose Killings. And, of course, I wouldn't smoke in that wonderful, historic room you've put me in, but is there any way I could have the nicotine gum that's in my purse?"

Al stopped in his tracks and gave my request some consideration. I hoped that, as a smoker himself, he'd help me out. He shrugged. "Can't hurt," he replied gruffly.

"Oh, thanks ever so much, Al," I gushed. "It'll help me relax. If you dig around in my purse you'll find it. You'll also find some notes I was making about Margarita's death and my camera, with a photo on it that can prove—" I didn't have a chance to finish.

"Stop it, Professor Morgan! I will give you your precious gum to assuage your addiction—you won't be so lucky when the Federales are in charge of you—but that's it! I will not buy into your tales anymore. Now come on, back to your . . . accommodations." He grabbed my arm and more than steered me back into the little room, where he slammed the door and locked it, violently. A few moments later he pushed a pack of gum through the grille in the door. "Here—chew your jaw off! You'll be pleased to know that the Federales will come early. They will be here to collect you both at 9:00 AM tomorrow. I have spoken to the officer heading the Rose Killer case, and he will be coming here himself, straight from the latest dump site. Make the most of your last few hours of comparative 'freedom.' It won't be long now until I can prove my worth as a detective!"

When I'd checked my watch by the light in the bathroom, I'd seen that it was midnight. Nine hours, that's all I had! Nine hours to use my brain to figure out what had really happened since Bud and I had arrived in Punta de las Rocas. I popped out a square of nicotine gum and chewed furiously. Within a few moments the craving for a cigarette had passed. *The gum really works!* I knew that I'd be able to concentrate better without feeling the terrible pangs of my addiction, which had become very strong again, very quickly. I chastised myself for having given in to buying cigarettes at all, and I saw again, in my mind's eye, the picture of the wonderful *In Search of Reason* on the Malecón in Puerto Vallarta. *Apply yourself, Cait!* As I visualized myself clambering up Bustamante's unsupported ladder, the first clap of thunder boomed above my head. Seconds later I could hear fat drops of rain slap against the metal bars that encased the window. I opened the casement just a little and drew in deep breaths of the metallic air: rain on sunbaked dust smells wonderful, but it was all I had to smile about.

I lay down on the cushioned bench in my little room and closed my eyes, releasing my thoughts to run free and form themselves into a reasonable explanation of all the facts I'd gathered and observations I'd made. The answer had to be in there ... somewhere.

Usually when I'm using the wakeful dreaming technique, my thoughts whirl about in no particular order to begin with, then various aspects of my findings gather themselves about a person or a place. This time, things went a little differently. I allowed the process to take the path it had chosen for itself, because, after all, that's the whole point, but it seemed to be leading me into a world where Edward Lear had laid his hands on everything I saw, and I felt uncomfortably like a very confused Alice.

First I saw Bud, *dear Bud*. He was running around in his cell with a giant watch face hanging about his neck. He looked panic-stricken and shouted, "I'm out of time, I'm out of time!" He kept bouncing off the bars of his cell, and, as he did so, they transformed into giant rose stems, the thorns cutting into his flesh until he was covered in blood. But he didn't stop running, around and around, bouncing and bleeding. I felt sorrow, and anguish, gripping my stomach.

Dorothea appeared next. She was a red-cloaked giant, swooshing into the municipal hall demanding that Bud be hanged. Her voice made the walls shake. She pumped her fists at the roof, which blew away to reveal dark thunderclouds. "Hang him, hang him!" she bellowed, and a gallows appeared in the corner of the hall, looming ominously, and growing by the minute.

I saw myself pop into existence in the middle of the hall, surrounded by a group of menacingly tall men. Al, Frank, and Dean crowded around me. As they grew ever taller, I felt as though I was shrinking. The foliage on Dean's Hawaiian shirt sprang to life and started to grow independently of the man. Sinuous vines crept across the floor of the municipal hall, which was disappearing and transforming into Margarita's flower shop. Suddenly the vines blew apart, and the insubstantial flower shop was full of living blooms. They were singing and weeping for Margarita, who lay among them, broken into pieces, but alive. "My children, I love you all," she was saying, as she gathered as many of the living, singing, weeping flowers into her arms as she could.

I reached toward the woman, who I saw had a golden scar running across her face, which she stroked proudly, but she turned away from me and screamed to Al that he had to save her, he had to make her whole. Al ran to her, his chest puffed out in his glittering dress uniform, which I somehow recognized as an ancient French general's style, and he gathered the pieces of Margarita together, but they kept slipping through his arms. He called, in French, for Frank to help him, but Frank was drinking tea with Ada. They seemed completely oblivious of everything that was going on around them, content to be in their own little world, with Ada pouring tea and Frank telling her how useless their children had turned out, but how much he loved her. Ada was pushing his hat off his head. Telling him it was rude to wear it indoors.

I saw a cigar in Frank's hand, but I couldn't smell the smoke.

I did smell an overwhelming scent of dampness, mold. I turned from the scene where Margarita lay to see Greg Hollins curled up on a big, moldy cushion on the floor in front of me. He was leering up at me and offering me a pack of cigarettes that I somehow knew were made of rose petals, not tobacco. "You'll enjoy them; they are very good quality; they are exactly what I tell you they are . . . you know you want them," he said greasily, with a sly look and a crooked smile. I pushed the packet, and him, away, and I turned again to try to escape.

Jean George sprang out of the ground in front of me. She scowled. "We don't want you here!" she screamed, but as she did so, her voice was drowned out by another, more piercing scream. I knew it was Serena. I would recognize her scream anywhere. She flew into the room, a bird with a giant female head and a bill that was wide open. She landed on top of Bud's prison cell, and her claws and beak tried to reach him inside. I ran to chase the woman-bird away, but Al grabbed me, dragging me back to Henry's house, where he pushed open the front door with one finger and said, "You should lock your door, Cait. It's too easy for people to get inside."

"Leave her alone," shouted Ada Taylor, suddenly beside me. "She's a Canadian; she can't have done anything wrong."

"She is *not* Canadian," shouted Al. "Like me, she is nothing, she is no one. We have no home, people like us. We are not one thing, not another. Look," he pointed at my face, "she has no face. No identity. Look around—no one has a face!"

I looked around, and I could see that Al was right. *No one* had a face. They were just blobs, with no bodies, no faces, no identities. One blob moved, and it immediately became Greg Hollins, but a new version of the man: this version was wearing a hat with corks dangling from it, and had the legs of a kangaroo. Now, instead of holding a pack of cigarettes, he was holding a bottle of tequila toward a blob I knew to be Dorothea. "G'day Dotty, strewth, you're fair dinkum. Have some of this . . ." he said, with a strangled Australian accent.

Tony Booth appeared next. He was in his chef whites, but instead of a head he had a Día de los Muertos skull, like the one popularized in the etching *La Calavera Catrina* by José Guadalupe Posada. His body was elongated in the same style, and he was tossing pepper around his kitchen and wailing, "I am going to ride the surf forever!" Beside him appeared a weeping Madonna, who I knew, instinctively, was his wife, Callie. She showered her dead husband with yellow sticky notes as she sang, "The numbers always tell our secrets."

Dean and Jean George rushed by on a white horse, being chased by Juan Martinez in his blue pickup truck, which trailed blood and water rather than exhaust. His arm was hanging from the window of his truck, and I could hear him screaming the name of his dead daughter.

Margarita magically appeared, alive and whole, filling her little white van with gas at a gas station, but the tank was overflowing, gas pouring down the hill, which was, I knew, the hill upon which the municipal hall was built. Then her white van transformed into a horse, still white because it was made of ice. It reared up and galloped away, and I was on its back. We passed grave after grave along the roadside until we reached Rutilio's Restaurant, which was now floating on a pontoon out at sea, with fish swimming away from it in all directions. I jumped off the frozen horse and found myself behind Margarita's flower shop, inside a tiny box that was so small I could hardly move. Rutilio stood above me, pouring tequila into the box from a tiny little bottle that seemed to pour forever. "Drink, drink, it is the good stuff—see, it is dark; that shows it has aged in the barrel."

"I don't like tequila—I hate it!" I cried. I burst out of the little box and stood in front of Rutilio, who was holding a giant bunch of white roses.

"For my dead niece, and for my dead friend." He wept.

Bob and Maria were now beside him, their individual faces mixed in my mind into one. They were twins, male and female. Then Miguel appeared, so very different from his brother. He slapped a big badge made of mirrored metal onto his brother's puffed chest. "Now he is my pretty baby brother policeman," he said. They all carried white roses.

Dorothea, appearing as a red cloud above us all, blew at our little group like a fierce wind, scattering the others away so that only Rutilio and I remained. The roses he clenched were white, his shirt red, and he was grinning so widely I thought his head would split open. Then he began to disappear. In a series of blinks, he and I were at his niece's grave, then at a church in Punta de las Rocas, then at a church in Puerto Vallarta, then back inside Margarita's flower shop. As we moved from location to location he kept getting dimmer and dimmer, until all that was left was his chef hat, his teeth, and the white roses, all hanging in the air. Margarita's store evaporated, leaving Rutilio standing in front of the rear wall of his restaurant, where his remaining features disappeared completely against the white of the wall

I jumped up from the cushioned bench with a start. Of course! White roses, yellow roses, red roses, blood spatter, too much gas, the frozen horse, the flowers for four masses, and the Cheshire Cat.

It *couldn't* be! I was *sure* I knew who had killed Margarita, and why. Except it meant that they had to have been in two places at once. I was so close . . . but there seemed no way I could be right! *Damn and blast!*

Time's Up!

I LOOKED AT MY WATCH. With the morning light streaming through the window of my cell, and rested eyes, I could make out that it was already gone 9:30 AM. Obviously my wakeful dreaming had become a full night of sleeping dreams! No wonder everything had seemed so complex and detailed—I'd been asleep for hours. *Damn and blast! I'd needed that time to think.*

It dawned on me that the Federales should have already arrived. What was going on? I told myself that maybe the Mexican attitude toward timekeeping applied to the police force as well. Besides, it wasn't as though I was looking forward to their arrival. I needed to get to the washroom.

I popped a piece of gum into my mouth. *That's a bit fresher, but not much.*

"Al. Al? Any chance of using the washroom, please?"

Al was outside my door immediately. *Good grief, he is always so stealthy!*

"I wondered when you'd wake," he said thickly. "Though I don't know how you could sleep at all. You and . . . *that man* . . . have no shame. You don't seem to feel the weight of your guilt at all."

A riposte of any sort was beyond me, let alone one as acidic as I'd have liked, so I just contented myself with heading toward his bathroom as fast as I could.

When I was as cleaned up as I could be, I opened the bathroom door and said, "Is there any chance I could use the brush that's in my purse? And maybe the lipstick . . ." Al was about to explode, I could tell. "I don't want to use the lipstick to make myself look better. I don't think that's possible. But my lips have dried out, and they are cracking." I licked them as I spoke. "It would help. Please?"

Al tutted loudly, slammed the bathroom door, and shouted, "Don't move!" as he stomped away.

What was I going to do? Where could I go? How would I get there? I looked at the woman in the mirror, and my mother looked back at me. I shook my head at my mirror-self. When had I become my mother's age? I didn't have my glasses on, but my eyes were rested enough that I could see many wrinkles. Most from laughter, some from frowning at students, or worrying over grading. Probably many of them from smoking too much for too long. As I chewed my nicotine gum and thought about how I yearned for Bud and I to be together, I promised my mirror-self that if we got out of this, I'd never smoke again, I'd stop drinking, and I'd lose fifty pounds. It would be a new beginning. I could do it.

Al knocked on the door and opened it a crack. *I wonder what he thinks I'm doing! He's not like a real cop at all.* "I'm passing things to you," he announced. He handed me my hairbrush and my lipstick.

"Can I have my specs too, so I can see what I'm doing?" It seemed reasonable. I could hear Al rooting about in my purse, and my glasses appeared. "Thanks," I said.

Five minutes was all it took, but I felt like a new person when I emerged—ready to face my accusers and the rest of the world. Which was just as well, because when Al and I walked back into the municipal hall, the FOGTTs were there.

"Good," said Al, unsurprised. "You're early."

I was puzzled. My watch had clearly said 9:50 AM in the bathroom. If the Federales had been due at 9:00 AM, what was it that the FOGTTs were early for? I couldn't help but speak up. "What's going on, Al? Why are these people here, and what's happened to the Federales? They should have been here nearly an hour ago. Are they not coming?" *I could hope.*

"They have ten minutes yet," said Al abruptly. "They'll be on time." *Am I losing my mind?* "But my watch says it's 9:50."

"Haven't you changed it?" interrupted Dorothea in her booming voice.

I knew I was in a terrible situation, but I wasn't going to take that from her. "Yes, Dorothea, I *have* changed my watch. I changed it on the airplane when we arrived in Puerto Vallarta. They announced the local time before we got off. We're two hours ahead of Vancouver here."

"No, we're not," the horrid woman snapped. "You don't know *anything*, do you? You come here, poking your nose into *our* business and doing *terrible* things, but you have *no idea*." She puffed up her chest, encased this time in magenta, and said, "Here in Punta de las Rocas, we're in Nayarit. And Nayarit is an hour behind PV. *Everyone* knows that!"

I could see Ada and Frank Taylor, *and* Dean and Jean George, nodding in agreement with the annoying Dorothea. Greg ignored her. I sensed that something had happened between him and Dorothea—something had made him angry with her. *Not unusual, in all probability.*

At least now I understood why Dorothea had said that Margarita's murder had taken place at 11:00 AM. I must have heard a clock from outside Nayarit chime twelve that day.

"*Whatever* the time, why are you all here?" I snapped out of my thoughts and asked an obvious, if somewhat rude-sounding, question.

"I invited them," replied Al gruffly. "I want everyone who has been touched by the death of Margarita to be here when the Federales come to take him, and you, away." *More like you want an audience so you can show off,* I thought.

"You can wait in your cell until the Federales arrive. I have put some bread and some coffee there for you. I must make myself ready."

After Al locked me into my little room once again, I consumed my breakfast with gusto. Still glugging coffee I peered into the hall, where I could see Ada and Frank with their heads together. Poor things, they were obviously feeling very uncomfortable about the whole situation, and I wondered if they'd stick it out. Meanwhile, from my vantage point behind the grille, I could see Dean and Greg hauling chairs into a semicircle facing the end wall of the municipal hall. Ada shooed Frank away to help out, and sidled toward the door to my personal prison.

"How are you doing?" she asked.

"Not too bad, thank you, Ada," was what I said. *How on earth do you think I'm doing?* was what I really felt like saying. But it wasn't poor Ada's fault that I was in this state. I couldn't take it out on her. That wasn't fair.

"I talked to Frank last night about whether we should get in touch with the Canadian embassy—or someone like that—about you being arrested. I even talked to my son about it, you know, on the internet. They both said I should leave it up to Al. But I'll do it if you like. I could go outside and phone them now. I put the number into my cell phone. Would you like me to do that?"

My heart softened even further toward the woman. "Let's see how things go. If I shout out to you for help as they drag me away, maybe you could make that call?"

Ada nodded and scuttled away. I wondered, just for a fleeting moment, if she was the operative in the area that Jack had referred to. He would likely know her, and if she was undercover, she was making a good job of it. I could tell from Ada's body language as she made her way back toward Frank that she hoped no one had seen her, but I also noted that Al's eagle eyes hadn't missed a thing. He cast a suspicious glance toward Ada as she began to help out with the chairs. While the seating arrangements were being made in the hall, as if for a civic meeting, the rest of the gang showed up. By the time the Federales arrived, everyone was there: the FOGTTs had been joined by Bob and Maria, Rutilio, Serena, and, of course, Miguel and Juan, who arrived together. Nobody looked as grim as the Federales.

I hadn't been sure what to expect. What I saw was an intimidating sight. As Al greeted their arrival by saluting and fussing about them, I could see him, more clearly than ever, as a relatively young man, with the softness and eagerness of the graduate student who loves art, literature, and poetry etched on his face. His federal colleagues, however, were a different breed altogether. Militaristic in appearance, they were dressed in black, wearing ball caps, Kevlar vests, and gun belts that dwarfed Al's. Several of them had automatic weapons slung over their shoulders as well as pistols in holsters. They were all business. Five of them surrounded a shorter man, who looked as dapper as he did forbidding in a more formal, but still highly militarized, uniform. If the number of gold stripes on his uniform, and the uprightness of his stance, were anything to go by, this man was pretty high up the food chain. I guessed he was in charge, and the way that Al, Miguel, and the other cops were deferring to him made that clear.

What was also clear was that Al was setting the stage in such a way that *he* would be the star. The body language among the Federales told me that they were being faced with a situation they had not expected. They'd marched through the main entrance to the municipal hall, so they hadn't seen Bud in his cell, and no one seemed to have noticed the room I was in, let alone me in it. Unfortunately I couldn't hear anything that was being said, because everyone was way down at the far end of the hall. I didn't have to wait long to know what was going to happen.

Al came to the door of my little room, unlocked it, and said pointedly, "They are here. Don't make a fuss, or they'll probably shoot you." *Nice!*

He put handcuffs on me, with my hands in front of my body, led me to a chair set to one side of the main group, and sat me down. Miguel was next to me, so close I could smell the tobacco on his clothes. I chewed my gum and wondered if I usually smelled that bad.

Al brought Bud from his cell. Upon Bud's arrival, two of the Federales stood beside him, one on either side, as he slumped onto a chair. Their automatic weapons were ready for action.

I looked at Bud, now no more than ten feet away from me. He looked awful. Al stood and cleared his throat. This was obviously an important moment for him, and he looked nervous. He began in Spanish, translating into English as he went.

He introduced the cop with all the braiding on his jacket as the man who'd been heading up the Rose Killer case. He also introduced the head guy's right-hand man, who looked pretty evil to me. Of all of them, he was the slyest looking. With this guy by his side, his boss could afford to sit and look imperious, which he did very well. The man with the most stripes was Captain Manuel Enrique Herrera Soto. The way Al introduced him made it quite clear that being a captain in the Federales was quite a different thing to being the captain in a tiny municipality. *Context!*

Al's introductions were over, and he was about to begin his explanation of why Bud was the Rose Killer. For his own sake, as much as for Bud and myself, I decided to try to stop him.

Before Al could begin, I shouted, "Al, please don't. Don't do this. You've really got it all wrong, and I can prove it!"

All eyes turned to me. The Federales didn't know the story yet; they just saw me and Bud in handcuffs and presumably assumed that *we* were the Rose Killer. Why would they be there unless Al had promised them their man? Captain Soto ran his beady eyes over me, and I clearly heard his right-hand man say in Spanish, "She'll be able to live off her waistline for a while in prison," as he smiled conspiratorially at his boss.

"I'm not listening to you anymore, Professor Morgan," replied Al. As he used my professional title I saw a look of surprise cross Captain Soto's face. *Not expecting me to be a professor, were you?*

I looked directly at Captain Soto and spoke to him in English. "Please Captain Soto. Captain Torres has misunderstood some facts, and I am sure I can explain everything to your satisfaction."

Now everyone turned their attention to Captain Soto, a situation with which the man seemed perfectly comfortable. He didn't stand; he didn't need to. We were all waiting for him to speak. When he did, it was in a surprisingly deep voice for a man of his stature, and, even more surprisingly for some there, it was in very good, if heavily accented, English.

"I have been invited here by Captain Torres of the municipality of Punta de las Rocas with the promise that he can reveal the identity of the Rose Killer, as well as the person who killed a florist in this area and poisoned a local chef. I have set out early and have traveled many miles to listen to his evidence and to take charge of his prisoners. This is not a court of law. This is simply one officer being courteous to another, and allowing him some latitude to tell us how he arrived at his conclusions. I have been told that Captain Torres is interested in a career with the Federales. Let's see if he's up to it. You, Professor Morgan, will have your chance to tell your side of the case in a courtroom. Captain Torres, please continue. You may do so in English; as you can see, I speak it very well. I am sure that Professor Morgan will not interrupt you again." His look told me it would be unwise of me to respond.

As motes of dust danced in the sunlight, and old wooden chairs creaked in the tense atmosphere, Al cleared his throat again and spoke. It quickly became clear that Al wasn't just bright, he was observant, logical, and ruthless. *Just what you want in a cop—but not one who's trying to put you in prison.*

"This man," Al waved toward Bud as he spoke, "was found with his hands around the throat of Margarita García Martinez on Sunday morning. I took him into custody, and he has remained here since, refusing to say one word. I have been able to use informal resources, without breaking any laws, sir," he nodded at Captain Soto, "to discover that this man has entered Mexico on numerous occasions during the last year, using different names and passports. I have been able to find thirteen visits where he flew into Puerto Vallarta airport. Here are the dates, his aliases, and the countries of origin of the passports he used." He approached Captain Soto, who motioned for his aide to take the paper Al was holding, which he did, passing it to his boss, who ran his eyes over it, his eyebrows rising by the second.

Al moved back to his original spot. "As you can see, sir, he has represented himself as Canadian, Swedish, and American. He has used various names. I found this passport in his accomplice's purse," he held up Bud's passport, "which names him as Bud Anderson of New Westminster, British Columbia. I suspect it's a fake, as are all the others he's used."

Captain Soto motioned to Al, who handed Bud's passport to the slimy sidekick. The captain whispered some instructions to the man. He took Bud's passport and the list and left the municipal hall. I saw Bud's shoulders sink and I could see him shaking his head ever so slightly. I knew that having his passport in the hands of the Mexican police was breaking protocol for him—I'd gathered that much from Jack before he'd upped and had a heart attack. I'd really dropped Bud in it. I hoped I'd have a chance to get him out of this mess.

Captain Soto motioned for Al to continue, which he did. "Once I'd established that this man had been making illegal entries into Mexico, I, of course, began to wonder why that might be. I also wondered if the reason for his trips here was what had led to him kill Margarita Martinez." I noted that Al kept things formal when talking about the woman for whom he'd had feelings—obviously wanting to look professional in front of a man who would probably be able to greatly influence any future career advancement Al might hope for.

Captain Soto was nodding as he listened. Al pushed on. "Once he was arrested, I knew I had to try to find out who he was, but I was sidetracked from that endeavor by the arrival of Professor Morgan." Al waved toward me. I nodded and smiled at Captain Soto. He didn't smile back. "I knew Professor Morgan by reputation. She is a criminologist, of sorts, from Vancouver." *You cheeky so-and-so!* "I was suspicious of her immediately, so I courted her company, to keep an eye on her." *It is true that he'd tried to make sure that either he or Miguel had been with me at all times, when possible.* "As I said, I knew of Professor Morgan by reputation, and I have read what she's written about observation techniques when building a picture of a victim. I have also studied such techniques as part of my advanced interrogation training, which I have already completed at the police training facility in Guadalajara." *Now you're really sucking up to Soto.*

Soto's body language told me that he was curious, but not impressed. If Al's skills were as good as he claimed, he, too, would have noticed this. It seemed that he did, because he went in for the kill. "When I first met Professor Morgan, at a local bar and restaurant—in fact, the site where the killing of Tony Booth took place—she had a sunburned nose and had clearly been in the sun for some time. I knew immediately that she could not have arrived in Puerto Vallarta only an hour before I met her, the day of Margarita Martinez's murder. Also, when I helped her with her luggage I noted she had two suitcases, which, even for a woman, is a lot for a week's vacation. Furthermore, one suitcase, battered and ugly, was hardly filled, whereas the other, better cared for and more elegant, was stuffed. That is not how one person packs luggage—in two very different bags and with such variances in weight distribution." He had me on both those points, and I saw Bud glance around at me.

"As I said, I tried to be with the suspect at all times. I knew that something wasn't right, but, at that time, I didn't know what. I didn't connect her to the slaying at the seafront, nor, at that point, did I connect the death of Margarita Martinez with the Rose Killer at all. As a good detective must, I persevered. I took Professor Morgan into my 'confidence' and invited her to work the case with me. She accepted eagerly. Too eagerly for someone trying to take a break from work. I could tell from her approach to the case that her agenda differed from mine. I wanted to discover the identity of the man in my cells—she was trying to hide it, throwing up a smokescreen of useless lines of questioning about the locations of different people at the time of the slaying, about the crime scene, about many things that were not relevant. She was transparent and foolish to think she was leading me astray. When she saw the man I had in my cells, she was shocked. Immediately I saw the way they looked at each other. I knew she knew him. With that lead, all I had to do was follow through." *Way to go Cait—you're obviously hopeless at hiding your reactions and emotions.*

There was a general rustling around the room at this observation, and folks shifted on their chairs. I suspected they were running through their interactions with me in their heads, thinking back on how I'd spoken to them, what I'd asked, and how I'd used them in my ruse to lead Al away from learning Bud's true identity.

Al looked pleased with himself. "As someone trained in these matters, and as a student of criminal psychology at Guadalajara University, I decided that I needed to find out what Professor Morgan was really up to. So, when I left Tony Booth at Amigos del Tequila that evening, I entered the house in which Professor Morgan was staying, and searched the premises."

Captain Soto held up his hand. "You broke into the place where she was staying to gather evidence?" He sounded annoyed. I wondered what the Mexican rules of evidence were, or whether search warrants weren't needed at all.

Al sounded proud as he replied, "The owner, Henry Douglas, is known to me. I had telephoned him to explain that I was deeply concerned that the tenant he had at his house was not quite what they claimed to be, and asked his permission to use the key that we hold at the police station to gain entry to his home to check that all was well. He agreed. I have his number for the records, sir." Soto nodded, and Al preened just a little. *You sly old dog, it was you who crept around me as I slept. I bet you never knew you'd put my shoes back in the wrong place!*

"Upon searching the premises, the only thing I could find amiss was that Professor Morgan's second suitcase did, in fact, contain male clothing. I couldn't find her purse, so I was unable to learn anything else about who the clothes belonged to, but, having witnessed their meeting, I was in no doubt that it was the man in my cells. The man who had ruthlessly killed Margarita Martinez." Al paused for effect, and he got what he wanted, because all eyes followed his to Bud, who sat with no emotion on his face, looking at the floor. *Even though your secret's out, you're keeping quiet, Bud?*

"Yes, Professor Morgan was in her bed, asleep, when I searched her temporary accommodation, but I believe she left later that night to carry out various nefarious tasks, to cover the tracks of her murderous partner. I believe she returned to Amigos del Tequila, using some excuse, and talked Tony Booth into drinking a beer she had dosed with a sedative. Once he had succumbed, having gone to bed not knowing he was drugged, I believe she roused Callie Booth from her already drugged state and made her drink from a glass laced with a sedative, on top of the one already given to her by Dorothea Simmonds. It wouldn't have been difficult for Professor

Morgan to gain entry to the premises as the Booths were not good at remembering to lock up, and she knew this. Also, Tony Booth was a good man; he was very hospitable. She would then have had access to the keys to Tony Booth's truck, which I believe she drove to the scene of the morning's murder, where she ransacked the flower shop and stole all of Margarita Martinez's photographic equipment—things she had noted and remarked upon to me when we had visited the flower shop together earlier that night. I saw her eyeing up the equipment, but she tried to sidetrack me with a pathetic story about her mother's wedding bouquet—a lot of rubbish designed to mislead my thinking. I saw what she saw, and she returned later that night to steal it, which made me wonder what it was she thought Margarita Martinez might have captured on her cameras. Professor Morgan had been asking everyone about Margarita's interest in photography, and I began to put the pieces together. If Professor Morgan had arrived with the man who'd killed Margarita, was Margarita's death, and the theft of her photographic equipment, all because she had seen something she shouldn't have? Was she dead because she knew something so damning, so bad, that she couldn't be trusted to not tell anyone? What could *be* that bad? Nothing bad happens around here. Nothing except the Rose Killings. I put those facts together and worked out what had happened. Margarita had, somehow, spotted that this man was the Rose Killer, and she'd had to be silenced for knowing that."

A wave of "Oh no!" and "How awful!" swept through the audience. Heads were shaken at Bud. I noted that Dorothea was clearly desperate to speak, but everyone could see that Al was not yet done.

"I decided to apply Professor Morgan's investigating techniques back to the woman herself: I knew she'd drugged the Booths, and I knew she'd raided the flower shop, but no one had seen her, and she had good reason for her fingerprints or DNA to be at both sites. I turned to her background. I checked out her university's website, and I found a photograph showing the man in my cell standing right behind her. I had *proof* they knew each other. It was the break I needed. When I asked for the help of a friend, the one who discovered the information about *Bud Anderson's* aliases and passports, I was able to match several of his trips to times when a murder had been committed by the Rose Killer. I am sure that when you get involved, sir, and have full access to all our immigration data, you will find that he was here on every occasion."

Captain Soto waved an imperious arm as if to say, "Maybe," but didn't strain himself by actually speaking.

"To be fair to Professor Morgan, I think I know why she has done what she has done. She is a criminal psychologist. She studies deviant psychological behavior. I am sure she has studied many cases about serial killers, and I believe that she met this man as part of her studies, or that he targeted her as someone he could bend to his will, and he has brought her under his power." I found it hard to imagine Bud as a Svengali-figure, but I understood what Al was trying to say. "I do not believe that she meant to kill Tony Booth, only to drug both him and his wife so that she could gain access to their truck to be able to do what she needed to do at the flower shop, and then dispose of the photographic equipment, which she has clearly done. In fact, Captain Soto, I have to admit that maybe if I had not stayed for a few drinks with Tony Booth that evening, he might have survived the drugs she gave him. I will always feel guilty about this. But I have brought you the Rose Killer, who is also the man who killed Margarita Martinez, and I have brought you his accomplice—at least on this visit to Mexico—who has, albeit unintentionally, killed Tony Booth." He saluted and bowed.

That's it? That's nothing! You don't know the half of it, Captain Alfredo Jesus Beselleu Torres.

"Very convincing," said Captain Soto, tapping his chin—a clear sign the man was thinking. He spied his right-hand man hovering at the entry to the hall, and called him over. He waved a hand to dismiss Al, who took a seat, and we all waited patiently—well, I wasn't feeling patient at all—while Soto listened to what seemed like a very long speech, whispered in his ear. I couldn't hear what was being said, but Captain Soto's face, and body, spoke volumes: his eyes gradually hooded over, his breathing became labored, his fingers began to drum on his armrest, his blinking increased. He didn't like what he was hearing, and the way he was looking at Al, who was glowing with pride and happily acknowledging the silent nods, grins, thumbs up, and attaboys from the locals, wasn't good . . . for Al. *I hope it's good for Bud, and me.*

Eventually, Captain Soto gave a couple of instructions to his slimy sidekick, who retreated outside again. Then the small, powerful man looked right at me and indicated I should rise. I did. Sharpish.

"You have heard what Captain Torres has to say. I think I am right in believing you would welcome a chance to put forward your version of events."

I nodded. "Very much so, sir," I replied in perfect Spanish. "Would you like me to address you in Spanish or English?" There were surprised glances all around.

Soto smiled. Again, he tapped his chin. He smacked his hand on his leg and said, "Very well. Speak. I will listen. English, please." I suspected that my Spanish accent was terrible.

I turned to Al and said, in English this time, "Al, I'm sorry about this. You are a good policeman, and I tried, several times, to warn you that you had all this wrong, but you *wouldn't* listen. Now that you've made these accusations against Bud and me, I'm sure that everyone in this room understands that I am fighting for our lives." Then I turned to Bud. "Before I begin, Bud, I have one question for you. Is there a name you can give Captain Soto, so he can get you checked out? There's no point sticking to protocol now. You know that."

Bud nodded. He cleared his throat—it had been a long time since he'd spoken. "Captain Soto, sir. If you contact Fernando Ramirez at the Ministry of the Interior, he will know me. Use the name Bud Anderson. It's the one he knows me by."

Soto nodded, held up his hand to indicate I should wait, pulled out his cell phone, spoke rapidly, put it away again, and then nodded at Bud as he spoke. "I know of Señor Ramirez, of course, though we have not met. His role in government is such that he does not mix with a mere captain of the Federales. Thank you, Mr. Anderson. Continue Professor Morgan." As he nodded at me, quite graciously, I caught a look of total confusion cross Al's face.

Oh boy—you ain't seen nothing yet, Captain Al!

Time for the Full Story

"WOULD YOU MIND IF SOMEONE took these off?" I asked, indicating my handcuffs. Soto nodded and Al did as he was told. I didn't dare ask them to do the same for Bud. "Captain Torres has examined the facts and come up with a plausible hypothesis," I began. I nodded toward Al. "But I'm afraid he gets an F when it comes to proving it. He has no proof that I drugged the Booths, stole their truck, burgled the flower shop, and disposed of the photographic equipment, or that Bud Anderson is the Rose Killer. None of it is true."

Meaningful glances were exchanged, though the messages were mixed.

"Here's the *truth*. Bud and I arrived to stay at an apartment at the Rocas Hermosas Resort on Sunday morning. Bud popped out to get some beers, and the next thing I knew, I was looking out of our apartment window to see him covered in blood and hauled off by the cops. That's the short version. The fact of the matter is I saw the whole thing, pretty much from the moment Bud left our apartment, until he was driven away to this very building. As I explain, I'll have a few questions to ask—is that alright with you, Captain Soto? I don't want to cross any lines."

Soto nodded. "Remember, this is not a court of law. I am being . . . polite, by letting you do this."

I nodded and continued. "Al, you were right about some of the facts: I did arrive here, in Mexico, earlier than I said I did, and I *was* in possession of luggage for two people. You did well to spot that, but you drew the wrong conclusions. Bud, I'm guessing you went into the flower shop and Margarita was bleeding out on the floor?"

Bud nodded. "You tried to save her because your training kicked in." He agreed.

I heard a loud whisper from Dorothea. "What training?"

I pounced. "Oh, of course, I didn't tell you how Bud and I met. You were right about that too, in a way, Al; it *was* through my work." Al looked smug. "Bud is a retired, decorated homicide detective, who was heading up the Integrated Homicide Team in British Columbia when we met, and he hired me as a consultant. His training as a law enforcement officer kicked in, and he tried to save Margarita."

"Why did he not speak up?" blurted out Al, who was visibly shaken.

"His last job was as a Canadian liaison for an international gang-busting task force, and there are certain protocols you follow when you're representing your country."

Eyes were widening around the room. Soto didn't look surprised. I guessed his guy had already told him who Bud really was and was now checking with the high-ups in the Ministry about how they should handle things.

I noticed that Al was sweating.

"Just because Bud's a cop, and a very well-respected one at that, it doesn't mean he absolutely *couldn't* have done it—but you have to understand he *wouldn't* have done it. Bud—did you see anyone make their way out of a tiny door in the back of the store?" Bud shook his head. "Okay. So, you all thought Bud was the killer. I *knew* he wasn't. That gave me an advantage. While you were wondering who the killer *was*, you were focused on Bud, but I was working out who the *real* killer was. I learned where pretty much everyone was in the few moments before as well as at the moment that Bud was discovered. I knew no one had entered the flower shop, except Bud, and no one had left it within the critical timeframe. I was able to discount certain people as viable suspects, but I was left with quite a few possibilities, all of whom had opportunity. Of course, there were two critical points I had to consider regarding opportunity—how did Margarita's murderer get into *and* out of the flower shop? Once I realized that there were a number of people not in the company of others at the time Margarita must have been murdered, I wondered who could have walked right in through the front door of the flower shop. And who could have *then* made their way out through the little door that Margarita had built into the back wall of her building, inside her refrigerated units? I had something to work with."

I turned and looked at Margarita's grieving father first. "Juan— you might have killed your daughter to be able to inherit her land and her water. You drove past the crime scene just as Bud was discovered. I saw you in your blue pickup truck. Others *said* where they were: Greg, you were in PV, but you could have been in Punta de las Rocas. Callie and Tony Booth too. Dean and Jean, no one knew exactly where you two were. Rutilio, you were in your kitchen, Dorothea was out of sight in Serena's massage room, and Ada was unattended in the salon."

"Now wait just a minute, dear ..." began Dorothea, about to launch into full attack mode.

I held up my hand. "Don't start, Dorothea. I've had quite enough of your bluster. Your attitude toward the people whose homes you live near has rubbed me up the wrong way. You have no sense of how tough it is for some folks here. You rail about being 'ripped off' without the slightest comprehension that people who rely upon income from tourism have to make their money while they can, in a short season, so they can live all year long."

"Exactly!" shouted Rutilio.

I turned on him next. "And you? You're just as bad as Dorothea. You see people on vacation, spending lots of money, and you seem to assume that's how they live all year round. You don't consider how hard they might have to save up to be able to enjoy a couple of weeks of spending as though it doesn't bother them. Bob, Maria—I think *you* get it. And, Al, I have great sympathy for the points you've made about how visitors don't respect the local issues, like water usage. You all live in an area that balances on a knife-edge: tourism changes everything—sometimes for the worse, sometimes for the better. But if an area has decided to embrace tourism, it must then work within a changed environment. I see some of you resolving this, and some of you not. It generates tension in almost everyone. And *that* tension contributed to *this* crime. Or, I should say, *these* crimes. I believe that the killer was under tremendous pressure, which might have contributed to their actions. But it doesn't excuse them. Another thing you were right about, Al, is that there are links between the Rose Killer, Margarita's killer, the person who drugged the Booths, and the one who stole Margarita's photographic equipment. So, Captain Soto, you *will* get to take the Rose Killer into your custody today—it's just not Bud Anderson."

Captain Soto smiled. I saw a gold tooth glint. *Perfect!* "So, Professor Morgan, who *is* the Rose Killer?"

"I'll get there," I promised. "But, first, a couple of sidebars. When I was at the Booths' home, awaiting the ambulance to take them away, I found some notes that Callie Booth had made about accounts that she was working on. A couple of them were crossed out, as though they'd been dealt with; one looked as though it had yet to be addressed. One of the 'canceled' notes related to the price of wax at your spa, Serena. Callie had noticed that your costs for wax had decreased considerably in recent months. I am guessing you've found a new supplier and decided to, shall we say, *compromise on quality*?"

Serena blushed. "You are right," she replied. "People do not spend as they used to. Even when there is a big wedding at the resort, not all the women come beforehand for treatments, and to make themselves look nice. These are difficult times. I have to save on what I can." She smiled at Ada and Dorothea, who were, as I knew, good clients of the spa.

"Thanks, Serena, that clears that up. Another of Callie's notes related to the extraordinarily good mileage that Margarita was getting from her little van"—puzzled looks were exchanged—"and the third, the one that looked as though it had not yet been dealt with, mentioned 'barrels and bottles' at Hacienda Soleado. Would anyone like to comment on that matter? *Anyone?*"

Dean spoke first. "I'm sure it's nothing, Cait. Nothing. It's probably an oversight." I caught a glance he threw to me, and me alone. It was a warning. He was trying to *threaten* me into silence! I wasn't going to stand for that.

"But it's not 'nothing,' Dean," I replied, staring him down. "Callie Booth discovered that the tequila production facility run by the FOGTTs doesn't own enough barrels in which to properly age the number of bottles of 'aged' tequila it sells. I first suspected that it was this discovery that might have led to Margarita's death, and to Callie's and Tony's poisoning, but—"

I couldn't say anymore, because, at that point, Dean George stood and bellowed, "Enough!" He had an amazing voice; I could almost *feel* his deep bass resonate around the hall.

With all eyes on him, and the nearby guard dwarfed by his huge mass, Dean George turned to his wife, looked down at her, and whispered, "Sorry, my dear." He then turned to Captain Soto and said, "Captain, your indulgence, please. You need to take a look at this." He held out something that was small in his huge hand; the guard took it from him and passed it to his boss. The man with all the braids looked at what he'd been handed, puffed out his cheeks in surprise, rolled his eyes, and allowed the guard to return Dean's property.

"Professor Morgan, you need to let this gentleman speak." Soto waved me into submission. I knew when it was time to cede the floor.

As someone who reads people, I should have been able to interpret Dean's glaring at me better than I had. But in my defense, I'd been focused on clearing Bud, rather than on picking up on micro-expressions. That said, as Dean stood in front of our group, I saw a different person emerge from beneath the folds of his Hawaiian shirt. Jean rose to stand beside him, they held hands, and Dean addressed his expectant audience. Just before he spoke, a light bulb came on in my head. A retired government employee? Evasive when questioned? He and his wife giving each other a cover story? Dean wasn't the person I'd thought him to be. His larger than life persona was just that, a personality he'd adopted to keep his true identity safe. *Of course! Dean and Jean!* I'd worked out their identities, but too late to prevent myself from letting the cat out of the bag. *Damn and blast!* I wondered what damage I might have done.

Dean commanded our attention, and his voice, softer now but still as powerful, filled the chamber. "My name is not Dean George, and, although this wonderful woman *is* my wife, her name is not Jean George. Juan García Martinez, Dorothea Simmonds, and Greg Hollins—I'll call you that for now, Greg, though I *do* know your real name—you are all under arrest for multiple counts of fraudulent trading of falsely labeled tequila in the USA. I represent the US government, and before you leave this room—no, don't try to run, Juan, I'm sure that Captain Soto's troops will have something to say about that—we will be joined by members of the Mexican authorities responsible for the examination and certification of tequila, who will escort you all into custody, where you'll find that a long list of charges are due to be brought against you."

Frank and Ada Taylor couldn't have looked more shocked, Bud clearly had no idea what on earth was going on, and, of all the faces in the room that displayed disbelief, it was Al's that drew my attention: he looked as though he was about to burst into tears. I could sense the confusion that must have been running through his mind at that moment. Not only was I undermining him, but Dean George was doing the same.

Dean continued, "Captain Soto, I need to make a couple of calls, with your permission?" Soto nodded. Dean looked at me. "Don't worry, Cait, this isn't your fault. We were almost ready to scoop everyone up, but your comments about the FOGTT accounts mean we'd better do it now, before these three can get word to anyone else and spoil our entire case. I had no idea that the FOGTTs had given their accounts to Callie Booth—they've always had a guy we know about in PV do them before. With that information out there, it's best we do it this way, now. I only hope it wasn't this case that got the Booths into trouble and Tony and Margarita killed. I knew we were dealing with international criminals, but I didn't think for one minute they were killers. By the way," he added, "just so you know, Captain Soto, word has come down to me through . . . various channels . . . that this man is on the side of the angels." He nodded toward Bud. "I've been ready to get your back, sir," he said directly to Bud, who nodded in response. Dean didn't sound like a lower-ranked official for whatever agency he represented, and I wondered if his reference to Bud as "sir" was anything other than a general politeness.

"We had nothing to do with Tony's death, or Margarita's!" shouted Dorothea.

"Shut up, you stupid woman," spat Greg Hollins. "This is all *your* fault. I told you to wait with those accounts . . . wait until our regular guy in PV was back from his vacation, but you had to do it, didn't you? You had to give them to Callie. Why couldn't you wait? You always have to have everything done the way you want it! Damn you!"

Greg's accent wasn't Australian anymore. New Jersey was nearer the mark, to my ear. Juan Martinez spat out some choice phrases in Spanish, which certainly didn't need to be translated in order for Dorothea to know what he thought of her. Then all three of the culprits sat silently, glowering at each other, as Dean George walked toward the exit with his phone clamped to his ear, his hands waving, and a lot of "Sorry, ma'am" and "Yes, right now, please, ma'am" audible to the room.

Captain Soto motioned that I should continue, which I did, though I could tell that I didn't have everyone's undivided attention anymore. Frankly, that didn't matter so long as I had Soto's.

"So, there we have the explanation of Callie's note about the FOGTT bottles and barrels," I said, maybe a little too brightly. "Let's get back to Margarita's gas mileage, which was something else that the eagle-eyed Callie Booth queried. How many of us get into our vehicles and notice the mileage? Not many, I'm sure. But what about how much gas we have? Pretty much everyone. Margarita cycled almost everywhere, using her van only when she needed it. She was careful with money, she had to be, and she'd have noticed if, on any given morning, she'd climbed into her van and there was less gas in it than there had been the night before. Margarita was a woman who paid great attention to detail, but she might easily have missed the fact that hundreds of miles were being added to her odometer. Which they were. You see, the person driving her van without her permission, or knowledge, was refilling it with fuel after they used it. So when she gave her mileage and her gas receipts to Callie, the accountant was puzzled and made a note to speak to Margarita about the anomaly—that she seemed to be driving a lot of miles for the gas she said she was putting in. The notes were near Callie's phone, and the chances were that Callie had spoken to Margarita about this matter already, then crossed through the note to herself."

"Who borrowed Margarita's van and filled it with gas?" asked Frank, his hand raised. Ada pulled his hand down and tutted.

"Well, Frank, to answer your question, the Rose Killer was borrowing it, to transport and dump bodies. The same person was driving it the day that Margarita took photographs of her own van—not one like it, but her *actual* van—when she was out taking daybreak shots of the surf. I don't think she knew what she'd seen, or photographed, at first. But she eventually put it all together: the pictures, the idea that someone was using her van without her say-so, and a person coming to her store to buy two red roses on Sunday morning. She realized she was looking at the person responsible for killing Miguel's daughter and all those other girls. The killer's response, knowing they'd been found out, was to act instantly. That is why Margarita died."

"So who *is it*?" asked Ada plaintively. "Is it one of . . . us?" She looked around the room, wide-eyed. And she wasn't the only one.

"Preposterous!" exclaimed Dorothea.

"No, it's not," I said quietly. I looked at Captain Soto and said, "Ready?" He nodded and made a few signals with his fingers, and two of his remaining four guards stiffened to full alert. Anyone thinking of making a run for it would have several automatic weapons to consider.

"I think that the death of Miguel's daughter was an accident. A heavy drinking session resulted in her death, and the person she'd been drinking with panicked, identified Margarita's van as a convenient way to get the body out of the vicinity, and thought they'd got away with it. But the police pulled in Miguel as a prime suspect. A month of Federales buzzing about the area didn't go down well in many quarters for . . . many reasons. So everyone breathed a sigh of relief when another girl was killed and *everyone* around here had an alibi—they were all attending one of the crucifix of Requiem Masses that Miguel had arranged. Captain Soto—I assume you had all the men in this area under observation at that time?" Soto nodded. There were a few surprised expressions around the room. "But that day, with everyone heading off in different directions for religious observances, did you ease up a little?" Again, he nodded, ruefully. "The one day that Margarita's van was available in the daytime because she'd closed her shop, you saw the *only* daytime abduction of a girl who was killed. Unlike Angélica Rosa, the second girl was drugged. Her exact time of death was suspect, though you knew she hadn't been dumped before a certain point in time. Let me pose this question. If a young woman was alone, who would she trust enough to accept a ride from? What type of vehicle would she willingly get into? Especially if she felt she might be in danger?"

There were shrugs around the room. I answered my own question. "A police car. Despite the rumors about the trustworthiness of the Mexican police force—I'm sorry, Captain Soto, but even *you* have to accept that the evidence for some corruption is pretty clear"—Soto shrugged—"how could Margarita's van be mistaken for a police car? It's white, that helps, and I discovered that Miguel has a magnetic decal that can be attached to any vehicle, thereby transforming it into a 'police car' containing a person a girl can, psychologically speaking, trust. And that's what the killer did: put Miguel's decal on Margarita's van and used it to lure in girls who would then be plied with drugged alcohol and allowed to die. But why? There was no interference. No apparent sexual motive. Was the killer doing it for the simple pleasure of watching these poor young women die? If so, why lay them out with such reverence, wrapped in a sheet, their hands in prayer, holding roses?"

There were mumblings. I turned and looked directly at the Rose Killer.

"Because that's what you felt was right to do for your little niece, wasn't it, Rutilio? I've seen how you like to pour your drinks. I'm betting you gave little Angélica Rosa just one too many strong drinks the night of the Día de los Muertos celebrations, she passed out, and you found she'd died. You panicked, loaded her body into Margarita's conveniently located van. It's always parked in the lane behind your restaurant, and I'm sure you knew where Margarita kept her keys, and how to get to them. It didn't occur to you that your brother would be suspected of killing his own child. It was during that period that your business suffered—I suspect you were racked with guilt. You came up with a plan: on the day of the Requiem Masses you took Margarita's van, and, once you were away from this area, added your brother's police decal. You might even have 'borrowed' one of his spare uniform shirts to complete the look—it would have been easy enough for you to gain access to one. You drove around until you picked up your second victim, then you made sure you dumped the poor woman's body in a place where the time *after which* she was dumped, 6:00 PM in this case, would be known. You probably followed a cop car on its normal route, so you knew there'd be a clear, unequivocal timeframe for the dumping of the body, because that was the vital part of your plan. You returned to Punta de las Rocas for the service here, assuring that both you and your brother, in Puerto Vallarta, had watertight alibis."

Miguel shot to his feet. "My brother could not have done this. I was cleared because I could not have driven from the place where the poor girl was dumped to the church I attended in Puerto Vallarta—where many people saw me. My brother has the *same* alibi—he was at another service here." Miguel looked terribly distressed.

"What time was the Mass said here?" I asked Al, who I knew had attended with Rutilio.

Al looked puzzled. "It was at 7:00 PM, the same as in Puerto Vallarta."

"But Punta de las Rocas, and the whole of Nayarit, is an hour behind Puerto Vallarta. When it's 7:00 PM here, it's 8:00 PM in Puerto Vallarta. Rutilio had a *whole extra hour* to get back here from the dump site and still be at the church in time for the 7:00 PM service. You're all so used to the difference it didn't occur to you. I didn't even know about the time difference until this morning, which was why I was stuck. I couldn't work out how Rutilio could have been in two places at once that day, though I knew, by then, that it *was him* who'd killed Margarita."

"This is rubbish!" shouted Rutilio, leaping up from his seat. "I would not kill my niece. I would not kill all those other girls. Why would I do that? You have no proof. There is nothing that points to me!" Rutilio grinned at me with his big teeth. *Look out, Cheshire Cat—here I come!*

One of the cops motioned with his weapon that Rutilio should sit, and he did, grumbling.

I sighed. "Rutilio—you are a classic narcissist with sociopathic tendencies. The giant face sign you have? The way you present yourself as the star of your own show at the restaurant? The roses you like to give the women with their checks, so that you can flatter them and have them focus on just you? By the way, I know that's why, for the first time, you had to try to get the red roses from Margarita for this latest kill—you told me yourself, you don't have your own roses during the summer months. For the rest of the kills, you used the ones you had in bulk at your restaurant. I know you used Margarita's van, because it's refrigerated. The refrigeration is what threw off the coroner's ability to come up with an accurate time of death—it messes with the onset of rigor mortis. Sometimes rigor sets in more quickly because of it, sometimes it is delayed. After all the press coverage about the confused time of death, you might have put two and two together and worked out that, somehow, the refrigerated van could help you mask when you were really killing. You didn't target specific girls; you'd just drive until you found one who was ready to accept the offer of a ride home from a man driving a cop car. Enough young people walk in these areas, because they don't own a car or even a bicycle, so it wouldn't take too long. Your niece's death was an accident. You covered it up. Your first 'real murder,' when you resorted to plying a girl with drink and drugging her, was to clear your brother, and you, of suspicion. So why more deaths, Rutilio? Why continue? My assessment would be that you did it just because you *could*.

And because you *liked* it. It had become 'your thing,' and you don't have many of those, do you? You had to give up your apartment in Bucerias and move back to live with your mother and your brother's family. None of your past jobs have gone well for you—you have always been 'misunderstood' by employers. Even your own business, the restaurant, is failing. You are getting older, and whatever looks you once had are fading. It was one way you could reassure yourself you were a real man—not in a sexual way, but by showing you had power over people. You are your mother's 'pretty baby.' She and your brother have unwittingly enabled you to remain free of responsibilities. They have backed you up when you've said that past misfortunes have not been 'your fault.' You display a classic inability to take responsibility for any of your own failures."

Finally there was a gasp from Miguel. "No!"

"Yes," I replied. "When I saw Rutilio on the day of Margarita's murder, he was standing against a white wall, holding a glass of water and what I thought were two chopsticks in his hands, at exactly the time that Bud was trying to save Margarita's life. I could just about spot his white chef hat against the white stucco wall." I looked at the killer and saw his mask slip even further as I spoke, a snarl beginning to twitch at his lips. "Initially, it was difficult for me to make out the white hat against the white wall, but I did. *Now* I know that what I'd thought were two sticks you were holding were, in fact, two red roses, but I couldn't make out the red of the flower heads, because they'd disappeared against the red of your chef jacket, just like poor Margarita's blood, which must have been all over it at the time. You put on a clean jacket in your kitchen before you joined the crowd in the street outside Margarita's shop. And the knife? You might have had one in your pocket when you went to her shop, but I think it might be discovered that the knife used to kill her was Margarita's own. Florists have all sorts of cutting implements to hand; all you had to do was reach out and make one swift slashing motion."

The men with guns were now even more alert. Rutilio's mask of bravado had completely disappeared, but he still seemed to have his toothy grin because his dry lips had stuck to his teeth.

Al and Miguel were on their feet. But I wasn't done. "Here's how it went, Rutilio. You sauntered into Margarita's shop on Sunday morning, needing two red roses because you knew it was your time to kill again. She wouldn't sell them to you, right? She'd picked up a special order for a wedding, and they were all spoken for. You insisted, and your insistence and anger raised her suspicions. When I was in her shop with Al, I noticed that she had two buckets with red roses in them, and one with yellow. I even noticed that she had twenty-two red roses and twelve yellow. When would a florist buy in anything other than *full* dozens of roses? Two red roses were missing from Margarita's stock. When I returned to the shop with Miguel, I saw a newspaper, laying sodden on the floor, warning girls to be careful because it was Rose Killer time. She'd worked out that her van was being used without her knowledge. I think the penny dropped that she'd even photographed it in use. She probably accused you of taking her van. She must have mentioned that Callie had raised the issue of the extra mileage, because that's why you went after the Booths. When it comes to their drugging, I suspect it went much as Al suggested, but with you, not me, getting Tony to accept a drugged drink, waiting until he went to bed, then getting Callie to accept a drink from you in her already hazy state. But you got your doses wrong. You're used to drugging young women who are small in stature—Callie Booth is a healthy, fit woman, as I saw from her wedding photographs, and she has a bigger body mass than you were used to dealing with, so your usual dose didn't work on her. Tony was a fit, muscular man, and I'm betting you gave him some extra, just to make sure. You certainly meant to kill them both. It was *you* who headed to the flower shop to search for evidence. Knowing that Margarita had photographs of her van being driven without her permission, you didn't want to take a chance. You had no idea what they would show—maybe your face?—but you couldn't risk them turning up. That's why you checked through all her photographs, then took all her equipment. By the way, you scuffed the back wall with the black plastic cases when you pulled them out through the little door at the back of the fridge. We wouldn't have the photos that we do if Al hadn't known about Margarita's secret stash of extras in her glove box. The time and date stamp will prove the van was being used by someone other than herself at a critical time."

There were stirrings around the room. Ada Taylor was looking especially perplexed.

I pressed on. I was almost done. "The 'long hours' Rutilio worked at the restaurant, Miguel? They were a great cover. For example, on Sunday night, all he had to do was scrape down his grill, then wait until the coast was clear at the Booths', drug them, and head back to search Margarita's store. He still had time to drive off, kill another poor young woman, dump her body, return the van to its usual spot, and come home to bed. Al, you know that Bud was in your cell on Sunday night and couldn't have been out there killing this latest poor young woman. If the medical examiner knows what to look for, I'm sure they'll be able to determine her actual time of death. In any case, Bud was in Canada on Saturday, and in prison on Sunday, so clearly he didn't kill *this* poor woman. And, if you're still in any doubt about Bud not being the Rose Killer, in my purse there's a camera containing photos of an event Bud and I attended in Vancouver in December last year, with a giant dated banner in the background, that will prove that he wasn't here for that killing either. Captain Soto, I promise you, Rutilio is your man. He *is* the Rose Killer, he *is* the man who slashed Margarita's throat, and he *is* the man who drugged both Tony and Callie Booth."

I sat down and waited for it to all go off, which it did. Miguel was up on his feet, as were Al and Juan. All three made for Rutilio,

who fell to the floor and curled up into a ball. He started to cry and wail. "It was an accident, my brother, an accident. Angélica Rosa drank too much. I couldn't get her to breathe. I did my best. It was an accident! But, brother, when I saw how you felt—that she was pure and safe with God, that you were celebrating that she was with her Maker, at peace—I knew it was alright to take the others. I *saved* them, my brother. Like your daughter, Juan, all of them were saved."
Is Rutilio really trying to make it sound as though his multiple murders had been some sort of sacrificial act? I wonder how that will play out in a Mexican courtroom.

Captain Soto instructed his guards to break up the melee, which they did, quite quickly. It's amazing what a few automatic weapons can achieve when pointed at a person.

In a matter of moments, Bud's handcuffs were off, and he was being addressed, very formally, by Captain Soto. Rutilio was being hauled away by the Federales. Dean and Jean George were making a beeline for me, smiling from ear to ear.

"I'm sorry," I said to them quietly. "I didn't know you were 'the operative' that Jack White had referred to until we were here. Dean, when you threw me that challenging look, the penny dropped. But who do you work for?" I still didn't know who they *really* were, only that they weren't who they said they were.

"US government," said Dean quietly, and conspiratorially. "Let's leave it at that. Working with Mexican authorities, multiple border authorities, and US officials. I got a call from some 'friends' in Ottawa—I've been watching your back. I informed them of your arrest, and I'd been cleared to take action before the Federales took you two away. And, like I said earlier, don't beat yourself up about it. We were pretty well ready to move on this group. We might have lost a few drivers in the wind, but I just heard from my superior that we've got everyone important, both sides of the border, in custody."

I couldn't help but be curious, so I pressed on. "I'm pretty sure

I've worked it all out. I'm guessing it's pretty big?" I asked. I turned to find Bud at my shoulder. I smiled and hugged him. Good grief, he smelled awful!

"So, will someone tell me what's been going on here?" Bud asked.

"It's the tequila," I explained. Dean and Jean nodded. "The Hacienda Soleado is selling more bottles of tequila than they have barrels in which to age it properly. Tequila starts life as a clear liquid, is aged a little in vats, or for longer in barrels, and is then sold at a much higher price for the older spirit. Callie Booth spotted the discrepancy between the number of bottles of the older stuff being sold and the number of barrels owned by the FOGTTs in which the tequila needed to be aged. I'm guessing they're coloring it and selling younger tequila as añejo?"

Dean nodded. "They're breaking any number of the very strict laws governing the production of tequila on this side of the border, and because so much of it is sold in the US, it's creating all types of fraud cases over there. We were sent in because it's the Americans who are running the show down here."

"Greg's not Australian, is he?" I asked, knowing the answer. *He couldn't be — he was too Australian to be real.* Dean shook his head. "It's him, Dorothea, and Juan?" I asked.

Dean nodded. "Juan's the one with all the local contacts; he knows which palms to grease to get the right certification. Of course, once it's off the hacienda it's a lot safer to transport than drugs: you get caught with a truckload of tequila that's been incorrectly labeled, there's deniability . . . not the case when you're talking about drugs."

"It's why we're here as a team," Jean said. "They wanted a couple on the case, so we could get to know what systems they were using, which locals were involved. And when poor Margarita was killed, and the Federales were bound to be called in, I just knew that something would happen to spoil our set up. They interfere. I guess that's their job, to be fair. We'd tried to build an atmosphere where everyone here supported Al as much as possible in everything he did, so outside forces were rarely called on. I was angry when I first met you—not with you, but because of the situation. I'm sorry I was hostile. You see, we've been at it a long time, on both sides of the border. It's not just these guys, and it's not just this plant, you see. It's big. Big money. At least the call from Ottawa gave us a chance to get everything sorted out." She gave me a huge hug.

"The Taylors—do they even know what's going on?"

Dean smiled and shook his head. "They don't have a clue. They're in their own little world. We'll protect them. Henry Douglas—the guy whose house you've been staying in? He's away in LA too often to have noticed anything. It's just Greg, Dorothea, and Juan, plus the officials who've been on the take. In a way, I'll be sorry to leave this place. We've liked it here. By the way, Cait, the reason I couldn't tell you where we were when Margarita was killed was because we were having a meeting with a local ... resource ... down on the beach at that exact time. Sorry that I," he squeezed his wife's hand, "that *we* must have seemed suspicious. I didn't dare break cover sooner than today—Al locking you up last night gave us just enough time to get things all lined up in case this happened." He gave an embarrassed smile.

At least I better understood what had been going on with the Georges. As I looked around I could see Captain Soto, Al, and a weeping Miguel moving toward Al's office. I turned to Bud and whispered, "Just one more minute, and I'm all yours, okay?" He shrugged.

I called to Al and gestured for him to come to me for a moment, which he did, carrying my purse. "Here's all your stuff, Cait. Mr. Anderson's things are in there too."

I took the bag and thanked him. "Sorry to butt in, Al, but one quick thing?" He nodded. "When are you going to tell the people around here about your rights to the García land?"

Al blushed and shook his head. "I don't know what you mean ..." he stammered.

I sighed. "Your Gram Beselleu? Her maiden name was Dubois. I looked it up. Juan Carlos García García, or should I say García Dubois, is not just 'the father of Punta de las Rocas' as you put it so passionately yesterday, he's also your great-grandfather, right?" Al nodded. "Are you due to inherit a lot of land?"

"I believe I might have a better claim than Juan does to the land that Margarita inherited from her mother's side of the family. Not that Margarita and I were closely related—it goes way back, and . . . well, it's complicated. The charter is clear—every child has their right. And I am one of those children."

"So it wasn't just fate that brought you here?"

"Not exactly. I didn't know at first, but I researched the area, and, of course, I knew my gram's maiden name, so I did a bit more digging. I was always pretty good at research." Al studied his shoes. "I don't think this is the time to make myself known as a García Dubois. I'm not even sure I'll stay. You know, maybe I'm not cut out to be a cop. Given everything that was going on in Punta de las Rocas, right under my nose, and I knew nothing! I'm feeling pretty useless right now, Professor Morgan."

I smiled. The poor guy looked pretty sorry for himself. "It's still Cait, okay?" He nodded. "Listen, I've learned in my life that not everything's for everyone. With Juan Martinez out of the picture, you might not just get your hands on that beautiful shoreline and save it for posterity, but there's likely to be an opening for mayor around here too. You'd make a good mayor. You should think about it. You love history, art, and literature—who knows, with time, maybe this wonderful old hall could become some sort of cultural center for the tourists who are thirsty for a taste of the real Mexico."

Al nodded, though he didn't look convinced. He said quietly, "I'm sorry about accusing you."

I cut him short. "It's alright. I understand." And I did. I didn't *like* it, but I understood it. "I'm off. *We're off*, okay?"

Al held up his hands. "Go. Stay. Do as you please. It's been a pleasure to meet you, Cait, but I wish it could have been . . ."

"You don't have to say it, Al, I know. Different circumstances? *Context,* right?" Al nodded. "Good luck, and goodbye," I called as I waved. I grabbed Bud by the arm and we both, *finally,* stepped out into the sunlight together and walked away from the strange building.

Bud threw his arms around me and held me tight. "I am so glad to be out of that place," was all he said, then he kissed me. It was a very bristly experience, but it was wonderful.

As we finally pulled apart I said, "So . . . *who* are you?"

Bud smiled. "What, not used to the beard?"

I hit him on the arm—not too hard. "You know what I mean, Bud. If that's your name at all. Who *are* you?"

Bud stepped back, holding on to my arms as he looked into my eyes. "When I was born in Sweden, which is where I grew up until I was all of ten months old, I was named Börje Ulf Dyggve Anderson."

"That's quite a mouthful," I replied.

Bud smiled. "*Exactly.* In my first Canadian school I was known as Bud, using my three initials, and I have always *thought* of myself as Bud. But it's not my real name."

"And what about the work you've been doing for CSIS since you 'retired'? Jack, with Sheila's help, let the cat out of the bag."

Bud paused. "I can tell you that CSIS sees me as a resource. I've got a lot of knowledge in this old noggin of mine," he said, patting his messy hair. "Of course, I'm not the brain-box that you are, but they do like to keep using what I know. But as for the details—you know I can't tell you."

"Is it over? Are they done with you? Or will you keep running off to foreign countries without me knowing about it?"

"Maybe after this they'll take more notice when I tell them I'd like to stop. After all, I'm pretty well known in these parts now."

I nodded. "Bud. We need to talk. Not today, maybe, but *soon.*

There's a lot I don't know about you. And that doesn't feel good. Understand?"

Bud nodded. "Cait, we will talk. And, yes, very soon. Right now, I need to decompress a bit, and . . . I don't know . . . have the holiday we've been looking forward to for weeks?"

We hugged again. It felt like I was home.

"Want a ride, you two? Then we can tell you some more background on our case against ingratiating Greg, domineering Dorothea, and slippery Juan." It was Dean George's unmistakable voice.

I didn't wait for Bud to answer. "Yes, please. Could we go to Henry's place, so we can check on how Jack is doing back at home, clean up, and collect our stuff? Then I suggest we take ourselves to one of those big hotels on the seafront in Puerto Vallarta for the next few days, get some sun, drink lots of cocktails with little umbrellas in them, and feast our faces off! I want to find some *good* food to eat—I know there must be a lot of it in the area. I want local snapper, fresh salsa, chicken with a light mole sauce . . ."

Bud smiled. "Hey, hold your horses! Getting clean to start with sounds great, and, of course, I'm anxious to know how Jack's coming along!" He hugged me tight. "As for your suggestion about staying in Puerto Vallarta and hunting down some excellent food, I'm all for that. My diet since we arrived has been, shall we say, 'bland'? Let's do it, Cait! Let's indulge for the time we have left before our flight home."

It was only as we were being driven toward the shimmering sea at the bottom of the hill that I remembered the promises I'd made to my mirror-self that morning about everything I'd give up if only Bud and I managed to survive our ordeal. But I told myself that what happens through a looking glass doesn't really count, especially if it happens in a world that's full of fake . . . *everything*. So I would allow myself to indulge for the next few days, then I'd make a fresh start when we got home. I'd make a list of things about myself that I could work on. *I like lists.*

An excerpt from *The Corpse with the Platinum Hair,*
the next book in the Cait Morgan mystery series

House Lights Down

The past few hours had been an indulgent blend of delicious food, engaging conversation, Bud's wonderful company, and some exciting wines, all in a setting I'd never dreamed I'd get the chance to visit—the owners' private dining room at the fabulous Tsar! Casino and Hotel on The Strip in Las Vegas. I'd left our table for a moment and had just finished using the washroom's fancy, if deafening, hand dryer, when there was an ominous clanging noise. The subtle lighting in the washroom cut out. Luckily, the pulsating neon beyond the floor-to-ceiling glass end wall provided some illumination. I pulled open the washroom door to check whether the restaurant, too, had been plunged into darkness. It had. Even the piped operatic arias that had accompanied our dinner had fallen silent.

A woman called out, "Everybody stay where you are, please. The emergency generator will come on in just a few seconds." It was Julie Pool, head of the legal department at the casino, to whom I'd been introduced before dinner.

"I not afraid of dark; I afraid of furniture. Is *moving*." Svetlana Kharlamova's operatic Russian tones had been heard and praised around the world for decades, but now she was simply whining.

"Please, Madame, stay still. The furniture isn't moving, you are. Ms. Pool is correct. If we wait a moment, I'm sure everything will be just fine." Jimmy Green, the Diva Kharlamova's assistant, sounded testy, which was hardly surprising, given the way the woman had been acting toward him all evening.

Everyone in the private dining room heaved a sigh of relief when the backup lighting kicked in.

Everyone except Julie Pool, who screamed, "Oh, no . . . Look! Somebody's skewered Miss Shirley to her seat with a silver saber."

Acknowledgments

My thanks to everyone I met on my travels in Bucerias, Mismaloya, and Puerto Vallarta who took the time to share their fascinating insights about life in their beautiful part of the world. To my mum and my sister, who, as ever, were the first to read and give feedback on my writing, as well as the sort of encouragement that can only come from those who truly love you. To my husband, who supports me in every way, through every day. To Ruth Linka, my publisher, who enables Cait Morgan to travel and solve mysteries. To every member of the TouchWood team, each of whom plays their unique part in allowing Cait to live, breathe, and get out into the world. To Frances, my editor, who has a true passion for, and impressive knowledge of, crime fiction, and always exercises a light, but effective, touch. Last, but far from least, my thanks to you for choosing to read this book and spend some time with Cait Morgan—as well as to all the printers, distributors, librarians, booksellers, bloggers, and reviewers who might have helped you find, and get your hands on, this book.

Welsh Canadian mystery author CATHY ACE is the creator of the Cait Morgan Mysteries, which include *The Corpse with the Silver Tongue*, *The Corpse with the Golden Nose*, and *The Corpse with the Emerald Thumb*. Born, raised, and educated in Wales, Cathy enjoyed a successful career in marketing and training across Europe, before immigrating to Vancouver, Canada, where she taught on MBA and undergraduate marketing programs at various universities. Her eclectic tastes in art, music, food, and drink have been developed during her decades of extensive travel, which she continues whenever possible. Now a full-time author, Cathy's short stories have appeared in multiple anthologies, as well as on BBC Radio 4. She and her husband are keen gardeners, who enjoy being helped out around their acreage by their green-pawed Labradors. Cathy's website can be found at cathyace.com.